Also By

Standalone

Called into Action

Love on the Winter Steppes

Three Keys Ranch Series

Hearts Unleashed

Wrangled by Love

Navy SEALs of Little Creek Series

Issued

Matched

Assigned

Hartford Minotaurs Hockey Series

Totally Pucked

Hearts Unleashed

Three Keys Ranch Book 1

Paris Wynters

For Sgt. James J. Regan

Your memory will live on and forever be celebrated.

RLTW

Chapter 1

KATIE

Sweet clover and cattle. Nothing like it.

Katie Locke breathed in the familiar scents wafting through the open kitchen window. The incongruous mixture meant one thing. Fall had arrived in Absarokee, Montana, the same way it did every year: swiftly and with vibrant color. A soft breeze fluttered around, gently lifting and lowering leaves of various shades of red, orange, and yellow. The air was cool and crisp, like a refreshing drink of chilled water after hours in a desert. But it wouldn't be long before winter hemmed in the ranch on every side. Just like it wouldn't be long before her ranch was hemmed in by the presence of the new foreman she knew they didn't need.

A third scent added to the mix: warm, ripe banana. Of course, she couldn't bake the foreman's intrusion away, but she sure was going to try. She hobbled over to the oven and peered in, ignoring the twinge in her ankle. The banana bread smelled wonderful but still looked soft in the middle. Sighing, she dragged her way back to the table and dropped into a chair, her gaze focused on the rich blue sky outside.

The back door opened. Nickel bounded in, paws sliding over the wooden boards of the kitchen floor.

She bent over and clapped her hands. "Here, girl."

Nickel had grown from a pudgy gray puppy to an awkward adolescent. Her ears and paws too large for her body. She tumbled to an undignified halt at Katie's feet, looked up, and waited for her ears to be scratched.

The puppy was nothing like her graceful and athletic Koda, who's probably running around the ranch, getting herself into some sort of trouble.

"You spoil that dog," her dad said, closing the screen door.

The complaint was so familiar it had lost all sting, becoming more like a greeting than anything else. Her gaze lingered fondly over her dad's weathered skin and thick graying mustache, to his shirt, fastened all the way to the very top button. No one did that anymore—but trying to persuade him of the fact was an exercise in frustration.

"Looks like a new pair of boots should be at the top of your Christmas list this year." She eyed his heavily scuffed boots, running her thumbs over Nickel's soft puppy ears. If she started dropping hints now, she might be able to persuade him to get a fresh pair of boots by New Year's.

"Koda's still running in the fields," he said, face flushing red. "Don't need anything else destroyed."

The Malinois, her protector and best friend, pulled down the screen door. For fun. The canine could be a furry psychopath without proper exercise. But what else would she expect from a retired military working dog. Little Miss Maligator never got tired.

Dad checked his watch. "New foreman should be here any second. Come out and meet him."

Black mist swirled at the edges of her mind, which started to fail, like an engine that turns over and over, never kicking into action. A salty tear dripped down her cheek, leaving a tight, dry feeling. "Already? Dad—"

"We need the help," he said. "You know we do. Even with both of us pulling twelve-hour days, we're barely keeping up. Katie, I promise he's safe. I ran a background check on him. He's a good guy."

"On paper." She gazed off into the distance, eyes unblinking. "We've been fooled before. Remember what happened to Snowbird? He still refuses to let anyone but me ride him after the last man—"

"You can't let one bad apple spoil the bunch," he said.

"Not just one bad apple. Ever since Bill retired, we've had nothing but a string of bad hires. Remember the one who stole from us?" Nickel nudged her leg. Absently, she stroked the dog's ears again.

"Rathborne's different. He's former army. Returned home after being wounded. He's really grateful to be offered the job."

Awesome.

Her dad was notoriously weak where sob stories were concerned. But she wasn't. Not after a new hire almost cost their ranch veterinarian her license. Not after some asshole abused one of the horses. Not after some guy snuck into the clinic and attacked her, leaving her unconscious with numerous fractured bones.

She shivered before pushing her shoulders back and inhaling, slowly and deeply. After a few breaths, the warning signs passed. Focus on the now, she reminded herself. Not the past. Right. The now. Her dad's latest down-on-his-luck find. Sorry, but no way some *Rathborne* was going to come in and have it easy just because he used to be in the military. "You should've talked to me before offering him the job. I looked at the books last night. We need someone with experience. Someone who can pull their own weight and then some."

She absentmindedly scratched at her forearm, taking deep, measured breaths. "Not to mention, I'll have to work with him, too."

A large hand gently landed on her shoulder. "Meet him before you make any assumptions."

Tires crunched on the gravel driveway, and the room closed in around her. She pulled at the collar of her shirt, attempting to cool herself down. "Sounds like he's here."

Her arm trembled when she hoisted herself up from the chair to peer out the window. "Are you sure his application wasn't bogus? What kind of ranch foreman drives a blue Civic?"

Her father joined her, his uneasiness palpable. She tucked a strand of hair behind her ear, hating she was the cause.

"Guess we're about to find out," he grumbled, both walking out the back door and leaving the comforting aroma of banana bread behind.

The big red horse barn was only a short walk from the main house, but it may as well have been on the moon. Her brain picked up her feet in an unbalanced gait, carelessly dropping the lead weights to the ground with each harrowing step. She smacked a clenched fist into her thigh, her nails digging into the skin of her hand. Why was it still so difficult to walk? It had been six months since—since she'd woken up screaming on the hospital floor, covered in blood, as the hospital staff tended to her wounds.

You've got to stay off that leg, Katie. Your ankle will never heal if you keep putting stress on it."

She laughed, imagining Dr. Patel shaking his head at their next appointment. Come to think of it, she'd said the same thing to her own patients—back when she hadn't been too scared to still treat them. But how could she rest when there'd been so much work to do? It wasn't just that they were short-staffed. Working on the ranch was the only time she fully relaxed.

Thanks to having Koda around.

Even during her nursing rotation, rest was a rare luxury.

Her dad reached the barn first, but paused, waiting for her to join him before stepping inside. A rush of fondness swept over her. Healing slower was worth it if it meant being home, working with him on the ranch.

They stepped inside the shade of the barn; the smell of sweet sun-cured hay and horse manure wafted toward them. Katie took a deep, appreciative breath. She'd tried to describe the smell to people before, telling them she'd actually missed it while attending college, but the word "manure" always made them balk. Only people who knew ranch life understood when she said that smell was comforting.

Today, it did little to calm her frayed nerves. Or melt the icy daggers surging through her veins, straight toward her rapidly beating heart. Down at the far end of the barn a car door slammed. A man walked into view and ambled toward them.

Aware of the crackling in the air the moment he stepped through the entrance, she snapped her spine straight and emitted a tiny gasp. This was not the dead weight she'd imagined. He moved slowly. Purposefully. As if he calculated every footstep. His eyes remained obscured by the shadowy light of the barn, making them impossible to read even as he stood right in front of her. She swallowed, her suddenly dry tongue sticking to the roof of her mouth. Whoever this man was, he was anything but innocuous.

Dad shook hands with the stranger, and then stepped back and turned to her. "This is John Rathborne. John, I'd like you to meet my daughter, Katie."

"Pleased to meet you, Miss Locke." His voice was rough but warm, setting off a wave of heat within her belly. He sized her up, his dark gaze lingering curiously on her face.

She lifted her jaw and adjusted her sunglasses, making sure they continued to hide her left eye. The man was broad-shouldered and tall. His close-cropped hair was speckled with gray, but he had the body of a man in his prime. Her cheeks heated, and she tucked a strand of hair behind her ear.

"Katie's been working on the ranch her whole life," Dad continued. "Even during college and nursing school. She even got the head nurse to adjust rounds so she could help during the cattle drive. But things didn't—work out. Now she's back here full time."

John's cool gaze swept over her, and Katie couldn't help but feel like she'd been judged.

"I'm sure I'll be able to learn a lot from her," he said. She wasn't sure she liked the sardonic arch of his eyebrow when he spoke, either, but a faint beeping sound cut him off before she could question him further.

Dad craned his neck toward the house. "What's that?"

Her eyes widened. "Oh, my gosh. The banana bread! It's burning!"

"Oh, I should've known." Dad simpered. "Happens every time. I'll take care of it. Why don't you two take a moment to get to know each other?" He looked at her and nodded, warning her to be nice. "I'll be right back."

She shoved her hands into her jacket pockets and looked around the barn—at anything except the man in front of her. But her eyes fell back to his muscled arms. An electrical zing coursed through her body. Her teeth sank into the plump skin of her bottom lip, attempting to fight off the faint tingling sensation occurring between her legs. Obviously, she'd been holed up at the ranch for too long, to get flustered over some new hire.

"Katie, is it?" He extended his hand. "It's nice to meet you."

She reluctantly accepted it. His skin was rough and calloused, yet at the same time his grip was gentle. She fought the urge to relax into the touch. He looked down at her with a polite smile that didn't reach his eyes—blue eyes, looking out from a face creased with faint lines.

Her breath caught, and every muscle in her body tightened. She'd seen this man before. His face, his voice—somewhere—*I know him*—

The beeping stopped and she pulled her hand away. "Looks like the banana bread crisis has been averted."

Where had she seen him before? Or was this just another trick of her over-anxious mind?

"Your father mentioned we'd be working together quite a bit."

"That's right. I keep the books, so the foreman goes through me for purchasing and payroll and stuff," she said, crossing her arms.

"So, you just do all the financial 'stuff'?"

She had to bite back a gasp. Wow, this man really knew how to get on her nerves, quickly. "No, not *just*," she lifted her fingers to make air quotes, "the financial stuff, although that's quite a task on its own. I also keep track of the vaccinations, the inventory, the calving records. But my preference, for your information, is being in the saddle out on the range. Alone."

He raised both hands in surrender and took a step back. "Hey, I'm just trying to make conversation."

"Yeah, well, in the future, maybe don't start by suggesting I don't pull my weight around here." She snapped her mouth shut before she could say anything else. Her heart beat too fast, too heavy for her to tell whether it was anger or something else making it race.

The front door of the house banged shut and she flinched. Dammit. She smoothed her hair and straightened her sunglasses. This foreman was not going to rattle her, or take advantage of her family. She needed to be strong.

What I really need is Koda. But the dog could be anywhere, and this was not the time to be unprofessional, or show weakness. Not in front of a possible new hire.

The drum of her dad's approaching heavy footsteps calmed her nerves. In no time he stood beside her, placing a hand on her back. "I think you'll do just fine here," Dad said softly to John. "If you need a good physical therapist—"

Physical therapist? She'd forgotten he was wounded.

"I'll be fine, sir," John said. "Thank you."

Dad nodded. There was a pause. "What do you say?" Dad again extended a hand to him.

John reached for the older man's hand and shook it. "Sounds damn good, sir. It feels pretty great to be out on a ranch again."

Katie frowned, irritated with both of them now. So much for her input. This was her ranch too.

"Call me Mitch." Her dad crossed his arms. "You mentioned your uncle owned a place, yeah?"

"My uncle Matt Lewis. He had a place north of Billings, but sold it years ago."

"I knew Matt," Dad said. "He was a good guy. What's he up to now?"

"Retired to Arizona, last I heard. Seemed he preferred deserts to mountains."

There was a sudden rustling in the bushes near the front porch of the house. Sure enough, a moment later, a pair of dogs tumbled out. Two Bits and Nickel up to their usual tricks. She smiled, watching the two dogs chase each other around the yard. She turned back to her companions and her smile faded. John grinned, watching the canines' antics, but for a moment, he spaced out.

"You like dogs?" Dad asked.

John's grin disappeared, leaving his expression unreadable. "I do. Used to have one."

He shrugged and didn't elaborate which made Katie eye him suspiciously. What dog owner would let the chance to describe their pet go? She was curious, but not curious enough to ask him any questions. The last thing she wanted was to invite him to share personal information and expect the same in return.

"Why don't I introduce you to the other ranch hands? Our veterinarian, Linda Taylor, will be here today, so you'll meet her, too. We still need to hire some more people, but that'll be part of your job. We're a fast-growing operation here. I wouldn't be surprised if we doubled in size by the end of next year."

With every word he spoke, Dad's pride in their ranch came through loud and clear. And she couldn't blame him. They'd worked hard to build the business. After years of overcoming obstacles, they'd finally made a name for themselves.

When she'd been a nurse, pride was a foreign feeling. Relief, sadness, and dread dominated the job. And on some occasions, happiness. But never pride. But now she was back at the ranch full time, responsible for its success, she felt the same pride her dad did. And she couldn't wait to see where the next years would take the business.

Katie loved contributing to the ranch's success. She just wished she didn't feel so hindered by her past.

John remained silent as they walked around the main part of the ranch, scanning his surroundings. He shifted yet again, fiddling with the keys hanging from the carabiner attached to his belt loop. She frowned. Did he find the open countryside unnerving?

"We keep the cattle in the west pastures during the summer and move them to the south for the winter. It gives the ranch hands working space to remove the darn spotted knapweed," Dad said, kicking a tiny rock with the toe of his boot.

"Uncle Matt had issues with the ubiquitous plant. I remember, and not so fondly, spending my summers pulling the weed out of the ground. Sort of a punishment whenever my final school grades were subpar."

"Never thought of using it that way. Then again, Katie here hardly caused any trouble." Her dad winked at her before turning to face the grazing cattle. "You'll notice the meadow is close enough to view from the house; I learned years ago it's better if I can see my herd."

"Makes sense," John said.

"Katie and I will probably move the herd in a couple of weeks since you can't ride. At least, not yet." He glanced in John's direction as if about to say something before continuing to the next barn. "We keep our saddle mounts in here, plus anything else needing to come in due to weather or illness or injury. And that's

Linda's truck parked out there next to your car. I want you to meet her because you'll work with her quite a bit."

A soft breeze kicked up gold flecks of hay and dust, which floated lazily in a stray beam of sunlight. She leaned against the barn wall, hiding in the shadows, grateful for their familiar shelter.

"Linda?" Dad called out. While the barn seemed cavernous, the sheer number of stalls swallowed up his voice.

"This place is so big, I'm surprised anybody could hear anything in here," John said.

A thickset woman in her late fifties stepped out from one of the many stalls that lined the inside of the barn. Her graying hair was pulled into a messy bun and she wore coveralls and a short-sleeved work shirt. "We're down here," she called. "Koda and I are just checking on your weanling."

"K–Koda?"

Katie turned. John had repeated her dog's name as though he couldn't believe it, and it was enough to make her speak for the first time since they started their tour. "Yes, Koda. It means 'friend' in the language of the Dakota Sioux."

But he wasn't listening to her. His eyes focused on the tan dog with the narrow black face, who emerged from one of the stalls with Linda. The big dog's long muzzle appeared to break into a huge smile. Katie's tension evaporated as her four-legged companion bounded toward them. Koda was more than a dog. She was Katie's strength. Her protector.

"Koda! Come here, girl!" She crouched to welcome her friend and give her a good scratch.

The dog ran straight to John, jumping on him. She whined and barked, trying to lick his face, her tail wagging so fast it was a blur.

Katie's jaw went slack, brain formulating no thoughts. She closed her mouth, then swallowed hard. "Koda?"

Her dog had never done this for anyone. She'd taken months to get used to Katie and her dad, and had only recently warmed up to Linda. Katie watched numbly as Koda fawned over a complete stranger.

John laughed, rubbing the dog behind the ears and going down on one knee to half-wrestle her to the ground.

"She certainly likes you." Confusion colored her dad's voice.

"Yeah, I guess she does. I–I like her, too." John kept his head down and scratched just under Koda's armpits, her favorite spot. Her foot thumped in the air in ecstasy.

"John's our new foreman," Dad said as Linda walked over. "I guess Koda's telling me I made a good choice."

John looked up, about to reply, and groaned. The dog had taken advantage of his distraction to wash his face with her tongue. Everyone laughed.

Except Katie. She was too busy trying to calm the turbulent roll of her stomach.

"You some kind of dog-whisperer, John?" Dad joked. "I've never seen that dog take to anyone so quick."

Katie watched while Koda stared up at John like he was a long-lost friend. Could he have known her before? No, that didn't make any sense. If he'd fostered her as a pup or something, he would say so—not act as though he was as surprised as anyone at the love the dog was showing him.

A whine brought Katie's attention back to the scene in front of her. Koda lay on her back, begging with shining eyes for a belly-rub. She felt an ache, remembering how long it had taken before the dog felt comfortable enough at the ranch to ask for belly-scratches. *If Koda trusts the man this much, he can't be that bad.* She pushed the thought aside. "Come on, Koda. Let's go inside."

The dog reluctantly rolled to her feet and trotted a few paces but then stopped, looking back at John.

"It's okay," John said, still resting on one knee. "You can go."

Color drained from her face as her inner peace shattered. Koda. *Her* Koda. The one being in this world that Katie could count on to put her first, no matter what, had just looked to a stranger for instructions. An icy finger trailed its way across Katie's neck. Her chest tightened. She knew she should try some anxiety exercises, and quickly, because she was close to losing her fragile grip on control. But she couldn't. Her dog—no, her *lifeline*--had just shaken off her command to seek reassurance from the new ranch hand.

How could Koda do this?

The trembling inside her grew into a tiny earthquake. In another minute, the panic would be a deluge of ice water surrounding every limb, creeping higher until it passed her mouth and nose, leaving her gasping for air but not being able to do a damn thing about it. And eventually it would shut down her body as fast as punching a reset button. She needed to get out of there. Before anyone saw her break.

"Koda! Come. Now!"

She spun and ran across the yard, her heart hammering like it belonged to a rabbit running for its life, Koda trotting along at her side.

Chapter 2

John

John pulled into the local dive bar lot and shifted the car into park with a sense of relief. No doubt his mother would have words to say about his drinking once he got home. But tonight, he was celebrating. He'd found Koda. He grinned, remembering how the dog's eyes had lit up and how she ran right to him. *She remembers. Koda remembers me.*

After their last mission, he and Koda had been unceremoniously dumped from the military. He'd wanted to adopt her, but by the time he'd taken care of the red tape surrounding his return to civilian life, she was gone, assigned to a civilian family.

He undid his belt, leaning back in the driver's seat as a wave of exhaustion hit him. He'd been holding out for this day ever since he'd left the hospital. Ever since Fort Bragg messed up and adopted Koda out to a civilian family. Handlers always have first rights. Unable to trace her adoptive family through his military ties, he hadn't given up. He'd turned to social media in an attempt to find his indispensable K9 partner. John closed his eyes, picturing the image he'd plugged into Facebook of him and Koda together. She lolled on the roof of a Humvee, tongue hanging to the side of her mouth as if she was grinning. He leaned up against the vehicle right next to her—the same vehicle that was destroyed by a cheaply made Improvised Explosive Device just a few weeks later.

He knew his chances were slim. His therapy sessions over the last three months revolved around his ability to handle never finding her. And after nine months of searching, he'd come close to losing hope. Until today.

Shutting his eyes, he replayed the moment when she bounded up to him, and he knew—knew she hadn't forgotten him any more than he could forget her. Her rough tongue scraped his cheek and he laughed.

I finally found her.

But he could still lose her. He winced, remembering that the Lockes were her legal owners now. And while Mitch was a nice guy—maybe even a little too nice—his daughter was another story altogether.

His mouth soured. Katie might look delicate, but her sidelong glances had been sharp as nails. She'd sized him up pretty quickly. He could make no mistakes around her—not if he wanted to be near Koda. It was clear from her outburst that his former partner was much more to her than a ranch dog. There was no way she'd give Koda up without a fight. Hell, she'd probably even fire him to keep him away from the dog.

He shifted in his seat. He needed this job. Thinking of Katie brought up a spark of annoyance. The way her dad treated her with kid gloves and doted on her—it reminded him a little too much of his ex. His short-lived marriage had provided him with enough exposure to spoiled daughters to last a lifetime. Her possessiveness irritated him, too—if she didn't know Koda was far more than just a dog to him. He could not see her taking the news that Koda was his canine partner well at all—hell, she'd barely tolerated him standing in their barn. She was clearly a woman used to getting her way. *Still, I know Koda's safe and happy—and working at the ranch, I'll see her every day.* It was enough—for now.

Like hail on a glass pane, the drumming of his fingers was as relentless as it was loud, trying to still his mind. Each thump on the dashboard echoed the tumultuous thudding of his heartbeat. Despite finding her irritating, he couldn't shake off her words—or her soft, inviting lips. Rich dark brown hair fell in waves around a delicate face, made even softer by the absurd sunglasses she wore. Her hand, so soft within his, was taut with a tension she refused to reveal. Her ass, outlined by her tight jeans, had swayed as she stormed out of the barn. A small fire ignited within his belly and his mouth went dry. She was hot. So what? No guy wanted to be shot down by a woman—particularly a beautiful woman.

But was it the fact she was hot that made it sting? *Or is it that you know she's right at I won't be able to hold this job down for long?* John stiffened.

He quickly climbed out of his car, but it was too late. His jubilation at finding Koda had faded, replaced with a feeling of dread. He made for the bar, pushing his shoulders back as he approached the door. He'd found Koda. Nothing else mattered.

The bar's wooden door creaked as he opened it. The sallow light of streetlamps trickled in through the windows. The stench of stale beer and body odor rose to greet him. Along the wall was every hue of amber liquid in their inverted bottles; every vice his therapist recommended he avoid. He took a deep breath and headed toward the large mahogany bar. *Not crowded. Good.*

A blonde perched on a stool at the end of the bar. Her eyes playfully danced over his figure, and he fumbled as he pulled up a stool in the middle. The woman might be interested now, but she had no idea what she would see if he took off his shirt—much less his jeans. He caught the bartender's eye. "A Yuengling. Thanks."

The beer went down easily. He ordered another.

"And I'll have an Orange Butterfly." The blonde climbed onto the stool next to him. "What's your name?" She lolled her head to one side, flashing him a flirtatious smile.

"John." He forced himself to breathe out. Like his therapist said, he had to start making friends. Now that he'd found Koda, maybe it *was* time to move on. "What's yours?"

"Melissa." Stacks of silver bangles covered her wrists, clinking together as she twiddled her hair in a seemingly absentminded way. "Whatcha celebratin'?"

"New job." *I'm so goddamn rusty at this.* He hadn't been with a woman in so long that even casual flirting was exhilarating. *And casual flirting is the most I can hope for.* He still enjoyed the female form and sex was on his mind as much as it had ever been, but since that mission last year, things had changed. Most nights he sat in front of the TV drinking—and with good reason.

The several surgeries following the explosion that wrecked the Humvee had saved his life at the expense of his body. His legs and hip were a mangled mass of scarring. Any woman who got one good look at him wouldn't be yelling for more—she'd be running for the Pryor Mountains, screaming the entire way.

"Lost in your thoughts?" Melissa interrupted as she inched closer to him, gently taking his wrist in her hand. "Must be quite some job."

A jolt of electricity shot through where she touched him. "Yeah. It is." He winced. *Way to smooth talk the ladies.*

"I noticed you limping. How'd you get hurt?" She swirled the straw around the half empty glass of her fruity vodka drink. "Car wreck? Snow skiing? Motorcycle accident?"

"Army." He took a long pull of the cold beer.

"Oh. Did you ever kill anyone?"

Why was that always the first thing someone asks? He would never get used to such a question. He pushed down his annoyance, summoning a jaunty wink. "Not yet."

"What happened?" She gazed right at him.

"IED."

"Well, that's no fun." She set down her drink. "Want another beer?"

He didn't have time to answer. She'd already waved the bartender over.

"Same as before. For both of us."

He raised an eyebrow as the bartender placed their drinks in front of them. "I didn't say I wanted another beer."

"You didn't have to. I know what a man wants." She lowered her mouth to her straw, sucking aggressively.

He was able to smother his laugh, but not able to hide his grin. He turned, taking a gulp of the Yuengling to hide his amusement, but he wasn't fast enough.

"What's so funny?" She pushed out her red lips just a little, looking up at him through her eyelashes. "I'm serious."

"I'm sure you are. It's just—" John motioned to the straw. "My ex-wife used to do the same thing."

Morgan had thought it made her look sexy, but the first time she'd done it, John had assumed she'd accidentally ordered something sour. When he told Dirk about it later, he'd laughed. From then on he'd referred to Morgan as "lemon-lips" and John had struggled to suppress a laugh every time she repeated her "sexy" trick. And Dirk—

Dirk.

Dirk's eyes crinkled as he turned his head toward John, lips moving to deliver a wisecrack. But the words never came. There was a flash of light and John threw his arm up instinctively—

The sound of crashing glass brought his attention back to the bar. He stared at the broken bottle on the floor in front of him. His chest heaved, as if his lungs were slowly filling with water. He sucked in air as if it were molasses, each rapid breath a stabbing pain in his chest.

"What the hell, soldier?"

It wasn't his commander, it was Melissa, her pretty lips grimacing as she drew back her chair. Her nose wrinkled as she wiped spilled beer off her stockings.

"It was an accident." He fought to get his voice under control. "Guess I just put my arm out without thinking."

Around them, the other occupants resumed their conversations. John suddenly realized how silent the bar had been. *Was everyone watching?* Heat crawled up from his chest to his neck, cheeks, and ears.

"No harm done." The bartender stepped out from behind the bar with a dustpan and brush. He cleaned up the glass, dropping a towel over the puddle of beer. "Want another?"

"No thanks." John stared at his hands, putting down a wad of notes on the counter. "Think I'm done."

"Hey—"

Ignoring Melissa's protest, he staggered out of the bar. Cold, crisp air blew through him, chilling his bones. Brittle red and brown leaves whirled past him in frenzied tornadoes. He lurched toward the car as if he were back in the hospital, learning how to walk. The cool metal of his mother's car was a welcome relief against the fire pounding through his chest. His lip curled with disgust. So much for celebrating ... or even making friends. Just one more bar he'd never be coming back to.

"Where are you going in such a hurry?" A warm hand touched his arm. "Don't you know it's rude to leave a lady hanging?"

The soft curve of Melissa's breast rested against his arm as she leaned into him, even as her perfume teased his senses. "I'm sorry. But I need to go home."

Her hand rested on his hip, her eyes raked over his body. "You did say ... ex-wife?" She licked her lips.

At any other time, the gesture would have sent his heartbeat into overdrive. A hot woman interested in him—he'd be a fool not to take her up on her invitation. "Look. Melissa. I'm not your type."

"Big, strong, tough—honey, you're exactly my type."

Strong? John swallowed bile at the back of his throat. "You're wrong. You don't know me."

"I know men." The soft pressure of her lips against his sent an ache through him. He struggled to hold back the hunger that overtook him. *It's been too long.* This had nothing to do with a certain rancher's daughter revving up his engine before he ever showed his face at the bar.

He shoved that thought away and tried to focus on Melissa's body pressed against his: warm, willing, eager. The memory of soft lips pressed together in a scowl jumped behind his eyes. Katie Locke's sharp appraisal of his weakness rushed over him. He stepped back, taking a deep breath. This wasn't right.

"What's the matter?" Melissa's tongue ran the length of her upper lip.

He winced. "I'm not who you think I am."

She stared at him. Her eyes were dark. "What do you mean?"

"I'm messed up. Big time. The IED was loaded with shrapnel. I've got burns, scars where they had to dig metal out of me." He swallowed, quickly. Now was not the time to remember that. "I'll make you sick."

She frowned. "You're sure about that? A lot of women find a scar sexy, you know."

He glared at her. "This isn't a beauty scratch. Even my own mother winces when she sees them."

She laughed, low and throaty, and—despite the situation—sent a wave of lust through John. "Well, I'm not your mother." She stepped back from the truck, snapping her fingers. "Show me, big boy."

He blanched. "What—right here in the parking lot?"

Her lip curled. "I'm not asking you to strip. Just take your shirt off. So I know you're not giving me the push—or are you scared of little old me?" She batted her lashes.

He fought the urge to roll his eyes. Morgan had thought that was an endearing habit too. "I don't need to prove anything to you."

But what if she was right? What if there was a possibility a woman could be interested in him, even with his scars?

His heart started to pound. He'd had one attempt at a hook-up, back when he was fresh out of the hospital, and hadn't tried since. Maybe this time will go better. His stomach twisted as he pulled his t-shirt and sweater over his head in one movement. The cold air prickled his exposed skin. He stood at attention, waiting for her to speak, to react—to do anything.

"Oh my god." Her voice was choked, faint. She stretched out a hand toward him, then abruptly snatched it back as if she'd been burned. "What is this?"

He swallowed. She was staring at his ugliest wounds–raised, bumpy, and aggressively slicing into his skin.

"I told you. An IED exploded near me," he growled, a sharp edge to his voice.

"You said scars! This—this is horror movie territory." Her voice rose. He averted his gaze, but not before catching the utter repulsion on her face. "Do you even have a dick left?"

Rage seeped through his veins, his neck corded. His breath was shallow and his nostrils flared. He needed to get out of here, away from the vile creature standing in front of him. Without another word, he opened the door of his mother's car, climbing inside.

He gritted his teeth, slamming the door shut. *Stupid!* He slammed his fist on the dashboard and pulled his belt on so viciously it dug into his flesh. As he backed out of the lot and onto the road, the memory of a warm hand, hesitantly resting in his, and softly curling brown hair framing a warm smile as she listened to her dad's words, returned.

He forced the image of Katie, looking up at him, her lips parted, a soft blush stealing over her face, out of his mind. It hadn't taken her long to realize he'd been damned lucky to get the job as foreman. If she suspected what he was hiding ... he swallowed. *Katie can never find out Koda was my partner.* Not if he wanted to keep Koda in his life.

Chapter 3

KATIE

The sun streamed in through the curtains like a flamboyant guest, not waiting for an invitation, hitting Katie right in the face. Time to get up. She wished she could be a kid again, not a twenty-five-year-old unable to sleep in. Not that she'd ever slept late. As a kid, most days she'd been awake before Dad. Always excited to tag along with him to check on and feed the animals.

Her body wouldn't move from the bed. Her muscles didn't ache. Nothing was broken. Her mind was the problem. Or more the fact she'd be working with John was the problem.

This is ridiculous.

She rolled over in her slovenly sheets as the morning light continued to hiss in her face. Her disheveled hair scattered across her pillow. In the basket at the foot of the bed, Koda stirred. Knowing the dog was present usually made her feel secure. This morning, the sound made her frown.

She couldn't get over how Koda had instantly taken to John. *Why am I jealous?* She crinkled her nose. It had almost seemed as if the two already knew each other. *But that's not possible.* If he'd encountered Koda before, during a tour of duty, surely he would have said so, right?

She tossed and turned once more, sighing as the image of him, his face creased in pleasure as Koda licked his hand, rose in her mind. Her body warmed up from the inside out before she realized what was happening. Her eyes flew open. How could she get mad at Koda when here she was, practically drooling over him? Enough. The last thing Katie wanted was to daydream about the stranger her dad had hired as new foreman. A man she knew nothing about beyond the fact that he was a military veteran.

A very attractive, very sexy military veteran. Who seemed to disapprove of her for some reason.

"Ugh." She pushed herself up and out of bed, throwing on a pair of jeans and a t-shirt before tying her hair back into a ponytail.

Koda sat up in her basket, tail poised to wag.

It never ceased to amuse her how ready Koda was to greet each new day. Her mind and body relaxed. In that moment it was just the two of them. No John. No Dad. No one to fear or pretend she was ok to.

"Ready to go?" Slipping her sunglasses into her jeans pocket, she headed to the kitchen. *No way am I dealing with him without a strong cup of coffee.*

Now to find where her dad hid the supersized mug she'd bought herself at college. Thank god the coffee was already brewed. She grabbed the mug from the cabinet over the stove and poured the hot liquid, breathing in the rich fragrance. She lifted the mug to her lips, savoring each sip. *That's more like it.*

She wanted to enjoy her coffee, but the sound of the cattle in the distance had her gulping the remaining liquid, and she winced as it flowed down her throat. She put on her sunglasses and grabbed her coat. She headed out the back door and over to the barn just as the sun crested over the mountains, the biting autumn breeze pinking her cheeks. The warmth that had been in the wind just a few weeks ago had either evaporated into the sky or leached into the earth.

Dammit. Her heart kicked into gear the moment she entered the barn to find *him* there already. Waiting for her. Warmth swept over her skin instantly, erasing the chill from the air with ease while the smell of bacon, dirty motor oil, and chassis grease flooded her nose.

"Good morning—" he began, but Koda quickly ran to him, jumping up to put her paws on his chest. He laughed, roughhousing with the dog. "Well, good morning to you, too."

"Koda! Come!" The dog returned to her a moment later, tail drooping. She couldn't help but be a teensy bit impressed by his work ethic. That didn't change anything between them, though. She'd still prefer to work alone. "You're here early, Mr. Rathborne."

He shrugged and offered a polite smile. "I've been up all night looking forward to getting started. I'm grateful to get a job like this. Not everybody would hire someone who's been—who's been injured."

She dipped her chin. "Why not?"

"Because they're afraid I won't be able to keep up. That I can't do the work. Don't want to take a chance. But I assure you—"

"You don't have to assure me of anything." When she was released from the hospital, people had held the same expectation—or preconceived notion—about her. But it was the farthest thing from the truth. In fact, she'd jumped back into work full speed the first chance she had. Anything was better than dwelling on what had happened to her.

She gazed at his face and some of the tension eased from her shoulders. Her heart softened. She understood how frustrating and hurtful it was when people underestimated you—especially when you were still healing from unseen internal wounds. Then she caught herself. Better watch out, before she turned into as big of a softie as her dad. The only thing that mattered here was the work. And if Katie had managed to pull her weight after her life upended, so could he. "Just make sure you do the work and we'll get along just fine. My dad might be a push-over when it comes to vets, but I don't care."

His smile vanished. "Don't worry." A trace of bitterness colored his voice. "I wasn't at all sure your father would offer me anything. I learned a long time ago not to expect much from the world."

She felt a twinge in her chest, wishing she could retract her previous remark. But if he was anything like her, pity would only make matters worse. No one wanted to be pitied. "Good. Now, if you'll come with me, I'll show you what I need done first."

She started him moving last night's shipment of one hundred hay bales into the separate hay barn.

"No haylofts for us," she informed him. "Fire hazard. And it blocks the ventilation to have the stalls covered up by a loft. My father won't permit hay to be stored in a barn, so somebody's got to move it a bale at a time into the hay shed and reload it as needed into the wagon twice a day for feeding. And that somebody is you."

"All right." He looked up at the truck parked outside of the hay barn. "How long do you think you'll want me to take care of moving the hay deliveries? I mean, I can't supervise anyone else if I'm—"

"As long as we need you to," she cut him off. "When you're done with this load, we've got some broken fence rails on a couple of calf pens that need fixing. There's a stack of boards at the far end and you'll find a hammer and nails in the equipment barn. After, the stalls in the main barn need cleaning. I'll turn the horses out so they won't be in your way."

He just stared at her. "Anything else?"

"I'll let you know. Come on, Koda." She turned her back on him and walked away, the dog trotting at her heels. Anything else? Ha! He would be lucky to even last out the day.

She hesitated, mid-retreat. Maybe she'd gone overboard, loaded him up with too many tasks. Then she huffed and kept walking. John was a grown man. He could take care of himself.

All morning, she went about her usual tasks around the pens and barns. Periodically, she glanced over to the truck where he unloaded bale after bale. And on a couple of occasions, she lingered more than she needed to, admiring his strength. The way his muscles flexed. The line of sweat soaking the back of his shirt was stimulating. Even that he wore Merrill boots instead of regular ones.

Stop looking at him.

There was no need to waste her time admiring him, he'd never stick around. Never look at her like a normal person. Not to mention she still couldn't shake the fact he was hiding something. Or the feeling she had as if she'd seen him before, heard his voice before. That made her uneasy.

He moved all one hundred of the ninety-pound hay bales himself, stacking them first in one direction and then the other so they wouldn't fall. After, she saw him moving the heavy boards into place in the calf pens. The regular sound of hammer and nail that followed indicated he was busy nailing them down tight. She had to admit, he was a hard and uncomplaining worker.

As her stomach rumbled and she stood up from her desk, she realized it had been a while since she'd heard the hammer. Glancing through the main barn, she bit her lip. It didn't look like he'd taken so much as a bathroom break all morning. *I should make sure he gets a proper lunch break.*

She walked to the house and grabbed a small cooler, stopping to pick up a well-chewed green tennis ball from the porch before making her way back to the barn. Setting down the cooler in the doorway of the barn, she took the tennis ball and began bouncing it on the hard-packed dirt. Koda immediately jumped to her feet and leaped for the ball. The dog grabbed it on the third bounce and ran outside with her prize—just as John shot out into the aisle.

He breathed heavily, still holding the rake in his hand, his eyes wildly scanning all areas of the barn. Almost the way she'd done the first time she spotted a strange man after the attack.

She shoved her hands in her pockets, rocking back and forth on her toes, attempting to keep those painful memories at bay. "How's your first day going?"

He barely spared her a glance before returning to his perimeter scan. "What?"

"First day," she repeated. "How is it?"

"What was that noise?" he said.

She paused and studied him closely, this time noting how his face was pale beneath his tan. The way his knuckles blanched of color on the rake handle. And his posture, like a cat. Ready to spring at any second.

"Hey, look at me," she said, in the sort of soft voice she might use to tame a wild animal. When she had his attention, she added, "It was a tennis ball. I was bouncing it on the barn floor. Koda grabbed it and ran off."

He exhaled and gave her a slight nod.

"Good," he finally said, his own voice gruff. "It's going good. Getting back into the swing of things is always tough."

He didn't offer up any explanation for his odd behavior, so she didn't ask. She'd avoided conversations enough herself to read the signs. "It can be. Give you another few days and I'll bet you'll have the hang of it again."

His eyes widened at the unexpectedness of her encouragement. He started to smile at the same time that she scowled. He wasn't a baby, and she wasn't her dad. That was all she needed—for him to think she'd gone soft on him. There was no time, or money, to waste on another bad hire. The business wouldn't survive. "You'd better catch on quick because you'll have to. With winter coming, we don't have time to bring you up to speed."

He held up his hands. "I hear you, loud and clear." He eyed the cooler. "You don't happen to have some water in there, do you? Or is that not for the hired help?"

Her breath hissed between her teeth. Without a word, she handed him a bottle of spring water.

He grabbed the bottle and drank it all without stopping, making guilt twinge in her chest. She should have thought to offer him water sooner. She might not want him here, but that didn't make it okay to have him collapse from dehydration.

"Look," he said, finally catching his breath, "I could use a break. Is that okay with you?"

"That's fine. I'm here because I brought you lunch."

"Lunch?"

"Yes. Lunch. You know, that meal you eat in the middle of the day." She winced at how sharp she sounded and rubbed her forehead. There was just something about this particular man that got under her skin. "I know you've been working hard and I thought you might be hungry."

"I guess I am." He glanced at the cooler next to her. "Thanks."

"Don't mention it." She picked up the cooler and took it over to the plastic chairs sitting in the aisle near the door, outside of the tack room. She pulled one chair a few feet away from the other and sat.

He leaned the rake against the stall door and walked over to the other chair. He sat down gingerly, as though it was agony just to move. His back and knees seemed stiff, like the joints had locked in place and refused to move any longer, but he didn't so much as whimper. When he reached out for the ham sandwich she gave him, she saw his hands were cracked in multiple places and new blisters were forming on his fingers and palms.

This time, the twinge of guilt was hard enough to make her wince. "I guess I forget to tell you there are gloves in the equipment room. Any time you need them, help yourself."

"Good to know."

She held out an ice cold can of soda. A sad attempt at a peace offering, but it would have to do. "Sorry. Your hands should toughen up pretty quickly. In the meantime, help yourself to the first aid kid we have in the house."

Already wolfing down most of the sandwich, he wiped his hands on his jeans before reaching for the soda. "First aid kit? Who needs a first aid kit? I'm still raring to go. In fact, I was hoping that you'd give me some tasks that'll actually get my blood pumping next. This was like a walk in the park."

He managed to say it with a straight face, but his eyes twinkled. She snorted, amused despite herself, and played along.

"You bet. I'll see what I can do. By the way, are those boots really functional for the ranch?" She frowned down at his choice of footwear.

"What, are my Moabs not good enough for you? They're super functional, even in stirrups," he said, food crammed into the side of his mouth, causing his cheek to puff out.

"Really?" She eyed the boots doubtfully.

"What? You don't think the military teaches us to ride horses?"

"I never thought about it before," she said. "Do they?"

He nodded. "Some units need to know a lot of things, and that includes how to ride." He finished a second sandwich, along with the bag of corn chips and a fresh peach. And two more cans of soda. "That hit the spot. Thanks."

"No problem." She noticed the way he still favored his leg. "You might want to try some ice on your knee tonight."

His eyes softened. "Thanks."

A warmth filled her chest—and immediately she dropped her chin, focusing on the ground. "You've got nothing to thank me for." She stood and briskly repacked the cooler.

Koda trotted back into the barn, tennis ball in mouth, and dropped it at his feet. John took the gift and bounced it on the barn floor. Koda's head bobbed left and right as she followed her favorite toy.

"Hoping I'll throw this for you?"

Katie watched, the feeling of irritated confusion returning. "Never seen her take to anybody so fast."

"One dog recognizes another." He reached down and scratched Koda behind her ears. He launched the tennis ball out through the barn door, sending it near the house. Koda tore after it.

"Now you've done it." She crossed her arms over her chest. "She's gonna pester everyone to keep playing. She doesn't stop."

He laughed. "She's a working dog, not to mention a Malinois. She needs the exercise." Koda came bounding back into the barn, dropping the ball at his feet. He chucked it farther this time. Koda ran off, barking happily.

"At least you can throw far and get a break before she comes back. Some days I swear my arms are going to fall off."

"She's a good dog. I'll be glad to play with her anytime. Always good to have a partner to get you through the workday."

Partner. Every muscle in her body tensed. The idea that Koda would abandon her to be *his* partner gnawed at her insides, filled her veins with an icy fear. She stood up and turned toward the door.

"Koda! Come!" When the dog ran over to her, still carrying the tennis ball, she took the ball away and dunked it into an open toolbox. She slammed the lid shut with a satisfying thud.

"Mr. Rathborne," she said, her voice shaking, "Koda is not, and never will be, *your* partner, because she's *my* partner. I need her. She stays with *me*." Katie swallowed past the gathering tightness in her throat. "In the future, I'd appreciate if you left my dog alone. She's a working dog, not a plaything for you to toy with."

Then, before she lost complete control over the panic threatening to engulf her and melted right there in the barn, Katie hooked her fingers under Koda's leather collar and hurried her back to the house.

Chapter 4

JOHN

John cut through the Veterans Administration's gym. On either side of the building, he could see other vets working with physical therapists. Many of the men looked up as he entered. A few nodded as he passed. He should make more of an effort to get to know some of them.

He winced, remembering the events of his failed bar visit. Since arriving back home, he'd kept his distance from others. Especially civilians. They were always talking about how proud they were of his service. How much they appreciated what he did for the country.

It was all bullshit. *Service—ha!* If only they knew how little he'd done. *They wouldn't congratulate me. They'd hate me—they should hate me.*

Reaching the reception desk, he grunted his name at the cheery redhead sitting behind the computer. He didn't want to talk about his feelings or what had happened. He was sick of discussing the thoughts in his head and the emotions rattling around in his heart. And now he had another of his mandatory Friday appointments with his psychologist. For his *Post-Traumatic Stress Disorder.*

The receptionist waved him toward the waiting area, and he sank into one of the blue plastic chairs. His body ached, muscles stiff. He couldn't think of the last time he'd worked so hard. Still. Despite the aches and pains, it was nice to feel useful again. He'd be sleeping soundly tonight, that was for sure.

He cracked his knuckles, turning over the possible topics of conversation today. They fell into two categories: things he was willing to talk about, and things he was *not* willing to talk about. Most things fell into the latter category, but he found himself edging toward the former on certain topics. *If we can stick to the new job, I just might be able to get out of this unscathed.*

"What happened to you?"

Startled, he looked at a little girl of about seven or eight, her long hair divided into pigtails, a cast on her arm. Her eyes showed blatant curiosity.

The girl's mother sat in another one of the uncomfortable plastic chairs lining the waiting room. She was curvy, with dark curly hair that stretched down to her elbows.

"Bethany!" Her mouth curled up into an apologetic smile. "She's curious about anyone who's here. She knows—"

"No problem," he said. "I got hurt while I was in the army."

Bethany nodded. "My dad was in the army, too. He's in the office right now. I hope you feel better!"

What to say to that? "Thanks." He scratched his chin. "You, too."

The girl skipped away back to her mother.

"Staff Sgt. Rathborne. Right this way." The receptionist stood at the open door, ready to lead him to the therapist's office.

First time I've been relieved to hear them call my name. He waved goodbye to the curious girl still watching him.

"John, come in! How have you been this week?" Dr. Evans started each of his sessions with the exact same question. Everything about the man was predictable. He always wore the same grey cardigan with the same pleated khakis. He couldn't imagine the doc was spending his money on tailored suits or Italian leather shoes. Judging from Dr. Evans's horn-rimmed glasses that were taped in the middle and white tufted hair, John didn't think his cash was being blown on luxury cars or wild trips to Vegas either.

"Not bad." He plopped down in his usual place on the comfortable navy couch across the room from the doctor. "I got a job."

"A job! Excellent. What will you be doing?"

"Ranch work." He kept his answers short. Therapy sessions worked better when he revealed as little as possible.

"Ranch work." Dr. Evans beamed. "How do you feel about that?"

He leaned over, resting his elbows on his knees. "Glad to be getting paid, having something to do instead of wasting away in my room. And I like working outside. Maybe I can even fix up my truck instead of having to borrow my mom's car."

Dr. Evans smiled. "The blueberry, correct?"

"Yes, sir. Can you imagine what I must've looked like driving up to the ranch in that thing?" John smiled, leaning back in his chair. "Talk about first impressions. Hell, not sure I would've taken me seriously."

"And how are things going with your mother?"

John shifted his weight, making the couch creak. His mom was the reason he was here. Partially, anyway. After a very nasty, very vivid dream, he'd smashed up the bedroom. Supposedly, he'd threatened his mother, too, which was why she called the cops. He didn't remember any of it. But the fear in her eyes twisted his gut. So, he agreed to "get help." After all she'd given up for him, meeting with Dr. Evans was the least he could do.

"All right," he answered.

"Last time we talked about how she sold her house and downgraded to a small townhouse, saying it was to help you. You were very uncomfortable with that. How are you feeling now?"

"I didn't need her help. I told her—I told her I'd rather rot in the hospital before forcing her to sell her own house. It's the house I grew up in. But I guess stubbornness runs in this family and she did it anyway."

Dr. Evans tapped his pen against his notepad, his eyes peering over his horn rims. "John, accepting help isn't a bad thing. It's a healthy sign of strength to know when we need it."

John ran his thumb over the knuckles of his hand, his chin dipped.

"Are you still feeling those spikes of anger we talked about?" Dr. Evans crossed his legs, pushing his glasses up his nose.

"Nope."

Silence. His eyes rose to meet the older man's gaze. A frown covered his therapist's face, his pen poised in the air. John felt like a kid who'd been sent to the principal's office.

"John, we've talked about this. It's important we work through the issues you've been having. Anger likes to build up. Letting it out in a healthy way can help us keep it from getting the best of us." Dr. Evans took off his glasses and set them on the desk. "John, what would you like to discuss?"

"Can't we talk about my new job?" John folded his arms across his chest.

Dr. Evans gave him an encouraging nod.

"Like I said, I'm working on a cattle ranch not far from here. I work with the boss's daughter. She keeps the books and such. She doesn't like me much, but I'm managing all right. And there are horses and there are—dogs. There are dogs." He stopped, hoping it would be enough. He didn't need the doctor prying into his feelings about finding Koda, or discussing his options of getting Koda back, especially when both topics were emotional landmines. For a long time now, his mission had been simple: find Koda. He'd never stopped to think about any potential complications. Like the possibility that Koda's new owner might be both super attached and sexy as hell—sexy, despite the fact that she clearly thought John was beneath her. Plus, he wasn't ready to lose the job that had gotten him out of the suffocating condo. Out of the small room he barricaded himself in to keep away from his mother's watchful eyes. And working on the ranch made him feel useful. At least the physical labor gave him back a tiny sliver of the purpose he'd felt in the army.

Dr. Evans smiled patiently. "The outdoors can be calming. And I'm confident you will find a way to win over your boss's daughter. You're a driven young man. You've accomplished more than most people have at your age."

John sighed, veins pulsing as if he'd downed thirty cans of Red Bulls. These goddamn sessions were too long. Like the-fact-I-even-have-to-attend too long. And there was no clock in the room. Dr. Evans's way of eliminating 'last minute of school before summer break' syndrome.

Wily old bastard.

"How's the ride to work? Any issues with driving?" Dr. Evans asked.

John was flown to Bagram after the attack. Three days later he had his first seizure. He remembered the darkness that had crept up on him and engulfed him. Later, one of the other guys in the hospital told him he'd started convulsing violently, but he didn't recall any of that.

"No issues whatsoever. Glad to have gotten my license back. I thought it would never happen, but it worked out. Maybe other things will change, too."

Dr. Evans didn't say anything. He didn't need to. The look in his eyes as he polished his glasses told John all he needed to know—the answer was still the same. The life he knew, the one he'd dreamed of since he was a boy, was gone. He was never going back to the Sandbox.

My place is with my men, not here. God, I'm such a fucking failure.

"With the new job, I'm concerned about you getting enough rest. Especially for what seems like physically demanding work."

Pain flared in his chest, burning its way up his throat. Dr. Evans looked mild-mannered, but the doc never hesitated to probe the darker parts of John's life. The ones he locked down deep and wished he could forget.

"John, are you still having nightmares?"

The image of Dirk's mangled body snapped into his mind. Bile rose in his throat.

"You know what? I'm done with this shit!" He stood up, aware his actions proved he still needed Dr. Evans's help, but he didn't care. He just didn't care anymore.

"What is it you feel you're running from?"

"Fuck you. I don't run from anything." John shoved his chair over as hard as he could. Without another word he thrust the door open and left the office. Tears welled in his eyes as he tried to suppress the images of Dirk's dead body.

"Mommy, where's the army man going?" The young girl's voice broke through the storm in his head.

He fumbled for the door. He didn't want to wait to hear the answer.

He reached for the driver side door handle and his reflection greeted him in the window. *Goddammit!* He looked shaken—like a man on the brink of breaking down. *Can't even keep it together for one lousy session!* He was a failure—and it was becoming increasingly harder to hide it.

He kicked out, striking the edge of the curb with his foot. His bad leg screamed in protest. *Good. I deserve to hurt. I deserve to break every bone in my foot. I failed.*

Failed to protect his brother.

Chapter 5

KATIE

Katie took a deep breath, looking across the yard to the equipment barn. Going over the month's financial records with John was not how she wanted to spend the afternoon. She'd rather gouge her eyes out with a red-hot poker, but as her dad said, John had been at the farm a week and it was high time he learned how to keep the books.

She pushed her sunglasses back up her nose. This time, she wouldn't let her guard down. She was prepared for his good looks. But there was something about his combination of strength and the air of sadness around him, along with those too-brief glimpses of happiness, that pulled at her, drawing her in.

The steady clinking of dog tags filled the quiet hall. Koda stood beside her, tail wagging, tongue hanging out.

"Not this time, Koda." While having Koda around made her feel secure, the mystery of her dog's reaction to their new foreman threw her off guard. She couldn't risk Koda getting attached. "I won't be long."

Feeling as if she had cruelly deprived a puppy of a treat, Katie shut the screen door behind her.

The afternoon breeze tugged at her hair. Balancing the heavy ledgers on one hip, she tucked a stray strand behind her ear. No luck. The wind pushed it back in her face in mere seconds. With a sigh, she readjusted the ledgers beneath her arm and kept going.

At least it's only John. Her mouth twisted. There was no "only" about it. Any meeting with him was a confrontation. He might have charmed her father and Linda, but she wasn't so easily convinced. People were untrustworthy until proven otherwise, and she could tell John was hiding something—and she had every intention of figuring out what that was. Her father had been pleased when she'd offered to go through the ledgers with John, taking it as more proof he'd made a good hire.

So, here I am. Filling her lungs with as much fresh air as they could hold, she straightened her spine and stepped inside the equipment barn.

The well-lit space smelled of machinery and motor oil, not the hay and grain and horses she much preferred. A couple of farm bikes were parked in the center of the barn, with an ancient, rusting tractor in the back. The rest of the equipment was either leaned against the wall or stowed away on shelves. At the far end, light peeked through the crack below the door. Her dad had built the private office a couple of years ago, specifically for the ranch foreman.

She set the ledgers on the nearest shelf and smoothed her hair into place as best she could with her fingers. She ran her sweaty palms against her jeans, her breathing rapid and shallow. *Not now. Calm down.* Inhaling through her nose, she picked up the ledgers and held them tightly against her chest as if they were a shield. Placing one foot in front of the next, she made her way to the door and knocked loudly before walking in.

John jumped to his feet, phone in hand, as she pushed her way inside. His face was pale, and he seemed to be catching his breath as he stared at her.

"Um. My dad wanted me to bring the general ledger out here so we could go over it."

He took a deep breath, a hand against the back of the chair he'd just been sitting in. "Okay."

A battered tan baseball cap hung on the back of his chair, an earth-toned American flag patch on the front. "My dad wants you to look over the way we balance the different accounts. So, you'll become familiar with them for ordering and whatever." She dropped the ledgers on the desk between them.

"Makes sense." He pulled the ledger across the desk, taking a deep breath, as though trying to get himself under control. He looked at the ledger and sat, meticulously thumbing through the book.

She crossed her arms, leaning back against the door to watch. Did the ledger make him nervous? Or had something else rattled him, right before she'd come in? Concern crept into her awareness before she dug her fingers into her sides to shake it away. Enough, already. The jerk had probably lied on his application and had no idea what he was looking at, that was all. No wonder he needed to get himself under control.

Sitting at the desk, he didn't seem as ridiculously big as he usually did. And while he didn't have many wrinkles, those that lined his face were marked, as if whatever caused them had gone in deep.

She'd asked her dad to show her his job application. His birthdate put him at thirty, but something deep in his eyes looked much older. He moved like an older man, too. It wasn't the stiffness, the legacy of whatever injuries he'd suffered. It was the heaviness in his movements. As if living was becoming too much of an obstacle.

She watched him skim each entry, trailing a finger across the page to ensure he took in every detail before moving to the next. *Meticulous is not the word.* He applied his attention to their financial records the same way he'd applied himself to the tasks she'd set him.

The demanding day of tasks didn't end with the results she'd hoped for. Quite the opposite. Every job was completed. No complaints were uttered. And her dad was delighted with the way their new foreman was shaping up. While she found herself begrudgingly impressed with his skills, she was also worried that it would be even harder to get rid of him now. And she still wanted him to go. His presence sent her nerves into overdrive.

She swirled the ends of her hair around her finger, toe tapping the ground. More like beating the ground.

He glanced at her feet and then lifted his brows at her. "Do you have somewhere you need to be?"

Realizing how loudly her shoe had been assaulting the floor flooded her cheeks with warmth.

"We both have jobs that need to get done. And the cattle aren't going to feed themselves." She fought off the embarrassment, making sure each word's tone was perfectly measured.

"We've got time."

Easy enough for him to say. He didn't seem at all bothered to be stuck in close quarters with her, whereas being around him filled her with this itchy, antsy sensation that she couldn't quit pin down. To relieve the restlessness, she started pacing back and forth in front of the desk. The distraction didn't keep her from noticing every little move he made, though. Like the way he thumbed through the ledger. When her father licked his finger before turning over a page of the accounts, she found the motion endearing. When John did it? Her skin tingled, and she found her thoughts drifting to other ways he could put his tongue to use.

That unwelcome thought stopped her in her tracks. What? No! Not okay. Gritting her teeth, she pivoted toward the desk and began drumming her fingers on the worn wood. "So? Thoughts? You do have those, right? What do you think of it?"

With a smirk that infuriated her, he lifted a few pages of the ledger and let them riffle through his fingers. "Not a bad start. I mean, you've done a good job with the accounting, but this seems pretty basic for an operation of this size."

Her nostrils flared. "There's a section for each account. And we keep track on the master. It's exactly like every other general ledger for every other ranch around here." She leaned across the desk, turning the leger to the next section.

"You sure about that?" He gave the page in front of him a cursory glance and looked directly at Katie. "Hate to break it to you, but paper and pen is pretty outdated in this day and age—even in Absarokee."

She sat primly on the edge of the chair. When he looked directly at her, she felt exposed, like all her weaknesses were on display. She put a hand to her face, making sure her sunglasses were still there. "Are you saying we're behind the times?"

"Have you guys considered converting to a computer program? There's lots of good, easy-to-use software out there. A lot of it's free. I could—"

"Look." She cut him off as sharply as she could while alarm raced down her spine. Ever since the attack, changes rattled her. Even small ones. "My father sent me out here so you could learn how we do our bookkeeping—not so you could critique our system. We've been doing it this way for years and it's been perfectly fine. What makes you such an expert anyway?" She barely recognized her voice, as high-pitched as it was. "When was the last time *you* added up anything other than a bar tab?"

Both anger and uneasiness flooded through her—and then he laughed. A deep down, gut-busting laugh that had him leaning forward on his desk as he tried to catch his breath.

That laugh, the way the sound vibrated through her with the force of a rollercoaster. She'd heard it before. She'd definitely run into him before, but where? Right now, however, his amusement was irritating.

"What's so funny?"

"You are," he gasped, trying to catch his breath. "You're a real piece of work, you know that? You're acting like I set fire to your house when all I did was suggest you upgrade your accounting system. I didn't realize anyone got this hot and bothered over numbers."

Her mouth hung open. Hot and bothered? Was he messing with her now? Had he somehow peeked into her brain and witnessed the kind of deviant thoughts about him she'd been having? She pushed up from the chair so quickly its leg skidded on the floor. Her ankle gave a sharp spasm of pain, and she tried to hide it.

"Hey, wait," he called, as she yanked the door open. "You forgot your stone tablet, I mean, paper ledger."

She turned around to see him standing and waving the book at her, with a good-natured smile on his face. She took two steps forward, snatched the book from his hands, and turned to leave.

As she did, he added, "Think about what I said. You know, about the computer program. I'd be happy to teach you."

She froze in her tracks, her fingers digging into the ledger. This. This...*disruption* to her orderly life was exactly the kind of thing she wanted to avoid. "When I want instructions from a has-been soldier, I'll ask for them. Which means, if I were you, I wouldn't hold my breath."

The air in the barn practically crackled. "Whatever you say, princess." The edge to his drawl probably should have warned her to back off, but she was too riled up to care. How dare he judge her! He had no idea what she'd been through. What she'd survived. Zero.

"*Princess?*" She whirled to face him. "What, do you think I'm helpless? That I can't pull my weight around here?"

His folded his arms while he gave her a slow once-over. When he finished, his lips quirked up into an insulting smirk. "I don't know about pulling your weight, Princess, but you seem pretty happy throwing your weight around. If this is how you treat the people who offer to help, I can't wait to see what you do to the peasants who really piss you off."

Her chest burned at the unflattering picture he painted. She wasn't like that! How dare he judge her like that. "I don't think of people as peasants and I didn't ask for your help on updating the system. If you would just do as I asked, we wouldn't be having this argument in the first place!"

"You don't treat people like peasants, yet you want me to follow orders with only a yes, ma'am or no ma'am? Sure thing, Princess."

She sucked in a furious breath. "Quit calling me that."

The smile vanished from his face, his eyes locked onto hers. Piercing through her. "Then quit acting like the name fits. I might not have been born in the saddle, but I work hard and do my fair share and more. Even if I am a *has-been* soldier." He paused. "Although, you have a point. Maybe Princess isn't entirely fair, seeing as how you do work around here. How about I call you General instead? Since you sure as hell seem to enjoy ordering me around."

Shame flooded her, kicking her into defensive mode. "You may have fooled everyone else, but you'll never fool me. I know that you're hiding something, just like the others. And I'm going to find out what it is."

"Just what are you saying?" There was no mirth in his voice. His eyes were flat. How had she ever imagined them to be kind?

There was no way she was going to let anyone threaten the ranch. "You heard me. I'm watching you." She whirled around with the big heavy ledger stacked up in her arms—and promptly caught her foot on the doorstep.

The ledger went flying as she grabbed and missed the doorframe, slamming into the dirt floor of the barn. She spat out straw as she heaved herself onto her hands. Her body shook and she couldn't make herself move.

Strong hands settled on her shoulders. "Are you okay? Look, I'm sorry. I was just trying to dish out some of what you were throwing at me. Wasn't trying to get you hurt."

As if the fall wasn't bad enough, he has to go for my pride too? She snapped her head around to face him, determined to let him know what he could do with his pity.

But her eyes found worry covering his face. Like he actually cared. Her heart thudded. If she could see his regret—what did he see?

"I'm fine, just please, let go of me. Here, take the books." She thrust them at him, relief filling her when he released her shoulders. "I can get up myself."

She took a deep breath and pushed herself to her feet. Her body protested, but after what she'd been through, a little twinge of pain wasn't about to stop her. *Princess, her ass.*

"Here." He held out the books, almost like a peace offering and for a moment, when their eyes met, things seemed okay. Until he tugged at the collar of his shirt and started to smile again. "You know, a computer program would weigh a lot less than that heavy ledger. You wouldn't have to lug it around and risk tripping. Just saying."

She ripped the ledgers from his hands and only just refrained from whacking him with them. "How about I keep my ledgers, while you take that computer program of yours and stick it where the sun doesn't shine?"

"Is that an order, General?"

She stomped out the door and made her way across the yard, heart pounding and chest tight while his laughter trailed behind her. It wasn't until she was back in the house that she could breathe again.

She threw open the kitchen door and flung herself into the nearest chair. Tears welled up in her eyes, momentarily blinding her.

Koda's muzzle intruded into her vision as the dog laid her head on her leg. Her fingers ran through the coarse fur, and she buried her face into the dog's neck. "Always there when I need you."

The dog's tail scraped the kitchen floor as it wagged.

Taking a slow deep breath, she wiped her cheeks free of tears. Once the storm of emotions subsided, she was left with her parting words and the sound of his laughter echoing through her head. To her utter astonishment, she found her lips twitching. What was it about him that made her sound and act like a middle schooler? Had she really told him to stick his computer program where the sun didn't shine?

She laughed and groaned at the same time. And then she remembered what he'd called her, and her smile faded.

Princess. If he only knew.

Chapter 6

JOHN

John leaned a hand against the doorway of the equipment barn as Katie stormed back to the house, leaving him adrift in her wake. She might be small, but damn, if that slim form didn't conceal one heck of a verbal punch! *Hurricane Katie.*

Had he imagined the shine of tears in her eyes as she'd turned to go? His gaze lingered on her rapidly retreating figure. And how afternoon sunlight made her tawny beige skin glow. A soft breeze lifted her wavy hair.

His blood sizzled. Being confined in the tiny office with her had been a struggle in self-control. When she'd leaned across the table, he fought to keep his eyes on the ledger. Now, as he watched her walk away, the heat he'd been battling solidified into desire.

Dammit!

He rubbed his temples. He shouldn't have allowed the boss's daughter to rattle him. Not to mention, she already suspected he was keeping something from her. *And what would happen if she found out I'm Koda's former handler?* From what he'd experienced, she'd throw a fit and fire him. Mitch might force her to give Koda back and he would become the person who took away her friend, the one who ripped the dog she loved out of her life. Under that outer layer of bossiness, he'd started to notice that Katie was anxious. That she relied on Koda, for something more than just companionship. If he took the dog away, John would become the asshole she already thought he was.

But he'd learned some valuable information. The ranch had had some undesirable past hires. Mitch had mentioned an employee stealing some Ketaset from Linda. Almost cost the veterinarian her license.

John wasn't like that. This job meant something to him. It was an opportunity to start over. But it wasn't just her lumping him in with past hires that bothered him.

Old man—where does she get off? I'm not that old!

He sank back into the office chair with a loud groan and then shook his head. So maybe he did feel a little creaky for his thirty years. His time in the Middle East had drained some of the life out of him. He didn't just feel like he'd lost his youth. He no longer remembered what it had felt like to be young and free, without the burden of responsibilities weighing him down.

His phone buzzed with a message notification. He glanced at the screen and swore—his mother interrogating him about the new six pack of beer sitting in the fridge. He just couldn't catch a break. He loved his mom but sometimes, her concern was stifling. He stood and made his way outside.

The jingling of metal tags cut through the air.

"Koda?"

His black-and-tan partner ran over to him with her tail wagging.

He groaned as he took in the bright green ball gripped between Koda's teeth. "Not now, Koda. I have work to do."

Koda tilted her head inquisitively, her brown gaze hopeful. And of course, he caved. He never could resist those soulful eyes.

"Come here, girl." Dropping to one knee, he held out his arms. "It's good to see you."

He spent a few moments with his face buried in her thick fur. Koda was a much-needed distraction. Just the smell of her brought back a barrage of memories—not all of them welcome.

Dirk.

He stood and threw the ball as hard as he could. Koda raced after it, disappearing over a small rise.

He walked back along the row of pens near the horse barn. Most of the saddle horses had been turned out for the day to enjoy a little fall sunshine and they all turned to look at him. He filled his lungs with the fresh air. *Pure Montana air—nothing like it.* So far, the hardest part of the job had been leaving it to go and sit in that tiny hole of an office.

He kicked at a small rock. His foot connected harder than he intended. The rock ricocheted off a fencepost and hit a water trough inside one of the pens with a loud clang.

A couple of the horses spooked at the sudden noise. They trotted away, setting off a chain reaction amongst the others. Thundering hooves sent sod flying in an arching spray. Their heads extended forward, ears flat back, puffs of moisture escaping their nostrils.

Way to go. Can't even go an hour without scaring something. He stopped, resting his hand on the fence, waiting for the horses to settle down.

"Everything okay?"

He turned to find Linda, the ranch veterinarian, standing beside the barn, watching him. Great. Now he looked like an idiot in front of someone else. "Sure. Just looking at the horses."

"Did Mitch get a chance to assign you a horse yet?" she asked.

"I'm not going to be riding much."

"Oh? That seems highly unusual for a foreman." She smoothed back the few grey hairs that had escaped her messy bun while she'd been working, the wrinkles at the corner of her eyes deepening when she gave him a lopsided grin. "Especially since some of the tasks rely on you being able to ride."

He shrugged. "I was hurt during my deployment a while back. My legs are still recovering and I have some balance issues from time to time."

She walked over and stopped at the fence next to him. "If you can't ride, why would Mitch hire you as a ranch foreman?"

Straight to the point, this one. "He feels I have some other skills he can use." He shoved his hands into his pockets, resisting the urge to fidget. "Plus, my physical therapist said I'll be able to ride eventually."

She continued to study him.

His gaze fell to the ground—and immediately a burst of frustration erupted inside his chest. So what if she doubted his ability? Sure, the veterinarian had been working on the ranch for years, but she didn't have any say in his position. *Mitch is the boss, not her—there's no reason to feel like I need to convince her I'm right for the job.* Katie was already hassling him enough for the both of them.

Linda's comforting smile was at odds with her brisk question. "Well, there's no time like the present to find out whether or not you can ride. Come on. I have just the horse. Let's see how you do."

"Now?" His eyebrows shot up to his hairline, but she had already started walking toward the barn.

His heart sped up as they approached the barn. *It's just a little horse ride. You'll be fine.* The words weren't enough to stop the alarm rising in his chest. His doctors and therapists had spent so long drumming his limitations into his head that riding so soon felt like a bad idea. *But if I can't do it, there's no way they'll let me stay.*

As he walked inside the cavernous barn, she was already leading a tall gelding, his chestnut coat as fluid as water, out of the stall and into the aisle near the tack room. He had to be about sixteen hands.

"This is Redwood. You hold him while I get him ready."

Soft eyes met his, so still, they reflected promise. Redwood seemed quiet and patient like the horse his uncle Matt used to ride. *Maybe this won't be so bad.* He could only hope.

He ran his hands along the horse's neck as Linda curried, brushed, saddled, and bridled Redwood.

"I'll let you do all this next time," she said, leading the horse outside. "Right now, we just need to see what you can do in the saddle."

"Okay." Time to get his head in the game. If he psyched himself out before they even started, he had no chance.

Linda led Redwood into one of the empty paddocks. "This will do for your first practice ride. Not too big, not too small. Now, do you think you can get up by yourself? Or do you want to stand on the fence while I hold him for you?"

John hesitated.

"Koda? Koda!" He heard Katie's voice in the distance.

Pride kicked in. He hadn't ridden a horse since high school, and his knee sent a shot of pain through him whenever he bent it too far—but he was not about to let anybody know. Especially not the veterinarian who held his job in her hands.

"I can get on him." He walked around to the horse's left side and began gathering up the reins.

"Of course. Just take it slow." Linda rested her hands against the fence.

He snorted. Like taking it fast was an option. "Are you a veterinarian, or a physical therapist?"

She cocked her brow again. Must be her signature look. "I had a pretty good fall off a horse years ago. I've been through extensive physical therapy, too. I'll look out for you."

His face heated with embarrassment, yet a weird gratefulness for her understanding coexisted with it. Not knowing what to say, he forced his left foot up into the stirrup, and grabbed the saddle horn. He took a moment to gather his strength and pulled himself up into the saddle.

It was a clumsy mount-up—he could feel Redwood stepping over to keep his balance—but he was up and he'd done it by himself. His chest puffed out in response to his elation.

Settling into the saddle, he allowed Linda to adjust the stirrups for him. His grandmother had done the exact same thing when he'd learned to ride as a kid, and the warmth of the memory put him at ease.

She stepped back from her handiwork with an approving look. "Give it a go."

He nudged the horse with his legs. Redwood began walking around the pen. The motion was both familiar and foreign. Wave after wave of childhood memories flooded over him with every long rocking step the horse took. He eased back in the saddle and let his body become part of the horse's gentle movement.

The forced bend in his knee caused him no small amount of pain. He ignored it. He was riding a horse! A few months ago, this would have been impossible. But now—a wide grin stretched across his face and stuck there.

Take that Dr. Evans and your PTSD! And you, bastard terrorists—you think your piece of shit IED was gonna stop me? For a second he could feel the heat and smoke of the desert. He swallowed as the desire to go back and make things right rose in his chest, even as he knew he'd never be able to do it.

Dirk's image raced through his mind. A shudder traveled the length of his spine. He tried to concentrate on the horse as he began jogging him around the pen, but the memories came on thick and fast.

"That's enough." Linda's words jarred him out of his dark thoughts. "Let's bring it in."

He guided the horse to a stop and gingerly swung himself off the saddle. When he landed on the packed dirt, he winced. His knee had stiffened considerably. He took a careful step. To his relief, his foot held, more achy than painful.

Linda opened the gate for him and motioned him to lead Redwood through. She watched his progress with a sympathetic smile. "You'll need to practice every day, but I'll tell Mitch you aren't hopeless."

Pride reared up, and his hands clenched into fists before he eased them open again. *Relax. She's just trying to be helpful.*

He hated the idea of being anyone's pity case, though.

"How many other guys work here?" he asked as they made their way back to the barn. His knee still ached, but he'd be damned before he let her see his discomfort. He'd made too much progress.

"Four—including you. Mitch would like to hire at least three more. Last year winter came on early, but every forecast we've had suggests this year will be milder, which means more work can be done. Winter's our slow season, but Mitch wants to be ready."

"Apparently, I'll be the one doing the hiring." A slow smile crossed his face. It felt good to be in charge of something again.

"Fine with me. I'm much happier working with the animals and not the humans, for the most part."

Koda reappeared, ball in mouth. She barked, dropping the ball, and frisked around at John's feet.

Linda paused to watch. "Koda does seem quite taken with you."

"Nice dog," he replied as nonchalantly as he could. Katie was suspicious enough for two people. He didn't want to make Linda wonder, too.

"I think she's got some degree of PTSD. We know she was a military dog, but we don't have too many details on what might have happened to her. All I know is she sometimes seems startled by certain loud noises—things that don't bother the other dogs."

"PTSD? In a dog?"

"Yes. I've seen it in dogs and horses both. Is it something you're familiar with?"

He realized her bluntness was part of her manner, not personal—but that didn't stop the sense of failure from rising in his chest. People might say PTSD, but he knew what they meant: broken. Why couldn't people leave him alone? Whenever he met someone new, they tossed around that word as if they were all licensed psychiatrists.

Lucky dogs, though. At least they didn't have to suffer through useless therapy sessions.

"I'm only familiar with it in people. *Other* people." They led Redwood into the barn and stopped outside the tack room, hooking the left stirrup over the saddle horn so he could loosen the girth.

"Just figured you might be able to help. As a veterinarian, there's only so much I can do. Katie's been committed to rehabbing Koda—but when I saw the connection the two of you had, I figured it couldn't hurt to have one more person in her corner," she said, handing him a curry comb.

Is she talking about the girl or the dog? He rubbed his forehead. He was getting a headache from trying to follow the vet's conversation.

"I like dogs. That's all." The moment the words left his mouth he felt like an idiot. All he wanted to do was get out of there, but he still had to get Redwood unsaddled. "I've got to go up to the house and report to Mitch."

"See you tomorrow," she said, tipping her hat.

Once Redwood was curried and eating his hay, John set off toward the house. He took his time walking up the winding driveway to the Three Keys Ranch homestead. It was a rambling white affair with a wraparound porch. Large prairie grid windows dotted the outside of the house and a gigantic oak tree spread its thick limbs over much of the roof.

He had to admit he liked the look of the place. He could envision peacefully sitting out there on the porch after a long day's work, just gazing out over the twilight with a cool drink in his hand and Koda at his feet.

Goddamn. His lips quirked. *I am an old man.* Fantasizing about sitting on the porch, watching the grass grow? *Just as well it's not my house.* He took a deep breath, raising his knuckles to the door. It was Katie's house, and he'd be lucky if she'd so much as let him knock on the door.

And that was *before* she found out that Koda was his dog.

Chapter 7

Katie

Katie stopped when she saw John in the doorway, regretting having changed out of her oversized work shirt, heavy Levi's, and boots. Work clothes were armor, warding off unwanted attention. But a simple white t-shirt and fitted jeans might put her in a situation she wasn't ready to be placed into. Especially with the sexy foreman. *Stop thinking of him that way.*

She kept the screen door closed between them. "Can I help you?"

"I need to talk to your father."

"He's in the kitchen."

"Thank you," he said, pulling the door open.

The small entryway wasn't big enough to hold both of them. Taking a large step back, she ended up against the wall, leaving nowhere to run. She was trapped. Not the good trapped.

Panic set in like a cluster of spark plugs in her abdomen. Her breathing became more rapid, more shallow. Heat traveled up her neck and covered her face. A thick lump formed in her throat. Her brain synapses fired like a hyped-up internal aurora borealis. She couldn't speak. She couldn't swallow.

Closing her eyes, she internally repeated, *"I'm ok. I'm home, I'm safe. I'm ok."* Her breath fell into a steady pattern. The heat retreated from her face and her shoulders slumped forward.

A panic attack. In front of John. This night can't get any worse.

Her eyes opened to meet his face, taut and full of concern. She tried to swallow but her throat stuck, waiting for his response. Her head tilted sideways and brows creased in confusion as he backed out of the hallway and onto the porch.

He raised his hand to the door. "Knock, knock."

She stared at him, a small smile tugging at the corner of her lips. *Is he serious?* "Please tell me you don't expect me to follow with 'who's there?'"

"Kanga," he replied with a straight face.

She huffed an exasperated sigh and folded her arms, but when he continued to stand there and sigh, she gave in. "Kanga who?"

"KangaROO, not who. Duh."

She blinked. "That is literally the stupidest joke I've ever heard in my entire life."

"Yeah? Then why are you trying not to laugh?"

"I'm not!" But he was right. Her lips were twitching. His obvious ploy to ease her distress had obviously worked, and Katie couldn't help but be grateful for the unexpected kindness. "Okay, maybe I am, but only because it's so stupid."

The skin next to his eyes creased invitingly as he smiled. "Whatever you say. But I do still need to talk to your father." His eyes roamed over her face.

Her *bare* face, she realized. Shit. No sunglasses and hair tied back. Even worse, she was standing under the light. She stiffened and stumbled back while turning her head away to hide. "I told you, he's in there, so just go in already! Please!"

The heavy creak of floorboards filled the still night air as he walked past without saying another word.

She placed a hand to her face. *How could I have been so careless?* She ran her fingers over the scarred cheek and slightly asymmetrical eye socket the fractures had left. Her face had healed as much as it was ever going to, and the doctors had told her from the start she would never be entirely the same.

She'd never for an instant forgotten how she looked. Until now.

All because she'd allowed the new ranch hand to rattle her. Again. Yanking out the rubber band, she brushed her hair down near her face with her fingers. He might have caught her off guard, but she was not going to leave their ranch foreman wandering around her home unaccompanied. Especially since she hadn't figured out what he was hiding.

She found him standing alone in the living room as if he'd gotten stuck on the way to the kitchen, and she didn't blame him. A strength filled the room, originating from the wooden walls. The large bay windows—Nickel sleeping underneath—faced the east so the warmth of the morning sun filled the room in the morning. And they offered a beautiful view of the purples, blues, and golds of the evening sunset. Like a Salvador Dalí painting. Everything in the room had been built, made, or bought through the hard work of her ancestors. This home had sheltered the Locke family for four generations.

It was old, heavy, and rustic, but comfortable and inviting, too. Gleaming wooden floors lined the entrance hall and continued up the stairs. Plush carpet runners ran down the hall leading to the kitchen. Framed paintings of herding dogs, Black Angus cattle, and stock horses lined the walls, while the wooden beams expertly framed the darker wood of the roof.

"Cozy." John's raspy voice danced through the air. "Makes a nice place to relax after a long day on the ranch." He laughed a little. "The only thing my mother's house makes me think of is an explosion in a Laura Ashley knock-off store. She's stoic most of the time, but has this inexplicable fondness for florals and delicate little designs."

Katie didn't realize she'd started to smile until a clatter of dishes caused Nickel, ever hopeful for food, to take off like a shot. She firmed her lips back into place. before following the puppy into the kitchen, motioning to John to come along.

"Come on in!" Dad smiled, clearly pleased to see John following behind her.

She watched as he studied everything in this room as well. Hadn't he ever seen a ranch kitchen before? A sizeable stove with eight burners was set up along the wall, while a gleaming wooden island held a basket of fruit and a few trays of desserts. Shining copper pans dangled above the island. The main window in the kitchen opened onto a stunning vista of one of the pastures.

A faint smell of acrid smoke lingered in the air. "Oh no."

"I'm afraid somebody's burned the banana bread again." Her dad stepped away from the stove and held out a loaf pan. He looked almost comical with the floral oven mitts on his large hands. "Too bad, because Katie makes the best."

"Maybe I'll get a chance to try it sometime," John said.

She glared at the back of his head. *You should be so lucky.*

Her dad dumped the burnt bread into a trash can. "So, John. That you I saw putting Redwood through his paces?"

"Other way round." John stood stiffly at attention, like he'd only just stopped himself from adding "sir" to the end of the sentence.

Dad offered a bemused smile. "How did it go?"

"Seemed to go fine. Linda said we'd practice every day. I should get the hang of it faster than I thought."

Katie's eyes narrowed as she crossed her arms. Somehow, she'd become the third wheel in her own house. What was it about this man, that allowed him to insert himself here with such ease? "Linda can be persuasive, can't she?"

Both men spun around, as if finally noticing her presence.

"I'm not sure that's the word I'd use," John said.

"Maybe not. But she always has your best interests at heart. That's what I've learned over the years." Dad turned to wash out the hot pan. A sizzling sound erupted from the sink, followed by a cloud of steam. "By the way, I've got the list of five men who've called about the other positions. Do you think you can get the interviews done within the next couple of days?"

"Yes, sir."

She rolled her eyes. Such a good soldier, so deferential. And such bs, compared to the way he'd spoken to her earlier. In fact, John and her dad seemed completely at ease together. Not like the sparks that flew when she and John had to inhabit the same room.

Obviously, he was trying to impress his new boss. But he'd still have to go through her to negotiate pay.

"Glad to hear it. And I'm glad you've decided to come aboard. You'll fit in fine here," her dad said.

"I'll do my best," John said. "If that's all you need right now, I'll be going. Looking forward to some sleep tonight."

"Of course. See you in the morning. And Katie—walk him out to the porch, would you?"

"What? Why?" Her father just smiled patiently at her, turning back to the stove. With a sharp look at John, and Nickel at her heels, she headed for the door. Just as her father asked, she walked all the way out onto the expansive front porch and stopped.

John paused against the porch rail a few steps down. "Beautiful view."

She looked out over the pastures, at the dark silhouettes of Koda and Two Bits against a velvety sky as they trotted through the nearby fields. The last vestiges of the setting sun disappeared over the horizon, the copper hues giving way to a dusty purple glittered with stars.

"I'll bet you like sitting out here to relax."

She shrugged, not caring to discuss with anyone what she did to relax. Especially him.

But he tried again. "So, tell me. Are your dad and Linda dating? I can't figure out their relationship."

What did he just say? "Excuse me?"

"Just the way they interact. I was curious." He smiled.

Her eyes widened and her mouth dropped open as if he'd just produced a rhinoceros from his pocket. "That's none of your business. But—if you must know—the answer is no. Linda's been working here for eight years. She and my father are good friends. I mean, she's been like a mother to me, but I've never seen her and my dad act in any way that would suggest they were more than friends."

"So, I guess it's been nice you've been close to Linda, too. You all do seem like a family out here."

Her eyes narrowed. *This man sure is nosy—almost to the point of being intrusive.*

"Linda's done more for me than my own mother ever did and I wouldn't care if she and my father *were* dating. But they're not. And we are family. A tight knit one that doesn't easily let newcomers in. Especially ones hiding something."

Her eyes focused on him, waiting for a tell. But he just sighed and dropped his head. "My dad left when I was young. It was tough not having him there."

She flinched at his admission. *Nice one, Katie. Way to open old wounds.*

The twilight deepened, the shadows stretching further across the yard. "Sorry to hear that. My mother did the same thing. I was too young to remember. My dad searched for her. He thought she went back to Tongue River. But she wasn't there."

"Tongue River." He turned to face her. "You mean the reservation? You're Cheyenne?"

She raised her chin. "Part."

"I figured Crow, since the reservation for the Apsaalooke tribe is close by."

"You shouldn't make assumptions like that."

She'd shared enough with the foreman for one night. Maybe even a month. And it was time for this conversation to end. Stepping to the top of the stairs, she called out to the dogs.

"Koda! Two Bits! Come."

Two dark figures with four legs and ears raced across the field. Both animals tore up the steps, pushing past her in their rush to get through the storm door she'd left propped open. Knocked off balance, she squealed and collided with John's chest. His arms caught her. Kept her from falling farther.

For a moment, she relaxed in the security and strength of his large arms. It felt nice, being cradled against a rock-solid body. She couldn't remember the last time she'd been this physically close to another human being, with the exception of her dad. The next instant, her heart began to ricochet off her rib cage. Her body was reacting as if it was a horse being chased by a pack of coyotes. His arms turned into a trap. One that her pounding pulse urged her to escape, at any cost.

"Let go of me!" She yanked away, grabbing the railing to steady herself.

He released her, throwing up his hands. "Sorry. I was just trying to keep you from falling." He inhaled deeply. "Look, I get it. For whatever reason, you don't want me here. You've made that clear. But I work here now, and I was just trying to make polite conversation. To let you know me a little, so I'm not just some stranger."

"Maybe you should give up the attempts at conversation." She pinched the bridge of her nose, trying to suppress the bile making its way up her throat. *Breathe in. Breathe out. It's okay. You're okay.*

"I don't know what I did to get on your bad side, but I can see there's no point hoping we'll be friends."

He didn't understand. How could he when he had no way of knowing her past? It wasn't his conversation at all, but the way he'd grabbed her. In a split second, she'd gone from being in the present to getting sucked into the past. She'd overreacted, she knew that. But in that moment, instead of being the strong woman who'd survived, she became the frightened child, damaged and afraid, awaiting the next beating. And she hated herself for reacting that way. She hated that something so simple as a man touching her to keep her from falling could leave her feeling so weak.

But she wasn't about to explain all of this to him. Her past was none of his business.

"Look, I've got work to do tonight. You've got interviews in the morning. We both should just get some rest," she said, exhaustion taking over.

"Listen," he said, scratching the back of his neck, "I've got a deal for you."

"I don't do deals." She had no energy left to fight. To keep him away.

"Hear me out. I promise to stop trying to be friendly to you—if you promise to stop acting like I don't know how to do my job."

Her lips pursed. "No more questions about my private life?"

He nodded. "If you stop taking every suggestion I make like a personal attack."

Her cheeks heated. She'd actually looked up accounting software online and discovered some free tutorials—not that she had any intention of mentioning it. "All right," she said while eyeing him warily. "But you're new and we don't really know you. So, you're not entirely getting free rein to run things."

He sighed and raked his fingers through his hair. "Don't worry, Miss Locke. I'm not sure what sort of employees you've had in the past. But I can assure you, I take whatever job I do very seriously. Okay?"

His eyes were intense on hers while he waited for a response. Her mouth went dry. She licked her lips and his gaze followed the motion, sending a jolt sizzling through her. "Okay," she said. At that point, she'd have been willing to say just about anything, to get him to leave.

She remained on the porch as he walked to his truck. Her eyes momentarily settled on his round, muscular backside. She watched him walk for several long strides before she grimaced and turned away.

Stop, already. He's an employee and you don't even trust him. Or like him.

Did she?

She bit her lip and then cursed under her breath before slamming the front door. The stairway echoed the loud stomp of her boots up to her room. She was acting like an idiot. What difference did it make if she liked him or not, even a little? Nothing would ever come of it. Once he found out how broken she was, he'd run. No doubt he already thought she was unhinged, what with the way she'd freaked out over a simple touch. Even if his presence turned out to be on the up-and-up and he took an interest in her, how could she expect him to live the rest of his life like that? How could anyone?

Reaching her room, she closed the door, standing alone in the darkness.

Chapter 8

JOHN

For one panicked, gasping moment, John tasted copper in the back of his mouth. The shock of the initial blast faded, replaced by the acrid smell of the fertilizer used to create the explosive. Fire crackled as the Jeep burned. John knew he should move, but his body didn't respond to his commands. It was cold, clammy, as if he was already dead.

He jerked upright, shivering. His shirt was soaked. It took him a long moment to recognize the walls of the office or the desk in front of him. Feeling like he was sinking into a cavernous hole within himself, he leaned forward in his chair, resting his head in his hands. He'd fallen asleep waiting for the next interview to show up. His eyes wandered to the clock above the window. *Still early.* Taking a deep breath, he pulled out his phone and clicked on the social media app. He'd been meaning to post an update about Koda.

Thank you to everyone who shared this message. I found my canine partner. She is with a good family and she will stay with them.

He reviewed what he wrote, hesitating on the *she will stay with them* part. His heart filled with heaviness, but then he reminded himself of the way Katie relied on Koda. He clicked the post button before he could change his mind, scrolling on down the newsfeed.

Melissa.

His unsuccessful bar hook-up appeared in one of the pictures. A friend of a friend had posted a photo of a backyard barbeque. And another guy was holding her close. She was smiling at the camera, her arms entwined around the guy's neck.

Her latest looked like a classic meathead: buzzed haircut, oversized muscles, and the empty smile that made you wonder how many IQ points resided between his protruding ears. But hey, at least he didn't have the kind of scars that made women run. John grunted and continued to scroll past the picture, but not before blocking the friend of the friend who'd posted it.

He hoisted himself out of the chair to stretch his legs, making his way to the bathroom. For a few moments he stood in front of the bathroom mirror examining the lines and cracks on his face.

He looked worn. Beaten. What had been stubble just a few days ago was now a scruffy beard threatening to take over his face. He brushed his fingertips through the thick scruff, but as he did so he didn't feel hair. He felt desert sand and bits of shrapnel from the Humvee.

Maybe getting rid of the scruff would help. He grabbed the gel from the small bag of toiletries he kept in the bottom drawer of the vanity and rubbed it on his face, watching it turn to light green foam in the mirror. *That's a start.* Once his face was liberally coated with shaving gel, he picked up the razor. As he set the can of gel aside, he snorted at the label. Snakeskin scented. How do they come up with these things? Did a snake's skin really have a scent?

Suddenly there was a loud noise and he found himself staring into the mirror. The shaving cream can and the razor were both in the sink. He didn't remember dropping them. He gripped the sides of the sink so hard his knuckles turned white. Sweat beaded on his forehead as his breath came fast and ragged.

Panic attack. The moment he acknowledged it for what it was, he felt the familiar flush of shame and embarrassment.

After a deep breath, his heart rate began to slow. He hunched over the sink and splashed cold water on his face to rinse away the thick layer of gel. He felt sick and worn out even though he'd just woken up from an impromptu nap.

He scratched his chin. He could shave another day. So what if his stubble had become less 'sexy-devil-may-care' and more 'scruffy-but-who-cares?' He didn't. Care, that is. With a sigh, he exited the bathroom.

There was a light thumping of paws in the dirt yard outside the equipment barn. He turned his head toward it. Koda trotted through the open doorway.

"Hey girl." Some of the heaviness in his body eased. "Katie's not with you, is she?"

The dog wagged her tail. When Katie didn't appear, his entire body relaxed. The thought of dealing with the cantankerous Katie right now was almost more than he could bear. Things had been better since their "deal," but she didn't have to try to get under his skin. She only had to glance his way, and he felt as clumsy as a cadet on his first day of training. At least when she was openly hostile it had been easier to ignore the sheer perfection of her slight but curvy form. Now? He'd come dangerously close to getting caught checking her out more than once. *Ogling my boss. Yeah, that's a smart idea. Especially given the way she recoiled when you touched her on the porch—and that's without seeing your scars.*

Plus, keeping the secret of who Koda was to him meant he had to watch his interactions with the dog. He glanced around the yard once more before kneeling to pet Koda. He didn't want anyone else getting curious about why the two of them had such a close bond.

He stroked the soft, wavy fur and closed his eyes. This was stupid. He was stupid. Now that he'd found what he'd came for and made his decision about leaving Koda with her new family, he should leave. Sticking around would only make leaving Koda harder...and make his motives for working at the ranch more likely to be discovered.

To be honest, he was surprised no one had figured it out yet. Koda's eyes creased with pleasure and her tongue lolled out as he patted her. Her tail whacked the barn floor in pleasure. To him, the dog's happiness was obvious. But people had a habit of seeing what they wanted to see. Who would expect Koda's handler to show up at the same ranch where she'd been retired?

If the new owner had been anyone else, he likely would either have taken the dog with him or at the very least, told them who he was. But not with Katie. She was jumpier than a kangaroo, and she already saw him as a threat. No telling how she'd react if she found out about his ulterior motives. As irksome as she could be, she needed Koda. Anyone could see that. Only a completely self-absorbed asshole would take Koda away from her right now.

He got up, closing the office door before sitting on the floor of the barn to play with his friend. "I've missed you so much. I'm glad you're okay."

Koda licked his face and plopped down in his lap. Her tongue hung out of her muzzle.

Laughing, he rubbed her belly. "You're such a silly girl sometimes. I'm glad you're happy here."

Tires crunched over the gravel. His last interview had arrived. He quickly got to his feet, Koda springing up after him. He smiled to himself. Feels just like old times. He walked out of the equipment barn to greet the man with Koda at his side. Let's hope this guy is a better fit than the last three.

A short guy, square like a wrestler, with a perfectly tanned bald head and dark aviator-style sunglasses, got out of the car. He took his time looking around the ranch, before noticing John. The man ambled over to meet him, his hands hooked through the waist of his spotless jeans.

Oh come on. The last thing he needed was a wannabe cowboy. "I'm John Rathborne, foreman of the Three Keys Ranch."

The man gave him a once-over, never offering to shake his hand. "I'm Peter White."

"Let's head into the office." He turned on his heels and let the man follow him and Koda.

Back in the office, he shut the door and took a seat behind the desk. Koda settled next to his feet, but she watched Peter closely.

Peter's application lay on the desk. He gave it a glance, though he'd already familiarized himself with it. On paper, the man seemed like the perfect candidate for the job of ranch hand. He had experience with both cattle and horses, and knew how to clean stalls, mend fences, and chase down an orphan calf. But there was more to it than just a few barn skills.

"So, Peter. Tell me a little about yourself."

Peter shrugged. "I grew up in Billings, but went to a small private college out east. When I came back after graduation a few years ago, jobs were hard to find. I worked on a ranch over on the North Dakota border for a while."

He scribbled down notes as Peter talked. Private school, that explained his arrogant posture. Great. If he hired Peter, then he'd have two entitled workers to manage. He pressed his lips into a thin line over the fact he'd categorizing Katie that way. The more he was around her, the more he realized that his initial assessment of her might have been off. "Do you have references?"

That was a good way to weed out liars. Asking for a reference from interviewee number two had made the poor kid sweat and shake until he admitted he had no work experience and had faked his entire resume. He almost hoped Peter would have the same reaction to his line of questioning.

"Sure thing." Peter reached into his jacket pocket and produced a sheet of paper.

He scanned the list of several names and phone numbers. "What made you want to apply for this job?"

Mitch wanted all the applicants to answer that, but John would've preferred to ask tougher questions.

Peter frowned. "I saw a flyer. I need a job. Is that too honest?"

John laughed. "No. Not too honest. But seriously, what draws you to ranch work? From your references and from what you told me on the phone, the job in eastern Montana was your first experience on a ranch."

"I like horses." Peter smiled and leaned back in his seat. As he crossed his arms over his chest, he looked around the small space and again in an appraising way. Probably checking to see if the ranch was good enough for him.

John frowned. Peter White seemed like an ideal candidate for this job and they needed the help. He had to quit allowing his experience with his ex-wife to cloud his judgement. The one thing that gave him pause was the way Koda remained alert, like she was just waiting for Peter to make a mistake.

He sighed. From Peter's references alone, Mitch would want this man working on the ranch. If he didn't give Peter the job, he'd look like a fool trying to explain why. "I'd like to offer you a job here. After your references check out, of course."

Peter lit up in a smile. "That's great. Thanks, man." He reached out to shake John's hand.

"Why don't I call Mitch, so you can meet the boss? He has final say on all hires." John picked up the desk phone.

Impatience flitted across Peter's face. "Look—I didn't want to say anything because I didn't want it to look like I was looking for special favors."

"What are you talking about?"

Peter's face was unsmiling. "My father was Jefferson White."

John just gave him a blank look.

"Mr. Locke and he were business partners a while back. And friends. At least, they were until my father died several years ago."

"Oh. Well, you understand I'll have to talk to Mitch about your story."

"Go ahead. Like I said, I wasn't looking for special favors. But he won't turn me down."

John resisted the urge to rub his temples. Just what he needed—nepotism. "Alright, I'll talk to him. But remember—I'll be your boss, if you're hired. You'll have to answer to me." He leaned back in the chair, daring Peter to challenge him.

Peter shrugged and held his palms up. "I swear, dude, I'm fine with that. But you do know this is a ranch, right? Not the military." He eyed the army cap hanging on the corner of the chair.

"Yeah," John said curtly. "But I expect the same discipline from my workers as I did the men in my unit. Are we clear?"

"Crystal, sir." Peter shot him a mock salute. "Do I owe you some pushups or something?"

His blood boiled but John just sat very still, fixing Peter in his steely gaze without saying a word.

Peter sighed. "Sorry, bro. I was just trying to lighten the mood."

Bro.

This little frat boy wannabe was going to get on his last nerve. John closed his eyes for a moment. He wanted nothing more than to put his fist through Peter's overconfident face, but the small shred of sanity that remained told him to calm down and put the brakes on the anger. This ignorant little asshole wasn't worth losing his shit over. He obviously had no idea the kind of sacrifices he'd made. The kind of sacrifices Dirk had made.

He opened his eyes. He didn't want to do anything to jeopardize his job, so he counted to ten.

Stupid, but it worked.

Much as he hated to admit it, he needed to hire Peter. He was running out of options and if the guy's references were to be trusted, he was perfect for the ranch. Even if this kid was an entitled little shit.

"This is just probationary. Assuming Mitch gives the final okay. After three months we'll decide whether to keep you on permanently or not."

"Three months is all I need," Peter said, with a grin. "To prove myself to you, that is. Three months will do just fine."

Chapter 9

KATIE

The phone's soft buzz barely caught Katie's attention. She glanced at the screen and sucked her teeth as she saw the caller display. John. *Why's he calling?* For an instant, she debated answering it. If he hadn't been the ranch foreman, and if she hadn't been part owner of that same ranch, she would have let it to go to voicemail. But since he was, and she was—

"Yes?"

"Hey, Katie. It's John."

"Yeah, I know. What is it?"

She thumped her palm against the granite countertop when he sighed. She hadn't meant to come off so bitchy. "I need you to ride out with me. I have to take the new hire, Peter White, out to show him the ranch so he'll know where everything is when I send him to do something. We'll be covering as much of the ranch as we can."

"I know." Who did he think had done most of the training in the past when new hires came on? She'd even been there as her dad showed him around. The harder she tried to keep calm, the more her emotions shot up the proverbial finger. "Why do you want me to go along?"

"Because—" He sighed again. "Because I'd like to have your opinion about this guy. He's the son of your father's old partner, and your father wants him here. I'm not sure what I think about him. Thought you'd have a little more info and could help me out with this."

She blinked down at her phone. Was he asking her for help? "I don't want to be caught between you and my father. What if I'm fine with this guy—and so far I am—but you're not?" She bit her lip.

She could practically see him shrug. "You and your father are my bosses. He's already sure about the man. I just want to make sure you are, too."

She couldn't think of any good reason to disagree with him. Besides, this was the first time he was asking her for help. Since they'd made their deal, he'd kept his conversation brief and to the point, leaving no room for arguments. And they only interacted when necessary. Oddly, she almost found herself missing him. She grimaced. That probably indicated that she was overdue for a new hobby. "I'm on my way. And you can be sure I'll give you my opinion—on *your* new hire."

"I'm counting on it." And the weird thing was he sounded as if he meant it.

She grabbed her coat and sunglasses and headed toward the barn. As she did, she racked her memory for anything to do with Peter White. Growing up he'd been a cocky teenager, with more important things to do than entertain the wild tomboy of his father's business partner. And he'd gone to school out of state. The last time she'd seen him was four years ago at his father's funeral. At least the new foreman would be hiring someone she knew. Someone she didn't need to worry was the attacker who got away.

"Mornin', Miss Locke." A strange man stepped out of Snowbird's stall, and remained in the doorway so the large gelding wouldn't walk out.

She jumped back, a hand flying up to her chest. "Peter?" When he nodded, she gritted her teeth, frustrated at being startled. "What are you doing with my horse?"

"Just getting him ready for you, ma'am." Peter's eyes seemed to look everywhere except at her face. "John said the three of us were to ride out for the grand tour. So, I got your horse cleaned up and saddled for you."

"Thanks," she said faintly. Peter was not as tall as John, but neither was he the gangly teen she remembered. His bald head made him look older, and he'd bulked up in unexpected ways. *Is he seriously wearing True Religion jeans?* Then again, she couldn't recall the Whites ever wearing anything but brand name clothes. Despite the fact he wasn't a stranger, she found herself unable to squeeze past him to enter the stall.

When he moved away a couple of feet, she entered to greet her horse.

"Hey, big guy." The blue roan gelding swung his head around to greet her. She smiled as he lipped at her arm. "Sorry, but peppermints are for after we work. You know that."

"Nice horse. You ready to go?"

She turned to see John and Koda in the doorway of the stall. Her chest gave a now familiar squeeze. And the static, the crackling in the air that happened every time he stood near, was enough to make her a little afraid that if his hand brushed hers, she'd be electrocuted. "Sure. I'm ready. I figure we can show Peter what he needs to see inside of an hour. No need to ride all of the fences."

"I thought so, too. Want to take the dogs, or leave them here?" For once, John's expression was devoid of any hint of a smile.

"We'll just take Koda," she said. "Nickel and Two Bits can stay with Dad."

She led Snowbird out of the stall so she could check the bridle and saddle. She pushed her sunglasses up her nose. *This is going to be an interesting morning.*

She mounted Snowbird and led the way east, Peter trying to nose his horse ahead of John. "Let's do the near circle. We'll be going out just past the ranch buildings—the barns and sheds and houses—and along the fences where the pastures begin. You can get an idea of where everything is without having to cover every inch of the place."

"Sounds good, Miss Locke." Peter rode the small but powerful bay with the apt name of Bayberry. The stallion was a beauty, glossy as silk, and muscled with watch springs.

Peter looked as comfortable on his mount as she was on hers.

Pity I can't say the same for John. He sat stiffly on the tall and steady Redwood. The angle must be hard for his injured knee, but he never complained—or allowed so much as a grimace to cross his face. Any true sponger wouldn't pass up the chance to draw attention to his injuries. She stole a look back at John. *Guess Dad was right and I was wrong.*

He looked up, catching her gaze. He quirked an eyebrow in inquiry. She was confused until he jerked his head toward Peter.

She shrugged, turning her gaze back to the gently rolling hill in front of them. A narrow escape. He'd almost caught her checking him out. Something that'd become more frequent, and as unwelcomed as her feelings of "missing" their interactions.

Koda stayed close, often trotting off to investigate something interesting in the weeds but never going far.

"That's a fine dog you have there, Miss Locke," Peter said.

"Yes, she is." Her lips turned upward into a forced smile.

For the next forty minutes, she showed them both the main horse barn, as well as the two cattle barns—one for sale animals, one for anything calving or sick—the two bunkhouses, the equipment barn, the hay barn, and several smaller sheds to be used for storage or last-minute shelter.

"Three Keys ranch has been here in some form for at least the last sixty years," she told them. "There are some parts that have been torn down and replaced as time has gone on, of course, but most of it is still here and still operates much as it did when my great-grandparents owned it."

"And later on, too, when my own father and yours were partners here, Miss Locke," said Peter.

Her grip tightened on the reins but she just nodded at him and kept on riding, rolling her eyes under the cover of her sunglasses. *If he mentions his father again ....* She'd lost track of the times

Jefferson White had been brought into their conversation. It was clear Peter was intent on reminding her, John, and no doubt her father, of his father's association with the ranch every chance he got. They rode past the last stop—the north pasture, speckled with shrubby cinquefoil, where cows getting ready to calve were kept—and stopped at the gate.

"John." She beckoned him to join her, looking over the pasture. "Do you see anything unusual out there?"

He trotted over on Redwood. "Yeah, I do," he said, frowning as he took in the behavior of the cattle. "Why are they all bunched up out there at the fence line?"

"That's odd." Peter ambled over on his own horse. "They should be spread out all over and grazing."

"We'd better take a look."

"I'll get the gate." Peter started to dismount.

"No need." She reined Snowbird over and used a little leg pressure to stand him parallel to the wide aluminum gate. From there, it was easy for her to reach down, unlock it, and ride through it. She stood Snowbird parallel to it on the other side without ever letting go. "Come on in."

Koda trotted through first and the two men followed, one after the other.

"Nice trick," said John, watching as she closed the gate.

Peter stayed silent and rode on ahead towards the cows.

She smiled to herself as she watched him go. *Ha. That's what a lifetime on a ranch will teach you.* But a frown quickly formed. Something about Peter rubbed her the wrong way—something more than his bad habit of name-dropping. She rubbed the back of her neck and sighed. Or maybe those were her nerves, launching into overdrive again. It was equally likely that she was picking up on John's cues and running with them.

She urged Snowbird after the others while Peter sized up the herd. He turned his head to look at her. "Black Angus?"

She nodded. "Ideal for Montana. And the best beef you'll ever eat."

"Hey—hey!" John said. "The fence is down! That's why they're all milling around it!"

"What do you mean, the fence is down?"

He urged Redwood into a canter toward the cows, and both Snowbird and Bayberry instantly propelled forward to keep up. He began hollering at the cows and swinging the ends of the reins at them to drive them away from the fence.

He's right. She joined in chasing the cows away. Some fifty feet of the barbed wire fence was flattened. In a couple of places, it had torn away from the fence posts and lay curling and dangerous in the grass. But the cows seemed to have realized they now had a chance to get at the fresh new grass growing beyond the fence—right along the edge of a deep ravine.

"Go on, cow! Move!" Katie shouted, using Snowbird to drive them away from the broken fence. "Move out of here!"

Out of the corner of her eye, she saw Peter doing the same. Even Koda got the idea and helped push the cows away. Soon the four of them had the balky cows at a safe distance.

She kept a watchful eye on the herd as they regrouped. "I can't see any injuries. We're lucky they didn't want to step on the wire on the ground."

"That's right," added John. "Kinda like horses. They don't want to step on anything funny looking. But their greed might have gotten the better of their sense by tonight if we hadn't come out here today."

"So, let's get it fixed," Peter said, dismounting from Bayberry. "I've got a couple tools in the saddlebag."

"Me, too," John said. "I don't leave home without them. Not on a cattle ranch."

Katie stayed on her horse, holding the reins of the other two cattle while John set to work on the fence. She watched the cattle, Peter in her periphery as he worked. It didn't take much time, but it felt too long.

Finally, John gave the fence post he'd just finished a thump to check it would hold. "We'll have to come back out and do a better repair, but this will do for now. They'll be safe for at least a few days."

"Whatever you say, boss." Peter winked at her.

She rolled her eyes but made no reply. She was not going to be the center knot in their tug of war. Instead, she held out the reins of their horses.

Koda left off keeping the cattle from coming back and headed toward the three horses. Peter bent down and invited the dog over to him. Koda flashed him a brief glance and went straight to John. Her tail wagged rapidly as he scratched her ears.

She tried to hide her smile. *So much for being Jefferson White's son.*

Once they were back at the barn, John opened the door of the tack room—still holding Redwood's rein—and reached into the refrigerator by the door. He came out with two bottles of cold water. Peter glanced at him, but he pointedly ignored him and walked over to Katie with Redwood following along.

"Want some water?"

She took the bottle, her fingers lightly grazing his hand. "Thanks."

"You're welcome," he responded, and began leading his horse back to his stall to unsaddle him.

"What, don't I get any water? I just repaired a fence," Peter complained.

"Help yourself," John told him. "But if you don't mind, I'd like to have a word with Katie."

Peter looked around as if searching for a reason to stay. "What about Bayberry? Someone's got to remove his saddle."

"I'll do it," Katie said.

Peter looked uncomfortable. "I can't ask you to do that—"

"Fair is fair. You saddled Snowbird for me after all." Her tone was brisk, making it clear the subject was not up for debate. "Why don't you find my dad and tell him about the fence?"

"Yes, Miss Locke." Peter left the barn on slow feet, looking over his shoulder more than once.

"Nicely done," John said.

She took a quick gulp of water, before putting the bottle aside to lead Snowbird into his stall. "I am capable of dealing with ranch employees, you know."

"Never said you weren't." He followed her example. He drank in large gulps, clearly thirsty.

Should I have been nicer to Peter? Knowing her dad, he'd invite Peter to have a drink with him. "Well, you were right about Peter."

He choked on his water. "What?"

"Peter," she said shortly. "I don't know what it is, but he gets on my last nerve. There's just something about him...."

"More than bringing his father up every chance he got?" His eyes rested on her, waiting for her answer.

It was little things—the snide remark Peter had made after John's clumsy mount, the way he looked around the ranch as if he owned it. The way he smirked at them both, like he was in charge. "He doesn't strike me as a team player."

He sighed and rubbed his neck. "Let's not mention this to your dad. We need something more definite than him getting on our nerves before he'll consider letting Peter go."

"All right. I'll keep an eye on him."

"Me, too."

They resumed unsaddling the horses without another word. They were working as a team. Finally. One where silence felt comfortable, instead of uncomfortable. She found herself enjoying his presence. As she walked over to hang up the bridle, she laughed softly to herself. Maybe her need to keep safe, to keep strangers at a distance, had caused her imagination to run wild and lead her to believe that John was hiding some big secret. Maybe.

Chapter 10

JOHN

The day dawned cool and bright with a steady humming sound outside. *Cicadas.* John smiled. The sound took him back to his childhood. He stretched and winced as the sunlight gleaming into the bunkhouse hit him right in the face.

He'd been sleeping in the bunkhouse the past few nights. Between the work needing to get done, keeping an eye on Peter, and Katie piling work on to his ever growing to-do list, the hour drive back to Billings didn't make sense. Not to mention the pure exhaustion washing over him at the end of the day.

He actually enjoyed the bunkhouse. A pleasant smell of dried grass, sage, and pine tree hung around the building, even in the early morning. The wooden bunk beds and the too-firm mattress reminded him of deployment. If he closed his eyes, he could almost hear the soft snoring and heavy breathing of the other men stationed with him, the rustling sounds of their blankets as they tossed and turned, the occasional contented sigh from Koda. He opened his eyes, expecting to see her curled beside his bed and felt a pang in his chest when he glanced at the empty space. He wondered what kind of a bed Katie had for Koda, or if the dog slept with her. *She spoils her. Koda will get soft.* Surely even she could see Koda was no delicate lap dog.

He grunted, heaving his body upright. Despite knowing it was best to get up and get moving, he found it increasingly hard. Within a few hours, the sun would heat up the landscape until everything sizzled. His feet shuffled toward the bathroom, and into the shower. His hand fell to the lever releasing thousands of tiny drops, so cold at first, he almost cried out. The stream thickened, hot water enveloping his body. He began to plan the day ahead, ranking the chores needing to get done. But his thoughts slipped away, like the water coursing down his body.

Katie.

He shook his head, trying to stop picturing the way her jeans and t-shirt hugged her body, perfectly accentuating her curves. It was becoming increasingly hard to hide the effect she had on him, especially in those moments he'd caught her staring him up and down. The pit of his stomach stirred in response to her physical presence. Even now, he felt himself grow hard at the thought of her. Even the image of her scowling, hands on hips, did nothing to halt his body's response.

Am I a masochist? He needed to rid himself of this hunger fast before he did something he'd regret. Ruthlessly, he replayed his humiliating encounter at the bar, only this time it was Katie who flinched at the sight of him, her delicate mouth puckering with distaste.

His mind wandered to when he'd run into Katie at the house, and the faint scar he'd spotted on her cheek. He'd only caught a glimpse before she ducked back inside. The right side of her face looked somehow—off. Like the few men he'd known with facial injuries from war. Even long after healing, they looked just a little asymmetrical, as though the bones around the eye had sunken in and would stay that way permanently. And the way she hid behind sunglasses, or the way she wore her hair down when a ponytail would be more practical. The strange freak out once she realized he might have seen what she'd been hiding. The way she'd leapt away when he'd grabbed her so that she didn't fall.

The way she looked to Koda for reassurance.

He froze as all the pieces came together, forming a picture that he didn't want to see. God. What if Katie's injuries weren't caused by an accident?

Blood pumped hard through his body. Grinding his teeth, he resisted the urge to punch the wall of the shower, but just barely. Had someone hurt Katie? Had that been why she'd recoiled from him on the porch? Or was he just looking for an excuse for her eccentric behavior—and the way she'd rejected even his most innocent touch?

Taking a deep breath in, he placed both palms on his lower back and stretched. His muscles ached from repairing fences the day before, and his head hurt even worse from the strain of forcing himself not to punch Peter into next week. A groan rumbled in his throat at the thought of another day with the man. Mitch's former partner's son was a pompous turd, that was a fact. Peter was the kind of guy that John wouldn't trust to look out for anyone other than himself. He'd seen a few soldiers like that, in his army days. When the shit hit the fan, they were nowhere to be found. At least Katie wanted nothing to do with Peter and neither did Koda. The fact that the dog avoided him was all the confirmation John needed that Peter wasn't the type of person John wanted in his life. Dogs could sense these kinds of things, better than humans ever could.

He grimaced as he pulled on his clothes. Every muscle burned. His knee complained ferociously, stiff and unyielding as he worked his jeans on. He slid his swollen feet into his work boots and started across the yard to the horse barn. But even if he had somewhere else to go, some other employer willing to hire him, he couldn't leave now. Not with Peter there—not while he still had his doubts about the man's reliability. Not when Katie would be the one to suffer if the man bailed when there was an emergency. Plus, he wouldn't put it past Peter to take advantage of Mitch's sense of loyalty.

His mouth twisted. No doubt his senses were working overdrive. Peter was obnoxious, but likely not a threat. Still. Not a chance he was willing to take. And, exhausted as he was, he couldn't deny the sense of accomplishment buoying his spirits. It felt good, working again. Contributing to something larger than himself, instead of just sitting around and wallowing in self-pity.

He rubbed his aching back one more time and then set out. He hit the deep shade of the big barn and found Mitch inside one of the empty stalls, a hammer in hand, repairing the water bucket holders.

"Mornin', John," Mitch said.

"Want me to do that?" John scratched his chin, stifling the urge to yawn.

"No, that's fine. I like to do some of the hands-on work myself from time to time. Lets me keep in contact with the place." Mitch patted the nearest beam, a smile creasing his weathered face.

"What should I start on?"

"We'll know as soon as Peter gets back."

"Gets back?"

"He rode out an hour ago to check the repairs you two made yesterday and make sure they're holding. If the fences are good, I'd like you to start checking the rest of our fence lines. That's going to take a lot of riding, but it's got to be done. The dead of winter is no time to be repairing fences."

John's back stiffened. Had someone insinuated the repairs weren't good? Katie—no, it wasn't her style to go behind someone's back like that. Besides, she'd seen them at work. If there had been any problems, she'd have told John, directly to his face. Which left *Peter*. "If the repairs are faulty, I'll fix them right away. But they're good, Mitch. I'd swear to it."

"I'm sure they are," Mitch said. "Tell you what. You might as well give me a hand with these bucket clamps and feed boxes until he gets back."

John picked up a hammer, wishing he could tell Mitch what he really thought of the new hire—that Peter was nothing but a suck-up taking advantage of generosity and loyalty. But Peter hadn't screwed up yet. Even though his attitude was less than desirable, his work made him valuable. At least for now.

"Mornin', boss." Peter's voice drifted in with the breeze and dust.

John stepped out into the wide barn aisle. Sweat covered Bayberry, and the horse breathed hard. "How'd he get so hot? How hard did you run him?"

"Not hard. He's just a little soft from lack of steady work." A smile spread across Peter's face as he looked John over. "Looks like he's not the only one."

John clamped his teeth together, biting back the retort on his lips. "You don't need to worry about me."

"Good. Because we've got a long day ahead of us. The same section of fence is busted out again, up at the north pasture. And it's even worse this time."

John's shoulders tensed. "What are you talking about? You're telling me the fence we fixed yesterday is broken again today?" No way. There was no way his repairs had failed that quickly. His eyes narrowed on Peter's smug face, looking for a tell that the other man was lying. Although, for the life of him, John couldn't figure out why he would.

Which left the alternative—maybe his repairs hadn't been as good as he'd thought. His shoulders slumped. Maybe he wasn't ready for this job, after all. Then, he heard his therapist's voice in his head. Reminding him that everyone messed up sometimes, and not to let the little setbacks derail him. He straightened his spine. He was made of tougher stuff than that. If his work hadn't been good enough, then he needed to get his ass out there and fix the fence until it was. Simple as that.

"Except yesterday it was about fifty feet and today it's more like two hundred. I think we'd better get it fixed ASAP," Peter finished, with a glance at Mitch.

"Get that horse dried off and put up, and then you two take the truck and get out there and fix it. I don't know what the hell is going on, but I sure hope somebody fixes it right this time. Can't afford to have cattle dying for no good reason." With that, Mitch walked on down into the barn and disappeared into another empty stall.

John immediately started off toward the equipment barn.

"Hey," Peter called out. "Where you going?"

"To get the tools I need. You can stay here and help Mitch with whatever he needs done."

"Come on, man." Peter followed him. "You know you'll need some help. That fence will get done a hell of a lot faster with two guys instead of one."

John groaned as he reached the equipment barn, his muscles sore from fatigue and overuse. He stretched his arms down along his sides, feeling his neck and shoulders popping. Spending the day with Peter didn't thrill him, but neither did tackling the fence by himself. And Peter was right. Faster was better, especially where the safety of the cattle was concerned. "Yeah, all right," he said, grabbing his tool belt from where it was slung across the back of his chair. "Let's fix this bastard in time for lunch."

Peter laughed, his face registering surprise at John's sudden good humor. "Hey, man, we'd need a miracle to finish that fast."

The cordial exchange eased some of John's tension. Maybe he'd been letting his first impression of the other man get the better of him. Just because the kid was a little entitled and cocky, didn't mean he was a liar or involved in some inexplicable fence-breaking scheme. "Get Bayberry dried off and meet me here. I'll get my truck."

"Your truck? Hell, no. We'll take mine."

A few minutes later, they loaded wooden fence posts and wiring into Peter's truck. The brand-new black Ford F-150 gleamed in the sun. There was hardly any wear on it, only a light smattering of dust. He had to admit it was much nicer than his own beat-up old Chevy—not that he'd ever say so out loud.

"Got this baby brand new after I got hired," Peter said, as the two of them hoisted a roll of barbed wire into the bed. "As a gift to myself."

"Nice gift." So what if he found it odd the guy would drop thirty grand for a job that was paying him thirteen dollars an hour. *Who am I to judge?* The kid clearly wasn't hurting for money—that fact alone didn't make him any less valuable to Three Keys Ranch. Maybe it was time John got over his resentment of people who inherited wealth. His ex-wife didn't represent everyone in that demographic. "You said two hundred feet need to be repaired?"

"That's no exaggeration, trust me. It's seriously busted." Peter shook his head. "Like a herd of mammoths tore through the fence. Just like last time. All the cattle are accounted for, though, so I guess they either came back or it was something else."

"Something else." John chewed on that thought as he swung himself into the passenger seat. The situation didn't add up. What could bust through such a big section of fence overnight like that, in the absence of a storm or foul play?

Peter drove slowly through the north pasture, easing the big truck up alongside the broken fence, whistling slowly as they took in the damage. "Man, some fucker went crazy, huh?"

John's stomach dropped. That was an understatement. The barbed wire lay flat on the ground, barely held together by the broken fence posts.

Peter crouched by a shattered post, shaking his head, his forehead wrinkled. "It looks even worse now that I'm seeing it close up. I rode back fast the minute I realized it was out. We'll be lucky to repair this all today."

Almost definitely man-made. Uneasy, John glanced around, even though he knew whoever was responsible was long gone. The surrounding hills, decorated by western yarrow and lupine, were still and serene in the early morning calm. Somehow, the landscape's remote beauty made the damaged fence feel even more outrageous. "Some drunk assholes who thought it'd be a great idea to go for a moonlight drive, most likely." At least, John hoped that was the case—because the alternative was that the destruction had been deliberate. "Maybe a city hotshot with a new four-wheel drive and no idea how to handle it. See how the fence is crossed with tire tracks?"

Peter glanced over at him. "Somebody drove across it, for sure, but you're forgetting one thing." He pointed just beyond the flattened fence. "The reason the fence is here—that great big ditch. It's practically a cliff. If those animals got out, your problem wouldn't have been loose cattle—they'd all be maimed or dead."

John's hands fisted. The fence had been torn out on purpose. Someone wanted Mitch's cattle to get loose in the worst possible spot. How had he failed to miss such an obvious implication?

Peter's thick hand clapped him on the back. "No worries, man. It's easy to miss. But it looks to me like somebody's trying to mess with Mitch's operation."

His first impulse was to jerk away from the other man, but he held still. Peter was only trying to be helpful. "You think a rival ranch did this?" John hadn't considered this could've been a competitor. Mitch always greeted his neighbors by name when they met in town, and he was always met with smiles and handshakes. Of course, a smile could hide a lot of things.

Peter folded his arms as he leaned against his truck. "Hard to say. Jealousy and greed make people act crazy. And with the economy being what it is, Mitch's success could ruffle some feathers."

John nodded, scratching his neck while he surveyed the damage. Damn. He did not look forward to breaking this news to Mitch. "If Mitch sees us standing around chatting with a broken fence at our feet, it's our feathers that are gonna be ruffled. Let's get to work."

For the next couple of hours, Peter worked with him side-by-side, unloading the new wooden fence posts from the bed of the truck, and repairing the fence. The insistent sound of their hammering drifted over the valley, interspersed with the occasional grunt.

As they worked, John noticed Peter worked much faster than himself. With every swing of the hammer or the twisting of the fence's wiring, Peter became more and more energized. He, on the other hand, found it harder to raise the hammer with every swing.

Peter finally stopped, wiping the sweat from his forehead. "Hey man, you don't look so good. It's a hot day and these fences can be real bitches. I once spent an entire week re-fencing a pasture like this, and felt like I would drop dead when I was done."

John gritted his teeth against the implied criticism and continued to swing his hammer. No matter how hard it was, he was determined to pull his weight. Especially in front of Peter.

"What do you say, boss man?" Peter tried again. "Need a drink?"

John's throat became more parched in response to the question. He lowered the hammer and stepped back, catching his breath. *Dr. Evans is always saying I need to recognize my limits and accept help. And that I don't have to take it personally when people do offer assistance.* Accepting help from Peter was probably the equivalent of an entire therapy session. "What do you got?"

"A few light beers in a cooler. Nothing too good, but enough to take the edge off this god-awful job." The younger man laughed, dropped his hammer to the ground and sprung over to the cooler like he was walking on air.

Christ, this is probably like a morning jog to him. "A cold beer sounds awesome right about now."

Peter dug through a small toolbox near the cooler. "I've got some ibuprofen handy. Want some?"

John stared gratefully at the two little pills nestled in Peter's palm. He grabbed them and threw them into his mouth. He shook his head at the bottle of water Peter offered, taking a beer instead. After swallowing the pills, he pressed the cold can against his cheek and sighed.

The two men sat on the tailgate, taking swigs of beer as they assessed the work they'd completed. He had to admit, Peter was a conceited ass, but he was still one good ranch hand. Plus, he got points for thinking to pack a couple of cold ones. *Maybe I'm being too hard on the guy. Yeah, he's cocky, but maybe his attitude is earned.* John couldn't deny that the other man knew his stuff and had been working his ass off.

"What do you think of working on this ranch?" Peter took an extra-long swig of his beer and leaned back, letting the sun hit him in the face.

John readjusted his position, trying not to groan when his aching joints complained. He didn't know how honest he should be with Peter, especially since they seemed to have struck up some sort of nonverbal truce.

"It's pretty decent." His tone remained gruff and unemotional. "I like working with my hands. Never been the kind of guy who could sit behind a desk nine to five."

"I hear ya. My dad wanted me to go into business, but I've never been the corporate office type. My career path has always been what you might call non-traditional." Peter laughed and took another swig of beer. "But I do like it here. Mitch is a cool guy. So—what do you think of Katie?"

John was silent for a moment. He took another long drink of the beer before finally answering. "She can be a real pain in the ass, but I guess she's used to running things around here. And who can blame her? This is a job to us, but it's her home." He put his beer to the side, having worked up a nice buzz. "And I guess we need to get this done before we both end up passed out drunk—or worse—down in that ravine."

Peter laughed and hopped to the ground. "Good point, let's do it."

The two men fixed the last of the fence right as the sun dipped below the horizon.

John swiped the sweat off his forehead and stood back to survey their work with a sense of pride. "There's enough reinforcement in those posts that if anybody tries to tear it up again, it's going to be more trouble than it's worth."

Peter pulled off his work gloves. "That fence put up one hell of a fight, but I think we won."

"Yeah. I guess we did." Now that it was all said and done, John had to admit—he was grateful the other man had insisted on coming along. No way could John have finished this entire section in one day on his own. He flung the last of the busted fence posts into the cargo bed of the F-150. "Now let's get the hell out of here."

The two men climbed into the truck and rambled their way back to the ranch house.

The barns were deserted and full of shadows, but the farmhouse was brightly lit. As Peter slowed the truck, John spotted Katie's silhouette moving around in the kitchen.

When they pulled up, Mitch walked out of the front door onto the porch with a wave. "You boys come on in for dinner!" He turned and walked back inside the house, not waiting for a response.

"You staying?" John asked, as the truck rolled to a stop.

"Not tonight. I'm heading out for the evening. I have a hot date and I don't think she'll stay wet if I'm late."

John's lips tightened at Peter's crude talk, about some woman he didn't know. Then he forced himself to relax. Not his business, and anyway, he'd heard much worse in the barracks. Maybe he *was* turning into an old man. "Knock yourself out."

He hopped out of the truck and closed the door. Peter took off down the driveway toward the main road, spraying gravel in his wake. There was no denying that at certain times, Peter was prime, grade-A douchebag material—but at least he was a hard worker. John stepped up onto the front porch of the ranch house and knocked on the door, steeling himself. Time to forget about Peter. Dinner with the Lockes was going to be a challenge all on its own.

Chapter 11

KATIE

"Set two extra places, Katie." Her dad appeared in the kitchen doorway, heading for the sink. "I've invited John and Peter to join us."

A scowl covered her face as she continuing to wash the salad leaves. She'd heard her father's invitation through the window. Taking in hard-luck cases was bad enough without feeding them, too! She gave a cursory look at her meal. So much for having leftovers to eat tomorrow.

The sound of gravel careening off the ranch buildings tipped her temper over the edge. Flinging down the lettuce leaves, she darted through the passages, yanking open the front porch. "What the hell—"

John remained still, his hand raised to knock on the front door. "What's for dinner?"

"Was that you spraying gravel out there?"

John's eyebrows lifted and a faint smile formed on his mouth. "Not unless I suddenly have the ability to be two places at once. That was our newest ranch hand leaving. He has a date."

She looked behind him but found no signs of Peter. Thank goodness. "*Our*, nothing, Mr. Rathborne. My father wants Peter here, so he's here. That's all. But I can't forget you recommended him, and I found out yesterday just how charming he really is. Almost as charming as you."

He walked past her, heading straight to the kitchen. But he came to a sudden halt, and she narrowly missed colliding into him. He turned to look her in the eye. "I respect the fact that having an unexpected guest sprung on you last minute isn't the best. If I'm going to be in your way, say so. I'll tell your dad I just have time for a quick chat."

She scanned his handsome face. Large bags hung under his glassy eyes, which were at half mast. Neck and ears bright red from sunburn. He needed a rest before driving home. But if he passed up on dinner, behind the wheel was exactly where he'd end up.

"I'm serious." He took a step toward the front door, as if to prove it.

"I know." She bit her lip. Being forced to accept he was truly an honorable man made it harder for her to ward off her growing attraction. But she didn't know him. Not really. And she wasn't about to trust someone she didn't know. On the other hand, she'd never be able to forgive herself if he crashed because he fell asleep while driving. "It's no bother," she said. Then, just to make sure he didn't get the wrong idea, added, "Besides, if you eat with us, you can crash in the bunkhouse again and start earlier tomorrow."

He laughed wearily. "Always thinking about the ranch, huh."

"You two coming?" Dad called out a cheerful greeting from the kitchen. "Or are you planning on eating in the hallway?"

As John headed into the kitchen, Katie remained in the hallway for an extra second to catch her breath. Studying his face had sent her pulse dancing. Even dog tired, he was still easy on the eyes. Too easy. She cleared her throat and shook her head. *Snap out of it.*

"Peter's not joining us?" her father asked as she entered the kitchen.

"He apparently had other plans," she said.

Her dad turned to John. "How much did you two get done today?"

"Fixed the whole thing, sir." John pulled out a chair from the table.

Katie's jaw fell open, her eyelids blinking rapidly. "All two hundred feet? Was it really as bad as Peter said?"

John nodded, levering himself carefully into the chair. "I hate to say it, but the damage looks deliberate."

That caused the kitchen to go silent and stirred an uneasy brew in Katie's stomach. Her dad stroked his mustache as he absorbed John's announcement. "Nonsense," he finally said, shaking his head. "No one round here would do such a thing. Now, did you hear about the problems old Ted Frank is having, with his irrigation system? Poor guy, can't catch a break." He began filling them in on Ted's issues, turning the conversation away from the ruined fence.

Katie chewed her lip as she absently listened to her dad drone on, not liking that both times the fence had been broken so close to the ravine. Because if someone was breaking it deliberately, then they had to know that the risk to their ranch's cattle was high. Katie clutched the counter. Oh god. What if hurting their cattle was the point?

She released her grip. She was overreacting, as usual. Not making sense. Why would anyone want to hurt their stock? She forced her attention to the meal she'd cooked.

"Hope you've got an appetite, old man." She brought the pan of lasagna to the table, leaning over to place it carefully in the center, unaware until it was too late that her guest could glimpse down her shirt—white lace bra and all. But even once she figured out she was giving him a free show, she didn't try to cover up.

Why? Katie wasn't sure. She guessed it was because that ever since they'd called a truce, she'd somehow missed getting a reaction out of him. What the heck was wrong with her? How perverse was that? Cheeks hot, she turned to get the salad, conscious that his eyes followed her every moment. She remembered looking up from cleaning a stall, only to see him just turning away, with his own cheeks looking atypically red. *Has he been watching me this whole time?* An unfamiliar sensation flooded her body. Confidence. She'd almost forgotten what that felt like.

"Oh, come now, Katie. John isn't old." Dad laughed, taking a seat at the table. "I'm the old man around here."

"Dad, you know that's not true. You're just as young as me, especially when you're out in the fields with the horses and the cattle. I swear, you could pass yourself off as twenty."

"I appreciate that, sweetie." Her dad patted her on the arm as she took her seat next to him and began passing around the salad bowl.

As they always did at the dinner table, Katie and her father dove into conversation about the ranch. And for a few minutes, she forgot John was even there, genuinely surprised to look up and see he had hardly touched his salad or his lasagna. She frowned. "First time I've seen someone who claimed to have been repairing fences all day pick at dinner. Guess you don't care for my cooking, Mr. Foreman?"

He tugged his collar, seeming almost embarrassed. "If it's not any trouble, could I have a glass of water?"

"Sure, but you didn't answer my question. Is my cooking a problem?" Katie wished she could stuff the words back in her mouth. Why on earth was she pressing him on this and practically inviting him to ruffle her feathers?

"No, your cooking is fine." He glanced at his plate and cleared his throat. "It's just a little saltier than I'd anticipated."

Her face and neck heated. Her hands tightened around her knife and fork as she glowered in his direction.

He caught sight of her expression and winced. "What I meant to say was, maybe I'm used to my mama's recipe. And I'm feeling parched, is all." His eyes turned back to his plate and he cleared his throat. "Thirsty from being out in the sun all day."

Sure. Her chair screeched as she stood. Grabbed a glass from the cupboard, she filled it with water. She knew she wasn't a great cook. She could admit that.

It didn't mean that she gave him free rein to criticize her.

"Next time, feel free to cook for yourself, if mine doesn't meet your high standards." Katie knew she was being ridiculous.

She and her dad had often laughed about some of her cooking misadventures over the years, and she'd asked for John's opinion, after all. Still. He was in her kitchen, eating the meal she'd prepared. Would it have been that hard to tell a little white lie? She thumped the glass down on the table with so much force the water spilled.

"Katie! Take it easy." Her dad held up his hand. "He was just joking with you."

The kitchen became so quiet she could hear the grandfather clock in the hallway gently ticking away the seconds. No one moved. John sat perfectly still, his eyes locked on her.

Dad stood up and walked to the refrigerator, bringing back a chokecherry pie. *Figures.* Of all the fruits in the world, her dad loved chokecherries the best. She never understood why the indigenous fruit appealed to him so much since they didn't get their name for nothing. But every year, he and Linda would go to the festival in Lewistown and return with a myriad of chokecherry delicacies.

She disliked chokeberries. She disliked how tense this whole meal was—which fell on her head. But John kept dredging up her old feelings of inadequacy. First accounting, now cooking. Her self-esteem had taken a huge blow after the attack, and she'd worked like hell to get to where she was now. Then, John walked in, and suddenly her safe little world felt unsteady. Risky. And she didn't like it. Not one bit.

"Speaking of old people," Dad said, forcing a smile, "who's hungry for some dessert?"

Without saying a word, she grabbed her plate and dumped it into the sink. She turned to catch John flinching at the clatter of cutlery. The familiar reaction to surprise noises caused a pang of guilt to surface. So much for a pleasant dinner.

"Katie!" The fury in her father's voice made her guilt grow.

She spun on her heels and raced down the hall, pushing open the screen door with such force, it rattled the porch when it slammed shut.

She stood in the quiet darkness, chest heaving. Her breath shallow and ragged, and her limbs shaky. She leaned on the front rail and stared out into the night, letting the peace the cool air offered wash over her.

"I'm sorry, sir."

She could hear John's voice clearly. The small window over the kitchen sink. She must have left it open.

"I didn't mean to make her mad," he continued, sounding like a small child being scolded.

Her father responded in a tone that was at once gruff and surprisingly gentle. "It's not you. Katie's like the Montana summers. She runs hot one minute and cold as ice the next." Her father paused. "But when she's warm, it's like you never want the summer to end."

Dad. Tears pricked the edges of her eyes.

"I know people aren't perfect. That everyone has their own pain." John's reply was so quiet, she almost missed it. "My father was hardly ever around when I was small. He left for good when I turned ten. About the only real memory I have of him is the two of us playing basketball in our driveway."

Her father's voice was quiet but firm.

"Don't treat her any differently, John," he said. "She'll never forgive you if you do."

"I hear you. Well, seems like it's time for me to get back to the bunkhouse and crawl into bed. Thanks for a great dinner. I'd appreciate it if you'd pass that on to Katie for me." The scrape of the chairs against the wooden floor meant John was on his way out.

She could have left. Walked out back. Or over to the barn. But her feet wouldn't move. She held her breath as he stepped out onto the porch and came to an abrupt stop. His eyes darted between her and the stairs. He carefully inched his way past her, pausing a few steps down from her. Her eyes had adjusted to the darkness and she could see he was looking up into the black night sky.

"If someone had asked me what I loved most about Montana," he said quietly, "I would have told them it was the sight of jagged mountain peaks against the backdrop of the starry skies. When I was a boy I would count the stars in the sky until I lost my place, and then start all over again."

Air slowly passed through her nose and into her lungs. Her eyes scanned over his large frame. His shoulders slumped forward, as if the weight of the world were placed on them. And it was just too heavy to keep holding it.

"I tried to do the same thing in Afghanistan, during the nights when I couldn't sleep. And there were plenty of those. But without these fierce and jagged mountain peaks, it wasn't the same. I always knew that unless I came home, it would never be the same."

His words drew a warm rush of recognition. Of connection. Katie felt exactly the same pull toward her home state's rugged, majestic scenery. She put her hands in her pockets and scuffed one foot on the floor. She looked at him, before switching her gaze to the fields and the horizon She studied the stars gleaming in the ink black sky, until the porch creaked.

"John—wait."

She sucked in a deep breath when he turned around. His face remained in the shadow, his expression hidden. She couldn't tell what he thought. "I was out of line. I—know you didn't mean anything by what you said."

"I honestly didn't mean to criticize," he said. "Your cooking ranks way above what they served us in the mess halls most of the time, so I promise, your lasagna falls well within my standards. Hell, I'm so tired, that I would have been grateful if you'd served me a peanut butter and jelly sandwich. It's just...you asked, and in the army, being blunt is a virtue." He bent his head. "I'm trying to remember that being so forthright doesn't always work in the civilian world. But you know what they say about old dogs and new tricks."

Her chest constricted when he said *old dog.* "And I know I'm not a good cook. When my mom left, there was no one to teach me how. I taught myself through books and videos I found online. And you know my dad. He's not going to say my food sucks. He'd eat scrambled rotten eggs to spare my feelings."

A lump formed in her throat as she recalled sitting alone at school, tears pricking her eyes as she swallowed down a tasteless sandwich. She remembered how her classmates would whisper that her mom left because she didn't want Katie anymore. "So, I'm well aware that my cooking is nothing special—"

"Hey, don't sell yourself short," he interrupted. "That lasagna was tasty, and you know, a little extra salt here and there won't kill anyone." He winked, causing warmth to curl through her bare arms, despite the chilly air. "And it's especially good considering you taught yourself as a kid." He lingered on the step. "You teach yourself accounting, too? No—I know you did."

She went still as embarrassment flooded her. She slowed her breathing, calming herself so that she didn't lash out. She'd done enough of that for one night already. Time to give him the benefit of the doubt. "Are you mocking me?"

"No. I'm impressed. That's quite a damned feat for a young girl to do, go and teach herself how to cook and do the numbers on an operation like this. Your dad—well, he's a lucky man to have a daughter like you."

She studied his expression, searching for any trace of mockery, but sincerity radiated from him like light from the sun. As she stood there, soaking up his appreciation, something hard inside her bent. Cracked. No one had ever said those words to her before.

Until now, she'd never realized how much she'd needed to hear them.

"Thank you," she finally said. Her throat was too tight with emotion for much else.

He shook his head. "No need to thank me, it's the truth. But I should express my gratitude for dinner, Katie. Next time, I'll be a better guest."

She snorted. Happy for the break in intensity. "And next time—if there is one—I'll go light-handed on the salt."

"Sounds like a deal to me." John tipped an imaginary hat at her.

As she watched him amble away, she secretly hoped there'd be a next time. Which meant, she needed to find better videos on cooking. Low-salt recipes, too. Before she accidentally gave her dad high blood pressure.

Her lips pulled into a wide smile as she bounded up the steps to her room, feeling lighter-hearted than she had in months.

Chapter 12

JOHN

The following Friday, John left the VA hospital and walked into the twilight. He was tired physically and emotionally, having taken the last available appointment to not interfere with his job. But by the end of the day he had even less patience for Dr. Evans's probing questions. And the doctor appeared to be getting frustrated with his monosyllabic answers and refusal to discuss anything but his job. How long was he going to be forced to sit in an office, talking about the same shit week after week?

The sight of his trusty Chevy brought a faint smile to his face. The truck was a beat-up hunk of junk, but he loved it. He purchased it after his second deployment. His mother constantly warned him she was going to turn it into scrap metal, calling the

Chevy a death machine on wheels. The truck was far from perfect, but it was one of the few things John could truly call his own. That made it valuable to him.

His original intention had been to restore the truck, but between trainings and deployments he barely had time to keep the old vehicle in working order. Once he received his first paycheck, he'd put in some time to make sure his ride was reliable so he'd never again be stuck using his mother's car.

He drew in a deep breath before unlocking his truck. His mom had been a topic of conversation yet again with Dr. Evans. Her constant worried looks and handwringing whenever he was around had gotten so bad he preferred to live in the bunkhouse, even when his mother begged him to stay at her house so she wouldn't be alone.

Hopping into the driver's seat and starting the engine, he decided to head to Slingers. Slingers was a cheesy, cowboy-themed bar a few miles from his mother's house and even farther from the ranch. At Slingers, he could be anonymous. He could drink silently at the bar or shoot pool with the college guys when he felt up to it. On rare occasions, he might even chat up a pretty college girl. Though after the incident with Melissa, he tended to steer clear of women. No need to be humiliated again.

The parking lot was fairly empty, but the size of the crowd made no difference to John. He wasn't looking to make friends. Just distract himself until he was so tired he could fall into a dead sleep once he finally got home—wherever that proved to be tonight.

He sat at the long mahogany bar. The bartender took his order, handed him a beer, and left him alone. He took a slow pull of his Yuengling and glanced around the long, wide space. All the TVs were tuned to different sports channels. Watching silent coverage of a college football game, he settled into the easy, fluid atmosphere around him.

By his second beer, the crowd had grown. He headed over to the pool table in the back corner. The guys playing looked up, signaling him to pick up a cue. He tipped his chin in acknowledgement, grabbing cue and chalk. That was another thing he loved about Slingers. No one was big on conversation.

He played a couple of games before heading back to the bar for another beer.

"Wanna buy me one, cowboy?" A pretty redhead batted her lashes at him from the neighboring barstool. She couldn't be a day over eighteen, but her heavily made up face looked garish under the overhead lights. He almost laughed—at her look, at her request, at her assumption he was a cowboy even though he was—and shook his head.

She moved closer, her lips parting. Before she could get a word out, he grabbed his beer and headed to the other end of the bar. He wanted to escape his failures tonight, not set himself up for more. And when it came to women, failure was all that ever happened. *Just look at that dinner with the Lockes.* His teeth ground together forcefully. For once Katie had decided to lay off her vendetta against him. She'd been pleasant company—possibly even flirting with him—and with one dumb remark he'd ruined the night. For everyone.

He nursed the remainder of his beer while thinking about Katie. The more time he spent around her, the harder it was to hide his physical attraction. Especially when she wore her hair up. The sight of her carelessly caught up ponytail made his fingers itch with the desire to stroke her hair. And her eyes! It was a crime to hide them behind sunglasses. They were a rich brown, fluid with emotion. Sometimes, he got the sense that she was just as attracted to him. Just the thought sent a surge of longing into his groin.

That path leads to nothing but trouble. Steer clear.

He imagined her, stroking his back. Pulling up his shirt...and then screaming at the sight of his mangled skin. Katie, asking him if he still had a dick, like that other woman. Screaming at him not to touch her...disgust etched across her beautiful face.

His grip tightened on the empty bottle. He unclenched his fingers before he broke the glass, but the wound inside him didn't heal so easily. Like Katie could ever be interested in someone like him.

He stalked out of Slingers, ready to collapse into a bed and pray for the blessed oblivion of sleep. His head pounded with unwanted thoughts and images. To get to the ranch, he could either cut through the center of town or skirt around the outside of it on the quiet rural roads. The latter was a better bet.

As he drove down the endless black stretch of road, the slight throbbing in his head became an angry pounding. His fingers laced tightly around the steering wheel, his thoughts returning to the hospital visit. The anger he could never go back to combat. Never serve his country again. Never be with the men he considered brothers.

All his life, he'd lived and breathed the U.S. Army. As a kid, he'd known he would join up the minute he was old enough. During high school, when his friends had worried about college applications or had existential crises over what to do with their lives, he had been the only calm one. For him, it had been simple. He was meant to be a soldier.

But with the life he'd always wanted ripped away, he no longer had an idea how to get it back to normal. Working at the ranch helped, but going weeks seeing only the same five faces made the isolation close in on him, tightened by the stress of needing to learn life all over again. Even down to the way he spoke, since his bluntness offended lots of people. Especially Katie.

All the unfair things that had happened in the last year flashed through his mind. His foot pressed down on the accelerator. And the truck sped along faster and faster.

After flying around a curve, red and blue lights flashed in the rearview mirror. *Fuck!* For a moment, he considered ignoring the cop behind him. But he came to his senses and stomped on the brake, pulling onto the shoulder of the road.

I'm fucked.

He rolled down his window and waited until the officer came up beside him. The cop looked barely over twenty, peach fuzz still present on the kid's upper lip. "What seems to be the problem, *officer?*" His tone was more condescending than he'd intended, but hell. This little twerp likely hadn't lived through a fraction of the stuff John had.

The young officer's eyes narrowed. "I think you know, sir. I clocked you doing eighty-three in a fifty-five."

"That fast, are you sure? When's the last time you had your radar gun checked?" Now he was just being a smartass but damn. He hadn't really been going that fast...had he?

The officer's posture stiffened. "Is that alcohol I smell on your breath, sir? Have you been drinking?" The cop leaned down and shone a flashlight into his eyes.

John flinched as the light struck his pupils, throwing up a hand to block the glare. "Two beers only at the local watering hole. I'm fine to drive."

The officer looked unimpressed. "Sir, I'm going to have to ask you to step out of the car."

"Are you kidding me?" Rage uncoiled in the pit of his stomach, threatening to explode. John tried to remember the exercises his therapist had given him for just such a situation, but his mind went blank. He was so sick of everything being so damned hard all the time.

The cop bent his head toward his chest and murmured a few words into his radio. A static voice responded. A call for backup.

The officer issued his order again. John slumped in his seat as he watched the cop's hand stay right over his gun.

"I'm getting out now," he said, turning off the truck.

The other man stepped back, eyeing him intently. By the time he blew into the little breathalyzer, another officer had arrived. Under the legal limit. John felt like punching the air in victory but all he did was wave his fingers at the first cop. "See? Can we end this farce now?"

The two cops exchanged a glance before the first one spoke. "Sir, we're going to need to see your license. And just so you know--we retain the right to bring you in if we think you're driving under the influence, even if you test below the legal limit."

The cop's smug grin was what pushed John over the edge. On top of everything else. His anger boiled over, and before he knew it, his fist was slamming into the side of his truck. The impact made a dull, metallic thud. Both police officers reacted fast, and he found himself face down on the ground, spitting out dirt and gravel from the cold wet shoulder of the road.

The officer who'd pulled him over read him his rights while the other placed the handcuffs on him. His head continued to throb as the officers manhandled him into the police cruiser, his mind too clouded with anger and frustration to resist.

The ride to the police station was short, but long enough to realize he'd made a huge mistake. As he was led inside for processing, his breathing slowed and his heart rate returned to normal. His rage dwindled, leaving him exhausted.

The booking officer barely glanced up as his picture was taken and he was fingerprinted. He wanted to tell someone—anyone—he'd served in Afghanistan and done his duty to keep his country safe. That he'd helped to preserve freedom for all of them. Didn't it make a difference? Shouldn't he be allowed some leeway as he was forced back into civilian life—a life he didn't want?

John took a good look at the tight expressions of the cops around him. Tired, overworked, they kept passing him off from one to another. He was nothing more than a box to be ticked, a form to be filed.

The officer who led him to the holding cell was a squat, tough-looking woman with her curly black hair scraped back in a bun. As she shut the cell door, she said, "You're lucky. It's quiet here tonight."

"I still don't understand what you're charging me with. I wasn't drunk." He stood in the center of the cell, blinking at the police officer. He bit his lip. He didn't want to sound like an asshole. Maybe he could still get on the woman's good side. "You know, I was—"

"Disorderly conduct." The police officer marched away, her shoes clicking on the linoleum tile.

So much for winning her over.

He dropped onto the bench inside the cell and ran a hand through his hair. The last of his anger fizzled away when he realized he was going to have to call his mother.

Shame crept in and he pressed the heels of his hands into his eyes. He could picture his mother's face, her features dropping with disappointment and concern as she found out where he was. Now she'd turn into even more of a worry wort.

How could I have let this happen?

He sat quietly for a long time, lost in thought and exhaustion. The sudden jangle of keys when the officer came back to the cell startled him.

"Come on, buddy. Let's get someone down here to collect your sorry ass." She unlocked the cell door and grabbed him tightly by the elbow.

He took a breath through his nose and held it for a count of ten before exhaling slowly. There was no way he was going to lose control again. It was bad enough he was going to have to humble himself and admit he had screwed up.

The cop stopped alongside a phone that looked so old it was just one step beyond rotary. He was pretty sure he'd need a tetanus shot to hold the receiver up to his ear. "Does this thing actually work?"

From the look on the officer's face, she'd heard that joke before—and it hadn't been funny then.

"One call," the officer said. "And keep it short." She stepped back, crossed her arms over her chest, and waited.

Apparently, he was going to have an audience. With a sigh, he lifted the receiver and punched in his mother's number. The phone rang.

And rang.

And rang. Why wasn't the answering machine picking up? Where was his mother? She should be home. Her social circle was small and aging. All of them would be in bed by this time of night. And his mother kept a phone right by her bed on the nightstand.

He replaced the receiver and tried to think. If his mother couldn't bail him out, who could he call instead? There was no way he wanted to spend the night in jail.

"No one answered," he said to the policewoman. "Can I try someone else?"

Her jaw moved back and forth, and he could almost see the debate warring within her as to whether or not she was going to be a jerk about it. "Make it quick."

His mind raced through the names of the people he knew. *I really need to make some friends.* Mitch was the only other person he trusted, but who in their right mind would call their employer—especially their new employer—to bail them out of jail?

Not like I have any alternative. He punched in the main house phone number for Three Keys Ranch and waited while it rang. He took another deep breath, trying to keep calm.

"Hello?"

Katie.

He bit back a groan. Not the person he wanted to speak with. Not about this situation. The universe must really hate him right now. "It's John. Is your dad around?"

"Nope."

He waited for her to continue, but only silence followed her answer. He swore under his breath. Of course she wasn't going to make this easy. Hell, he was half-convinced the word easy wasn't part of her vocabulary. "Do you know when he'll be back? Or can you give me his cell phone number?"

"Why?" she asked, her voice laced with suspicion.

He sighed. "I need to ask him a favor."

"He's out of range. Won't be back until morning."

John squeezed his eyes shut. "Shit." Now what was he going to do? With his mom not answering and Mitch gone, he was out of options. It wasn't like he could ask Katie. She'd probably laugh, or just hang up on him and tell her dad when he returned to kick John's sorry ass to the curb.

"What's the problem?" Katie asked.

He hesitated, torn. Yeah, she'd likely to tell him to get lost, but on the off chance that she didn't? Was avoiding a night in the slammer worth the risk? "Um…" He cleared his throat, unable to get the words out.

"Are you okay?"

This time, he swore he detected a hint of worry in her voice. A tiny wobble. Not much, but enough to propel him to give her a shot. Besides, beggars couldn't be choosers. "I'm in jail. I need someone to come bail me out."

There was a brief pause. The cop watched him dispassionately while he tensed. Waiting for the rejection.

"I'll be there in half an hour." Then the line disconnected.

Stunned, he listened to the dial tone until the police officer told him to wrap it up. He slowly replaced the receiver on the phone. His mind refused to accept what he'd just heard. Katie was actually coming to bail him out?

She could've laughed out loud, telling him to have fun rotting in jail. Spit out an "I knew it" as she compared him to past foremen. Fired him on the spot. Instead, she'd told him she'd be there shortly. No questions asked. He could hardly believe his luck.

He followed the officer back to the holding cell, still stunned by Katie's response.

Although, just because she'd agreed to bail him out didn't mean she wouldn't hold this little incident over his head. No doubt he hadn't heard the end of it.

He grimaced as the door clanged shut behind him, but then shrugged. He'd worry about that when the time came. For now, he was too busy being grateful that he wouldn't be spending a night

in this cold, stark cell after all.

Chapter 13

KATIE

A short, heavyset policewoman thumped on the bars of a holding cell. She pulled out the keys and unlocked the door, metal hinges screeching when she pulled it open. "Your girlfriend's here."

Katie bristled at the words but didn't bother to correct the woman. Breathing in a liberal application of lemon-scented cleanser, she leaned against the white cinderblock wall. A familiar throaty grunt cut through the air.

"She's not my girlfriend."

The officer's high-pitched laugh followed. "You're about as good at lying as you are at driving. Now, move along."

Katie took a step forward, sucking in a short breath as John lumbered into the hall, somehow managing to look both disheveled and sexy at the same time. No fair. No one should look that good after spending time in the slammer. Although, when his eyes met hers, she noticed dark smudges beneath them. The moment he spotted her, he came to a complete halt, causing the smaller policewoman gripping his arm to be jerked backwards. "I was half convinced you wouldn't show," he said.

She narrowed her eyes. "Really? Which part of *I'll-be-there-in-half-an-hour* gave you that impression?" She didn't know whether to be insulted that he hadn't taken her at her word, or horrified. The thought of being stuck in jail without anyone to bail you out had to be terrible.

He lifted a brow. "The part where you were the one who said it."

The cop snickered in the background. Katie tried glaring at him, but her damn traitorous mouth kept twitching. "You're not funny."

"Never said I was.""This situation isn't funny, either."

"No arguments here," he agreed.

"Good." She paused, and then couldn't help but ask. "Were you really that surprised to

see me?"

He tilted his head and shrugged. "Can you blame me? I can never quite predict how you're going to react at any given moment—especially to something that concerns me."

She sighed. She wanted to take offense, but the man had a point. Her emotions tended to run wild whenever John appeared. "Well, I'm here. Now, let's leave. Please."

He nodded, stuffing his hands into his jacket pockets as they made their way to the counter.

"Is that all?" Katie said to the officer. "Can we go?" She must look half-asleep, like she'd rolled out of bed to come here—and she had. Her hair was scraped back in a messy ponytail and she'd grabbed whatever clothes had been on the floor.

"He has to appear in court. Disorderly conduct."

"That's all?" Katie asked.

"The court date is on the ticket." The policewoman passed a piece of paper over to her. "Other than that, Mr. Rathborne is free to go."

The cold night air bit into her skin as they stepped into the parking lot. After his call, she'd run out of the house so fast all she had was the Montana State University sweatshirt she kept in her car. But the cotton fabric did little to protect her skin when temperatures were this low.

When her body started to shiver, a heavy warmth enveloped her. John had pulled off his coat and placed it around her shoulders.

"Thanks," she said, tucking a strand of hair behind her ear.

"It's the least I can do. Thanks for coming," he muttered.

She turned her head to face him. His ears were red. *From the cold or embarrassment?* Katie suspected the latter. Looked like someone had left their false bravado back in the jail. When an involuntary smile pulled at her lips, she snapped her head forward.

"I paid your bail on the ranch credit card. Obviously, you'll have to pay it back." She increased her stride to make sure she remained ahead of him, wanting to keep the uncontrolled smile hidden.

"Never would have considered otherwise," he replied. "Even I can't fall much lower than this."

"Where is your truck?"

"Still on the side of the road. Do you mind dropping me off to get it?"

Katie shook her head. "Let's not. You smell a little like beer, and I don't feel like coming back down here to bail you out again." Or getting a call from the hospital, after he crashed. "You should just come to the ranch with me, instead of going to your mother's house."

John eyed her warily. "Figured you'd be glad to get me out of your sight and off your property for a while." His shoulders went back. "I don't want to put you out any more than I already have. I'm sure I'd be fine to drive. I was pissed about something, won't happen again."

Katie had to fight not to roll her eyes. The pride on this one, it was strong. "I told you. I don't want to have to bail you out again. Besides, we may need you in the morning to check the north pasture fence again." There. She had him. Now he'd feel compelled to ride with her, and she wouldn't be up all night, worrying about another phone call.

He hesitated, rubbing the back of his neck. "Peter's still there, isn't he?"

Though she'd grown up with Peter, having him at the ranch without her father there made her uncomfortable. Peter wasn't someone who had her back; he wouldn't protect her. And Koda didn't like him, which only unnerved her more. "Yes, he decided to crash in the bunkhouse for the night. He got in a fight with the girl he's been staying with or something. I didn't really care to listen. At any rate, I don't feel safer with him there."

Being at the station brought back memories she'd rather not dwell on. And with hardly anyone at the ranch, someone could sneak in and she'd never know it. Until it was too late.

"But you feel safer with me?" John rocked back on his heels.

The surprise in his voice echoed her own surprise. Did she? Feel safer with John? She wrapped her arms around her waist and decided, yes. Yes, she did. When that had happened, she wasn't sure. "Don't get a big head over it. I'd feel safer with just about anyone than Peter. He'd be too busy bragging about his dad's ranch to notice if anything was amiss."

John snorted. "You're not wrong."

A small grin appeared on his mouth. Katie could tell he was going to make some stupid comment about her trusting him more than Peter, so she spun on her heel and demanded, "Are you coming or should I just leave you here?"

He lifted his hands. A peace offering, even as his grin grew. "Sure. I'm coming."

She unlocked the doors to her red hybrid and climbed into the driver's seat. He was a little slower and more careful as he followed suit, until his long legs stretched into the floorboard from her passenger seat.

"Where's your dad?" he asked.

"He's at a ranchers' association meeting in Billings. A quarterly banquet. With Linda." The engine hummed while she fiddled with the heat.

"So, wait. You mean, there's nobody at the ranch right now, except Peter?"

She half expected a joke or another inquiry about the relationship status between her father and Linda. "That's right. Not even me since I had to leave and spend some time at my local police station tonight."

Fear crept its way in like a spider crawling up an arm, and she froze. Her eyes were unblinking, staring at the distant shadow under the tree, her throat bone dry. It appeared to be watching her.

"I know you don't like Peter. He's not my favorite, either. But he's a hard worker and your father trusts him. Maybe we should—"

Her foot slammed on the gas pedal and they peeled out of the parking lot, leaving the brightly lit police station—and the haunting shadow—behind.

"Hey, take it easy!" He grabbed the door handle to steady himself. "You just sprung me loose for crazy driving. If it's okay with you, I'd really like to skip making a repeat appearance tonight." He gave a low whistle while he side-eyed her. "Never saw anyone who had a lead foot for both the gas and the brake."

"Just hold on," she growled. The car jolted and swayed on the winding road, but she was desperate to get home. The police station. The empty ranch. The clinic, that one night...

Bile rose in her throat and a swarm of angry bats flapped around in her chest. Her hands were clammy, her knuckles white as she gripped the steering wheel. John offered some relief, but he seemed on the brink of exhaustion.

His sigh cut through the tension filled air as she turned off the road and up the driveway to the ranch house. "I'll be glad to turn in. Pretty sure the bench in that cell was designed to be as uncomfortable as possible."

Her lips pressed tightly together. "Just remember, you owe me."

"I won't forget. Thanks again for helping me out. Your credit card will be reimbursed first thing tomorrow. And I'll—"

A dark shadow ran across the field to her right and she slammed on the brakes.

"What on earth—"

Nickel, Two Bits, and Koda ran up to the car barking furiously. Her eyes locked onto the front porch.

"What are you doing?" he asked. "They'll move out of the way."

Her throat tightened, refusing to allow air in or out. She felt cold, as if all the blood had drained from her face and now pounded in the fingers gripping the car's wheel. Her eyes were wide and her body rigid.

"What's wrong?" John's voice was low. Out of the corner of her eye, she saw his body become rigid, scanning the ranch grounds, the alertness of his gaze at odds with his tiredness of a moment ago.

"The dogs. They shouldn't be out!"

She turned toward him, her eyes falling on his flaring nostrils. But his voice remained calm when he said, "Maybe your dad let them out."

"I told you. He's not here." She pushed the words out, her body beginning to shake. The house was dark except for the single porch light. "He went to Billings for that banquet."

"Could he have returned early, let the dogs out to pee, and fell asleep before he could call them in?"

"He's not back yet. His truck isn't here." Her hand clamped down on his muscular forearm, unwilling to let go. "The door—the front door is open!"

Barely visible against the pitch-dark interior, his hand reached over, put the car in park, and pulled the keys from the ignition. She never let go of him until he gently pried her fingers so he could exit the car.

Koda trotted up immediately, her ears perked. The dog cocked her head as if waiting for a command.

Bile had reached her mouth, the acrid fluid filling her mouth before spraying on the floor. Wiping her mouth with the sleeve of his jacket, she saw him wave a couple of fingers in Koda's direction. The dog ran up the porch steps, nose to the ground, checking the wood for scent. Curiosity momentarily replaced her fear. How did her dog know what the signal meant? Had he been working with Koda without her knowing?

John's large frame jogged over to the driver's side of the car, opened the door, and kneeled so they were eye level. "The front door is open. Katie, did you leave it open by mistake? Could the dogs have opened it somehow?"

She scrunched her nose, shaking her head as tears flowed down her cheeks. "Of course I locked the damn door and of course the dogs couldn't have opened it!"

His mouth hitched up in a half smile. He dropped the car keys into her hand. "Atta girl. Now, I'm going in with Koda to check things out. Why don't you let the other dogs in here with you and wait for us?"

"Wait? What do you—"

His whistle cut her off. Two Bits and Nickel came running, jumping happily into the front seat with Katie. He slammed the door and made a locking motion at her with his hand.

For once she did as he asked, locking the car doors.

Two Bits made himself comfortable on the passenger seat. But Nickel sniffed the vomit on the floor, sticking her nose and front paws right in the sour smelling liquid. As if a break-in wasn't enough, a vomit-covered puppy wouldn't be making the night any easier.

"Nickel, no!" But it was too late. The gawky pup had already licked the vomit.

Giving up, her body slumped into the seat. Her eyes scanned the house as she waited for John and Koda, hoping they'd be okay. She couldn't deal with either of them getting hurt. *No one else. Please,*

no one else.

Chapter 14

JOHN

John climbed the steps, his chest tight. He didn't like the way Katie reacted—like she was all too familiar with someone breaking in. His neck corded at the thought of someone harming her. He'd never allow that to happen. *But you let it happen to him. You let him die.*

His eyelids slammed shut, hoping to drown out the voice. This wasn't the time. Stepping into the hall, he flicked the light switch on. Nothing. He progressed through the house, room by room, flipping on the lights. Koda, a few feet in front, kept her nose to the ground.

He surveyed all windows and doors. No signs of damage. The kitchen was in order as well. Or so he thought. The glimmer of moonlight cutting through the window danced around in waves as it hit the water sitting on countertop. He placed his palm down into the small puddle. Cold. Too cold to have been left hours ago.

Someone had been in here recently. But who? And why?

A creak erupted from the ceiling. Koda's muzzle turned up, a low growl emanating from her furry body.

"Koda. Go find." He sent his partner up the stairway. She slowed her pace halfway up, ears pricked and turning from side to side. She dropped low on her haunches and her hackles stood up. She circled the landing once more before lying down and barking.

"Good girl. What did you find?" He bent down and peered at the floor. Nothing was there. But Koda alerted and he trusted her training. She'd never been wrong before. A dangerous scent was present. He needed her to continue searching.

"Koda, *suche*."

Koda jumped up, continuing her search. They retraced their steps, searching every room and every closet for a second time. They checked under the beds, in the closets, patted down the curtains.

Still nothing.

Turning the hall, he pushed open the door to the last room. Katie's. He turned on the light, his eyes trailing his partner, waiting for her signal that nothing dangerous was in the room. When Koda returned to his side and sat, he exhaled. *Everything clear.*

He sauntered in, studying every detail. He swallowed, his heart in his throat. It was far too plain. A simple oak dresser, nightstand, and bed were the only pieces of furniture in the room. A thick book rested on the nightstand with a page earmarked. When he picked it up, the cover brought a smile to his face, despite the urgent situation. The not-so-brief history of World War II.

He set the book down. The house was empty. But something wasn't right. He chewed his lip, stroking Koda's head. No way in hell he was letting Katie spend the night without protection. At least, not until Mitch came back. "Come on, girl. Let's go get Katie."

As he approached the car, he plastered a smile on his face. She didn't need to know someone might have been in the house. Not when cold water was the only evidence he had to make such a claim.

She unlocked the car door and scrambled out. "Well? What did you find?"

"Nothing," he said. "Not one thing seems out of place." He hoped his voice sounded believable. He'd never been a good liar.

"I know I shut the door," she insisted. "And there is no way the dogs could have gotten it open. That's never happened before, not once."

"Peter could've come in to get a glass of water or something. Or maybe Linda stopped by to pick something up for your father."

Her mouth dropped open as if he was crazy. And maybe he was. But right now, he wanted her to get some rest. Her skin was pale and her face drawn. A slight tremble was still present in her body.

"So what do we do now?" she asked.

There was one person who could have opened the door—the only person left on the ranch. The only person who had raised his hackles from the moment they met. The one person on the ranch that Koda didn't like.

Peter.

"Do? There's nothing to do now. For you, at least. You get to bed. I'm going to talk to Peter and see if he heard anything unusual. Then I'll fix the door to make sure it can't open accidentally."

He turned on his heels, making his way to the bunkhouse. Koda followed, and he stopped, looking down at the dog.

"No, girl," he said softly. "Stay."

"Will you come back when you're done talking to Peter? Just to let me know what he said?"

He'd already planned to spend the night out on the porch, but her request caught him by surprise. She must be rattled if she wants his protection. He mustered a smile. "Sure. I'll come back. But go on in and lock the door. Take the dogs with you. I'll be back as soon as I can."

Once everyone was inside and he heard the deadbolt drop into place, he headed off into the darkness. Though his heart should be racing and his palms sweating, they weren't. His body was relaxed and calm. Just like before. Whenever he stepped foot outside the wire.

Always a soldier.

The bunkhouse was dark inside, and Peter most likely asleep. The kid was in for a rude awakening. He threw open the door, hitting the light switch. "Get your ass up and out of bed. We need to talk."

No response.

No one was there. Shit. If Peter hadn't gone into the house—who did? Who else would break into the main house without stealing or touching anything? Did someone even break in at all, or was he just imagining everything?

His eyes settled on his baseball cap, resting on the end of his bed. He swallowed back the lump in his throat. *Am I making shit up?* His guilt cut deep for not protecting his brother. His stomach twisted thinking of his fallen comrade. Protecting Katie wouldn't make up for his failure.

Did I think it would?

He checked the bunkhouse to make sure no one had broken into this place. Nothing amiss. Collapsing onto the bed, his head sank into his palms as he sifted through his thoughts. The ranch house's open door felt deliberate—just like the destruction of the fence at the place most dangerous to the cattle. As if someone had done it intentionally. Either to mess with them, or maybe even put Katie in harm's way. An open door would be inviting to an intruder. If she'd walked in on an unexpected guest, she could've lost her life.

Grinding his teeth, he made his way back to the main house. He might have failed Dirk, and maybe he wasn't as good of a soldier as he thought. But he wasn't going to sit back and let something happen to Katie. Failure wasn't an option this time.

Chapter 15

KATIE

Katie sat curled up in her usual armchair, her arms wrapped around herself. Her teeth chattered uncontrollably. She'd changed her sweatshirt for something more substantial, but the cold didn't leave. And nothing she did warmed her up.

Koda's short high-pitched bark made her jump along with every creak of the house, usually as familiar to her as her own breathing. When the dog trotted to the door wagging her tail, she relaxed to some extent. She breathed out, making her way to unbolt the door.

"Hey."

She caught a faint whiff of beer mixed with the pine scent of John's soap as he squeezed in through the door. A combination that shouldn't have been intoxicating, and yet somehow was. An overwhelming urge to stand even closer to him encompassed her. Her hand pushed the heavy wooden door shut, double-checking the deadbolt lock was in place. If only she could shut out her physical attraction to him as easily.

Her hair escaped her ponytail to fall down her neck. When she caught a glimpse of herself in the decorative mirror hanging on the wall, she flinched. Dark circles below her eyes were not her best look. Nor was the big flannel shirt that had replaced her sweatshirt.

Yet he had a way of making her feel entirely naked—and entirely gorgeous—whenever she was near him. Like now as she caught his eyes on her, and immediately her breath hitched. Once upon a time, she'd known what to do with a man's interest. She'd also been forthright about acting on her own attraction. But ever since the attack…

She shook off the memories and waved her arm toward the living room.

"Go. Sit. Can I get you anything to drink? Pop? Beer? Water?"

"Beer would be great." He nodded thanks, before heading into the living room.

She collected a couple of bottles of beer from the fridge and assembled a large plate of deli meats, cheeses, and crackers, along with a big bowl of green onion potato chips. After all, it wasn't exactly like either of them was going to sleep any time soon. Balancing the plate and bottles so she only needed to make one trip, she headed to the living room.

He looked up at her and took a plate. "Hey, thanks. Just what I need. It's been a long time since dinner."

She set the beers down on a couple of coasters on the large coffee table, while he placed the bowl of chips in the center. He took the cold bottle of beer and pressed it to his red face.

"So. What did Peter say?" Trying to sound casual didn't work. She failed to keep the tension out of her voice.

After a long pull of his beer, he unceremoniously stuffed a ham-and-cheese cracker sandwich into his mouth. She sat on her hands, fighting the urge to fidget. She rocked back and forth a little, aware he was deliberately taking a long time to answer—and that couldn't mean anything good.

She was about to repeat the question when he finally finished chewing and swallowed. "He wasn't there. Must have changed his mind about staying the night."

"Wasn't there? What do you mean, he wasn't there?"

John met her gaze before zeroing in on another cracker. "Just what I said. Peter's truck is gone. There was no one in the bunkhouse."

She bit her lip while her stomach churned. She'd been hoping that a quick chat with Peter would have cleared things up. Now what? "Nothing taken, or messed with?"

"No. Just like this place."

She tightened her grip on her beer bottle. "All we're dealing with is three loose dogs and an unexplained open door?"

"That's right."

Her teeth continued to nibble at her lower lip. *If that's all then why am I scared to death?*

She couldn't help but curl up tighter on the end of the couch, hugging her knees with her arms. A chill swept through her body, even as perspiration beaded around her hairline. Her skin felt oddly sensitive to the cloth touching her skin. All her alarms were screeching a warning. Triggering her body into overreacting.

"Look, I know your father likes Peter, and trusts him. But do you?" John asked.

"No." She pulled a face and grabbed a cracker from the platter. "Don't like him. Don't trust him. Then again, I don't trust many people." She held the cracker to her lips, nibbling on it like a small animal. It tasted like sawdust in her suddenly dry mouth.

"I don't like him, either, but don't worry." He took another swig of beer. "If he doesn't stay in his place, he'll be out of a job." He swiped a third cracker sandwich and inhaled it. "So, where's your father again, exactly?" A few crumbs flew out of his mouth and landed on the coffee table. "Sorry...guess that was a pretty *crumby* thing to do."

She groaned before giggling as he quickly brushed away the cracker remnants. "Wow, now that's a dad joke if I ever heard one. It's almost like you want me to call you a geezer."

His cheeks flushed an adorable shade of red as he shook his finger at her in mock anger. "Don't you dare start in with geezer. Unless you want to be known as Princess from here on out."

"Okay, okay, truce! Besides, I thought we'd settled on General for me." She scooted off the couch and knelt beside Koda and gave her a good scratch behind her ears. The dog groaned her appreciation. "Oh, and my dad is at the Cattle Ranch Association quarterly banquet."

"Sounds like an interesting evening. That a big deal locally?"

"Pretty boring, actually. But he and Linda seem to enjoy it. Guess it's fun for old folks." She bit her lip to stifle her laugh. "Maybe you'd like it, too."

She turned, hiding her grin until a fluffy pillow collided with her head.

"Quit calling me old," he said before packing more food into his mouth.

"I call it as I see it."

"Okay, *General,*" he teased. "And I guess someone needs glasses. I'm thirty, not three hundred. I'm not even in my prime yet."

"Oh, really." She hoisted herself up and walked to the hall closet. Her hands rested on the handles of the bi-fold doors and she took in a deep breath. The tension in her body left. She was grateful she didn't have to be alone tonight, not to mention surprised at how much she enjoyed his company.

Grabbing an armload of pillows and throw blankets, she kicked the door closed with her foot and made her way back the living room.

"You can stay if you want," she said, as casually as she could manage. "At least until my dad gets home."

"Yeah. Sure. I can stay if you want me to." He didn't sound too eager to accept the invitation, but she didn't care. Regardless of her attraction to him, his presence made her feel safe. Or safer than she would alone.

Better make sure he doesn't get the wrong idea. She tossed John a pillow and a couple of blankets, keeping a few for herself. She plopped onto the sofa on the other side of the room, grabbed the remote control for the television, turned it on, and started flipping through the channels. "Anything you care to watch?"

He bent over, untied the laces of his boots, and placed them next to the couch. "Yeah. The back of my eyelids. Keep the volume down, please." He sprawled out on the couch and closed his eyes, shielding them with his forearm.

"One beer too many?" she joked.

"More like your driving," he teased right back, stifling a yawn.

She lifted one of the throw pillows, poised to launch it at him just as he peeked out from under his arm and raised one hand. "Don't you do it."

She tilted her head and flashed him an evil grin. "Why not? Who knows, maybe you're the kind of guy who's into a mild beating-by-pillow."

Oops. That came out a little too suggestive. And John noticed, given the way his breath audibly hitched. He cleared his throat. "Careful now, General. If I didn't know better, I'd think you were flirting with me," he said before closing his eyes again. "You're kind of cute when you're not tearing me a new one."

Her mouth fell open. Did he really just go there? She studied him, looking younger than usual with his eyelashes kissing his cheeks, his body so relaxed....and a pillow, strategically positioned over his lap.

Katie's eyes went wide. The realization of what he was likely hiding with that pillow curled through her lower belly with fluttery warmth. She nudged her thighs more tightly against each other. Heat and wetness built where her thighs met.

A subtle creak in the floorboards squashed her mood as quickly as it had begun. Katie cleared her throat, tucking her knees to her chest. She turned her attention to the TV and hoped it would distract her from her fear. And from the echoes of her arousal.

Chapter 16

A soft moan cut through the silence of sleep. John forced his eyelids open, yet remained still. Some nights he heard sounds—sounds that weren't there. But it wasn't the firm mattress of the bunkhouse beneath him, it was the slippery surface of a sofa. Another moan reached his ears.

Did the intruder return while he was asleep?

A softer moan. This time a woman's.

Must be a movie. *What the fuck is she watching?* He inched his arm to his forehead to see what was on the screen. *Of course.* He should have known. *Why did it have to be* that *movie?* Why were people going crazy over a glorified porno with bondage? If he was lucky, Katie would be asleep and he could turn this crap off. Or at least switch over to another channel.

His eyes took a couple of seconds to adjust to the dimly lit room. He turned his body, hoping the remote would be on the coffee table. His muscles ached and he didn't want to get off the couch. As his shoulder hit the leather of the couch, his breath caught.

She was definitely not asleep.

His eyes widened at the sight—remote in one hand, while her other hand disappeared beneath the blanket spread over her knees. Her lips parted, and her glossy eyes focused intently on the screen. His eyes traveled down to her spread legs. Even covered, he could make out the circular motion of her right hand.

Just ten feet away from him, she was touching herself.

"Oh, *fuck!*" He gasped.

She squealed, dropping the remote like a branding iron that had just burned her. She scrambled to find the remote on the floor, tossing the blanket around and shooing away the startled dogs, still half-asleep.

"I—I thought you were out cold!" She yelped it like an accusation and reached for the remote, but with her legs caught in the blanket couldn't right herself in time. With another shriek, she rolled onto the floor in a tangle of blanket and dogs.

A short bark of laughter erupted from his chest. The scene was comical, but it wasn't laughter that had his pulse racing. Beneath the blanket on his own lap, his dick stood at full attention. The knowledge that Katie—the woman who lit up his body like a Christmas tree—had gone at it all by herself, without caring one bit he that was lying just a few feet away from her, spoke directly to the man in him. His muscles twitched from arousal, and he gripped the blanket on his lap tightly, fighting for control of himself.

He tried hard to smother his arousal, forcing his body to lie perfectly still, unsure about what to do. Her obvious embarrassment could send her into one of her hurricane tirades, and a squabble was the last thing he wanted.

A new wave of electricity rushed through him when she stood up, finally having freed her legs from the blankets. Her shorts were missing. He stifled his groan, disguising it as a chuckle. A real chuckle followed, even louder. He couldn't help it.

"What's so funny?" She whipped around, growling at him.

"Aren't you too old to be wearing white cats with pink bows on your underwear?"

Red crept up her neck and cheeks. She tried to throw the blanket around herself, but Nickel, thinking this was a game, tugged at the end of it. She stumbled and sat down hard on the floor.

Fresh laughter shook his body and burst from his mouth. He knew he shouldn't, but hell. This entire situation was too hilarious to hold back. She glared at him from the floor. "Seriously? What are you, twelve?"

He held up his hand as he tried to get himself under control. "You can't have it both ways. Either I'm an old man or a twelve-year-old boy—I can't be both."

She snorted. "That's what you think. Every man has a twelve-year-old boy in him. Why do you think women complain so much?"

"Whatever you say...*General*." He chuckled one last time, sucked down a deep breath, and walked over to her, extending his hand to help her up. As she reached up and grabbed his arm for support, he noticed her gaze fall and land on his crotch. Which, despite the moments of levity, was still engorged. As she stared, her breath hitched, making him swell even more.

When she finally stood, she closed the distance between them and pressed her body against his. Both their breaths shook. She pressed her tongue to the seam of his lips, delving inside his mouth with a fiery, desperate passion. *Holy fucking shit!* This was nothing like his fantasies. His blood sizzled every time she ran her velvety tongue over his. *Holy fucking shit.* He groaned when her arms reached up and tangled around his neck, feeling the beating of her heart against his chest. His own hammered as his hands rested below her ears, his thumbs caressing her cheeks as their tongues mingled.

A high-pitched whine broke through the passion-filled haze, causing her to jerk away. Her eyes flew open and she gasped, before sucking down two shaky, shallow breaths. Then, as if she were royalty, she pushed her shoulders back and smoothed her hair into place. That invisible wall of hers went back up—so solid, he could almost see it. Like nothing had ever happened. "I'm headed back upstairs now. Sorry to disturb you. Better get some sleep—you have a lot of work to do in the morning."

She grabbed the blanket, swished past him, and then flew for the stairs. The three dogs took off, right on her heels. They all bolted up the stairs together, as if running from something terrifying.

His head dropped down, eyes settling on the outline of his erect dick, visible through his jeans. Maybe she *was* terrified—of the heat he was packing. But the internal joke didn't calm his nerves. His hand ran over the nape of his neck, recalling how she'd stiffened at their first introduction, and how she startled whenever he took a sudden step in her direction. Many times he'd caught her standing with her arms wrapped around herself like a barrier.

Humiliation chased away his arousal. He knew better than anyone how to read the signs. Or at least, he should be able to, by now. This was just a re-run of the thing that had happened with the woman at the bar. The same thing that had happened more than once now.

No matter how bad he wanted to spin it, the truth was Katie Locke was repulsed by him. Maybe she'd caught sight of his scars somehow, or who knew? Maybe she could sniff out how broken he was, without ever seeing a thing. Or maybe she really was the Princess he'd originally called her. The queen of the manor, sneering down at him once she her moment of insanity passed and she returned to her senses to realize she was kissing the lowly foreman. A used-up, broken down one, at that.

Anger sparked within him, but that heat quickly flickered out, leaving behind a hollow chill. How could he be mad at her? She was only echoing what he himself thought. No doubt she'd regretted the kiss the moment after it happened. By now? Hell, she'd probably forgotten the whole thing. Best if he did the same.

Determined to do just that, John twisted his neck until he felt the bones crack and release a flood of relief to the rest of his body. *God, I really am getting old*. And soft.

He needed a distraction, so he reached into his pocket and pulled out his phone. He opened his email, clicking through messages he hadn't checked for days. Some of them were from men he'd deployed with. Most of those messages simply read, "Miss ya, buddy." Or "Do you want to create a memorial for McDonald?" Or "How are you handling recovery?"

The emptiness in his heart, the numbness pounding in his brain, the sheer nothingness that took hold of his soul threatened to engulf him entirely. His fingers gripped the phone so tightly the case creaked in protest. He swiped the program closed without responding to anyone. He couldn't answer those questions. Not yet anyway.

And maybe never.

Chapter 17

KATIE

Sunlight danced across the kitchen's glossy stone floor, reflecting onto several objects and familiar furnishings. The cheerful light promised a good day ahead. But a nagging anxious feeling wouldn't release its grip on Katie. The possibility of an intruder left her unsettled, even after the embarrassing encounter with John. Her arousal had consumed her the previous night, and the movie just tipped her over the edge. And that kiss, dear god. That had only fanned the fires of her attraction to him even more. Between that and the unsolved mystery of the open door, she'd spent most of the night tossing and turning. And based on John's grumpy mood this morning, she guessed that he'd done the same.

"I'm trying not to worry about Dad, but it's tough." She stood up on her tiptoes to peer out the front window of the kitchen, and then glanced back at John, who stared into the depths of his coffee cup. Since last night, his expression had taken on a strange iciness. Or it could be her imagination, working overtime again. More likely, he was embarrassed by catching her in the act, and the kiss that followed, and trying to get things back to some semblance of normal. The exact thing she needed to do.

She cleared her throat and refocused on the view outside of the window, deciding the best way to handle her faux pas and the resulting awkwardness was simply to brazen through it. But she couldn't push their kiss from her mind. The feel of his lips, the way his heart hammered against her chest. How his pure strength felt soft and tender. And how she wanted more of it. Which was a terrible idea. In addition to the fact that she was essentially his boss, the strange feeling that John was hiding something remained.

To her surprise, he made no reference to her moment of abandon, instead simply nodding at her without uttering a word. She heaved a shaky sigh of relief even as her gut gave a sharp twist.

"He should have been home not long after we were. I've never known him to stay away all night," she said again. Partly to fill the awkward silence.

"You're sure he's not here?" John didn't bother to look at her when he spoke, choosing instead to continue perusing the interior of his mug.

"His car's not here."

"Well, yes, but maybe Linda dropped him off for some reason." His broad shoulders lifted and fell. Something about the careless motion dug beneath her skin.

"No, she did not." Her words came out clipped as she shook her head. "The door to his room is sitting half open. His bed hasn't been slept in."

He yawned and held up a finger, signaling her to wait. His obvious lack of concern set her teeth on edge. "Any chance he might have stayed over with Linda?"

Her eyes widened and her mouth dropped open. "Oh my—no! I told you already, it's not like that with them. You're like a broken record."

His brows lifted and a corner of his lip curled. "Hate to break it to you, Princess, but just because your love life is a sad state of affairs doesn't mean everyone else's is."

A gasp flew from her mouth. Of all the nerve! Then, a new thought shot into her mind. "You mean, like yours?" Did he have someone else? That would explain the cold shoulder she'd gotten all morning—guilt. The idea that he might have a girlfriend tucked away somewhere turned her stomach sour, so she poured more milk into her cup.

His jaw tightened before he relaxed. "Now, Princess, I'm pretty sure that falls under the things-you-aren't-allowed-to-ask category of employee questions."

Heat flew to her cheeks, but thankfully, he moved on before she had a chance to respond. "When was the last time you tried his cell phone?"

"About an hour ago. It just went straight to voicemail." She pulled her phone from her pocket and punched in her dad's number. The line rang and when it hit voicemail, she hung up while goosebumps prickled along her skin. "I'm getting worried."

"Did you try calling Linda? You said she went with him last night." He opened the fridge and began searching through it. "You must have something in there that would make a decent breakfast. Oh—now we're in business." He returned to the counter with a slab of bacon. "Perfect."

She scratched at her forearm. "We could try Linda, but I don't have her new number."

"Wouldn't your dad have a copy in his office?"

She ducked out of the kitchen, making for the small back room her dad fondly referred to as his office. The little desk and bookcase were almost dwarfed by his varied collection of treasures. Family mementos too hideous to be displayed in the rest of the house, but too dear to part with. Pictures she'd scrawled in crayon in her preschool days. Even parts from his first truck, the one she was conceived in. "Dad, the secret sentimental packrat."

Standing over the desk, she inhaled her father's usual aftershave. The file she needed was already on the desk. But after scanning the pages, she came up empty handed.

"It's not there," she said, returning to the kitchen to find John pouring himself another cup of coffee, the French vanilla aroma filling the air of the room. "I guess he updated the number in his phone but not in her file."

"We'll go down to my office. Her number's got to be there somewhere. And if it isn't, we can always—" He stopped.

"Always what?" She prodded, and when he didn't answer, she filled in the rest herself. "Call the cops and check for accidents?" At his reluctant nod, her mouth went dry. "You think...something's happened?"

For the first time since she'd seen him this morning, his eyes softened. "Katie, if anything bad had happened someone would've called. The hospital. Or the police. Or Linda. Your dad's fine." He rolled his neck and then shrugged. "I still say they stayed over together somewhere."

Not that again. "I told you, they're not—"

"Okay, I've got it, whatever you say." He lifted his hands in surrender, a motion that didn't match his skeptical expression. "Come on, we'll go out to the foreman's office and see if her number's in there." The chill returned to his voice, but at least he was relaxed. That helped to calm the barrage of terrible what-if scenarios that kept flying through her head.

A curt, sharp whistle cut through the air. Irritation stung her as Koda trotted into the room and stood at John's feet. Koda wasn't just her pet. She needed Koda. Both she and the dog had suffered horrible traumas and now, they protected one another. When Koda had first arrived, some of the ranch hands had become overly interested in her, not understanding the dog's need for space. But after she worked with the dog, Koda began to rebuild the confidence to interact with people. The dog had been a godsend, making her feel safe and protected—and she wasn't about to lose her to this man who simply walked in and took over as though Koda belonged to him.

They grabbed their coats and walked outside into the brisk mountain air. Although autumn was upon them, the fields seemed greener than ever before. The herds of cattle grazed in the distant pastures. A few hundred calves had been born this year. Some would stay on and become replacement cows, but most would go on to dinner tables as some of the finest beef on the country.

They reached the equipment barn and entered the small, cramped office. Immediately, John went to the vertical cabinet in the corner and pulled out Linda's employee file. "Here's her new number. Do you want me to make the call?"

"No. He's my dad, I can handle it." She might be thankful for his presence, but she wasn't about to let him know—especially since he had a bug up his ass about something this morning. Plus, even grumpy, she valued the way he didn't give her special treatment but acted the same way with her as he did anyone else on the ranch. She didn't want to risk ruining that with pity—or worse, disgust at her weakness. She grabbed the phone on the desk and punched in the number.

After seven rings, someone finally answered. "Hello?"

"Linda! It's Katie. Um, I was wondering if you know where my dad is." Her eyes fell upon John's, even as she listened to Linda's reply, instinctively seeking support.

"...poker game with some of the other men—"

"I'm sorry, what?" She struggled to hear Linda's words over the pounding of her heart.

"He went off with some of the other men after the banquet. Said they'd be playing poker at the hotel."

"Okay," she whispered. "Sorry I woke you up." She gnawed at her inner cheek, hanging up the phone.

"What did she say?" he asked.

"He stayed up at the hotel with some of the other men at the banquet last night. Linda heard something about a poker game. His truck was still there when she left."

His stiff, soldier-like posture relaxed at the news. "There. You see? He's fine. Just a little poker game he probably doesn't want anyone to know about."

"But—it's not like him."

"Are you sure?" He glanced down at her, his gaze never diverting toward her scars. "Look, your father works way too hard around here. He's allowed a little time to himself once in a while, don't you think?"

His words seemed to buzz around her like a fly you couldn't swat. He hadn't tacked on a *Princess* this time, but she could almost hear the word anyway. Mocking her. Suggesting that she was the reason her dad worked too hard. Her spine stiffened. "You think I'm overreacting, right? But I'm telling you, I know him better than you do, and—"

"Hold up. I don't think you're overreacting, okay?" He sighed and dragged a hand down his face. "If it were my mom, I'd be doing the exact same thing. I think we're both tired. And you're stressed—understandable, given the situation. Look, we got off on the wrong foot this morning, how about we start over?" To her astonishment, he held out his hand for her to shake. She eyed it suspiciously before extending her own. His big hand swallowed her smaller one, and the heat generated by his touch rippled across her skin.

She yanked her hand away and took a hasty step back. Worried that somehow, he'd be able to tell how such a simple touch from him affected her. His mouth tightened back into a grim line but didn't comment. "Come on, let's go back inside where it's warm, and I'll cook us some breakfast."

She latched on to the neutral topic with a wave of relief. "You cook? Don't remember seeing that on your job application."

Koda walked just behind the two of them. The dog barked and then let her tongue hang out, as if in appreciation of her quip. From the way John's back stiffened though, he didn't find the same humor in it.

"Yes, Ms. Locke. I can cook," he said. "Shocking as that may be for a man like me. I'm happy to prove it to you by fixing breakfast."

Katie sighed. Now what had she done to piss him off? She opened her mouth to tell him he didn't need to bother, before thinking the better of it. Why not let John make breakfast? Maybe he was the kind of guy who got grumpy when he was hungry. If so, then she was pragmatic enough about her kitchen skills to know that his bad mood stood a better chance of clearing up if they ate his cooking versus hers. If she didn't hear from her dad by the time they finished eating, she'd hop in her car and start looking.

When they reached the front door, John stepped aside to let her enter first, an old-fashioned gesture that reminded her of her dad. A ringing sound met her ears the second she walked in, and her heart leapt. *Dad!* She sprinted for the kitchen, sending Nickel and Two Bits scattering in her wake. She fumbled with the receiver of the old mounted phone, mentally cursing the fact she hadn't tried harder to convince her father to swap the fifty-year-old phone for something easier to handle. If she lost this call … "Hello?"

She listened—or tried to—as her breath caught in her throat.

"Hello, may I please speak to Katherine Locke?" A strange female voice responded.

"This—this is Katherine Locke." She nibbled at the frayed edges of her nails like a famished mouse.

"Ms. Locke, this is St. Vincent's Hospital. We are calling to inform you that your father, Mitchell Locke, is here. He suffered a minor heart attack. We need you to come down as soon as possible."

The news was an icy finger down her spine, with the chill leeching throughout her body until she was almost frozen to the spot. Her stomach filled with lead while her legs began to buckle. Strong hands circled her waist and kept her from collapsing, pulling her back against a warm, broad chest. But the contact did nothing to ease the pressure building in her own chest.

The receiver slipped through her fingers.

"What is it?" John spun her around. "Katie, what happened?"

The sympathy in his eyes was too much to bear. "I told you," she whispered, burying her face into his flannel shirt. "I told you."

"Told me what? Katie, who's on the phone?"

But she could not make herself say anything more.

A tiny echo emitted from the receiver. Her fingers felt as wobbly as jelly when she reached for it, but John was faster. "Hello?" he said.

Her fingers gripped the extra material of his shirt as she pushed her face against his body. After a few moments, John replied. "Ms. Locke's unable to speak to you at the moment." John's matter-of-fact tone took the edge off her panic. "Yeah, I'm a family friend. Tell me what's going on."

She drew in a deep breath. The faint smell of beer still lingered on his clothing. But she also smelled him. His scent. And a bit of sandalwood cologne.

"We're on our way." The receiver clicked as it connected with its cradle. His muscular arm shifted around her waist as he grabbed her keys off a nearby hook steering her out the door. "Come on. We're going to see your dad."

Tears blurred her vision, and her chest heaved. Her ribcage squeezed, like an elephant was sitting on her. She barely registered her legs moving or what was going on around her. Until the car door slammed. She jumped, her hand flying out. She sank into the seat when the car engine rumbled. Though she'd cleaned the vomit from the floor mat, a faint odor lingered, making her already unsettled stomach churn more.

Dad, please be all right.

Chapter 18

JOHN

John navigated the red hybrid through the twisty mountain roads to the main highway, hoping to reduce the normal hour and fifteen-minute ride into Billings by thirty minutes. But his attention was on the woman in the passenger seat beside him, slumped over with tears flowing down her cheeks. His stomach knotted. He should say something, but he didn't know what. How was he supposed to comfort her? Or even, if she would be receptive to his offer, after the way she'd run away last night?

When his mother had her heart problems, he'd taken a practical approach. Getting her healthy before his deployment had been his only goal. There hadn't been time to analyze his feelings about the situation. Maybe Katie could benefit now from his experience.

"My mother had some heart issues, too. I was about to deploy again when they started, so I just focused on getting her as healthy as I could before I left. I stayed with her at the hospital—"

Katie gasped. "*That's* where I know you from!" She whipped around in her seat, staring at him. Her tears had stopped.

"Huh?"

"The hospital." Her voice was an echo of its usual self, but there was growing confidence as she continued. "I met you at the hospital during my clinical rounds. It's been bugging me since you started working at the ranch. This feeling that I knew you, but I couldn't place how." She sank back in the seat again and released a loud sigh. "At least I know I'm not crazy. Not entirely, anyway."

"Shit. Seriously?" He tossed the information around for a moment, trying to remember the details of his mother's last hospital stay. Things were hazy, but bits and pieces began to come into focus. He'd been pretty stressed at the time, but now that she mentioned it, he seemed to recall a pretty nurse with dark hair and a sassy swing to her hips that looked an awful lot like Katie. He frowned. If he remembered correctly, that nurse always had a bright smile on her face. Had that really been Katie? He glanced over at her again, lingering on her profile. "I think maybe I remember you, but it's a bit fuzzy. Did you used to smile a lot more?"

She went still. "Yes. Probably." Then, she shook her head, like she was shaking off a dark thought. "So that *was* where I saw you. I knew it! But your head was shaved back then."

"Buzzed," he corrected. "I've never had a shaved head."

She snorted. "Whatever. We can agree that it was short."

While he drove, his brain worked overtime trying to figure out how to make her feel better without getting all soft and sappy. He knew he'd been stand-offish this morning, and now he felt bad. As much as the knowledge bothered him, it wasn't Katie's fault that she didn't find him appealing, with his scars and stiff body. He could still remember those moments when his mom first clutched her chest and complained of a crushing pain and dizziness, and the panic that flooded him at the thought of losing her. Once she was hospitalized, her friends tried to help, but their gushing reassurances only irritated him. His mom was the only family he had. Platitudes, no matter how well intentioned, didn't cut it. He knew Katie would feel the same way about her father. *If only I could take away some of her pain, even for a little while.*

"How does the moon cut its hair?" he asked.

At first, he thought she might not respond at all. Then she sighed. "How?"

He waited a beat. "Eclipse it."

His sideways glance caught her jaw dropping. "Oh my god. Apparently, I lied last time. *That* is the worse joke I've ever heard." But her lips upturned, briefly.

They pulled into the hospital parking lot. Once the car stilled, Katie began to shake, looking like a wild horse just arriving at the ranch for schooling and terrified of people. He laid a hand on her back when she doubled over and grabbed her knees, struggling to regulate her breathing.

"I—I—"

He cursed silently to himself. For all his experience, he was just like any other man—frozen, feeling powerless he couldn't come up with a solution to comfort her. "What can I do?"

"I can't go in there."

Not the response he was expecting but okay. She probably just needed a few minutes to come to her senses. "I know it's scary, but your father is in there. He needs you. Seeing you will make him feel better."

"No," she said, gasping sharply as she held onto the seat.

He blinked. No? Okay, so appealing to her emotions right now wasn't going to work. Time to try a new tactic. "You're his next of kin, so they'll need you to sign papers and stuff."

He glanced toward the sliding doors that marked the hospital entrance, his foot tapping his impatience. He glanced back over to catch loose tendrils of hair slapping her cheeks as she shook her head.

His foot tapping increased its tempo. His fingers curled around the steering wheel. He forced himself to calm him impatience. Reminded himself that she'd just had a big shock. "Looks like you need a couple minutes to get ahold of yourself. Go ahead, and then when you're ready, we'll walk in together."

"You don't understand—no, means no, I'm not going in. Not right now. Not in five minutes. Not at all. So quit harassing me!" Her voice gradually rose until by the end, she was almost screaming.

He reared back from her and felt his own temper rise. "I brought you all the way out from the ranch so you could see him."

Her fingers dug into her thighs. "Sorry," she said, in a softer voice this time. "I just can't go in there. It's too...hard."

He couldn't believe what he was hearing. "Look, I already said that I'll go with you. I know it's hard, but he's your *father*."

Bright red spots bloomed in her cheeks. "Thank you for that very helpful reminder. But you need to stay in your lane. I am staying in this car, and there's nothing you can do about it. *You* go. Don't ask me again."

Anger seared through his veins. He wanted to grab her by the shoulders and shake her. *You don't leave family behind, dammit!*

The image of Dirk's broken body flashed through his brain and he closed his eyes, but couldn't shut out the sight of his mangled friend.

Meanwhile, all Katie had to do was get up and walk through the hospital doors—a place where she used to work, for crying out loud—to see her father. Yet apparently the sight of her dad in a hospital bed was too difficult a burden her poor, precious self with. Never mind that her dad was probably frightened now too, and desperate to see his only daughter.

His mind went back in time. To the day his ex-wife told him that marriage to a soldier was too hard. And here he'd been thinking that Katie was different.

"Pardon me," he said, in a curt voice shorn of all sympathy. "I didn't realize that hospital visits were so beneath your highness. I'll just run on in and let your father know that his darling little girl can't be bothered to visit him."

Fuming, he jumped out of the car before he completely lost his temper and really let her have it, slamming the door behind him before he stalked toward the hospital entrance.

He heard Katie's sob as he walked away, but he didn't look back. She could drown in her tears for all he cared. She was probably mad because he'd called her on her entitled bullshit.

The brightly lit lobby of the emergency room and the astringent of antiseptic slapped him the face and gave him pause. Was he being too hard on her? After all, her father *had* just had a heart attack. Then he remembered the way she'd sneered at him, telling him to stay in his lane. Upset or not, she was acting like a child scared of an imaginary monster in her closet, rather than a grown woman whose father needed her.

He glanced over his shoulder toward the automatic doors, checking to make sure she'd hadn't followed. There was no one there. His ex had never shown up for him, either.

With a shake of his head, he ran a hand along the back of his neck and went over to the reception desk.

A nurse looked up at him and smiled. "What can I do for you, sir?"

"I'm here to see Mitch Locke," he said.

She glanced at her clipboard. "Are you family?"

"No. I work for him."

"Mr. Locke is in intensive care right now. I'm sorry, sir, but unless you're a relative I can't let you see him."

He resisted the urge to raise his voice and stared the woman down. "Ma'am, I'd love nothing more than to have his daughter come in to see him. In fact, I drove her out all this way to do just that. But she's camped out in the car, refusing to set foot inside for god knows what reason. I don't know what her problem is and frankly, right now I don't care." He took a deep breath to calm the anger brewing inside. "What I do care about is that Mr. Locke just had a heart attack and he's all alone. All I want to do is to let him know that someone cares enough to visit, and since she won't come in, I'm what he gets. I promise, I won't stay more than two minutes."

The nurse eyed him before giving a slight nod. "If he gives me permission, you can see him. Just fill this out."

He counted to ten slowly under his breath. *You need to calm down and stay calm.* Mitch needed someone he could rely on—and that wasn't Katie. And, if he didn't manage to restrain his temper, it wasn't going to be him, either. The form was tedious, but he scrawled his information and signed his name as quickly as possible.

"Thank you, sir." The nurse disappeared down the hall with the sheet.

The white walls, sterile chemical smell, and blinking florescent lights made him feel like he was hooked up to a cattle fence—not enough voltage to kill but sufficient to keep things uncomfortable. A movement outside caught his attention. A guy in the uniform of an ambulance driver leaned against a tree and lit a cigarette.

He slumped back, disappointed, shaking as if he were overcaffeinated. He really thought Katie might snap out of whatever snit she was in and come in. But that hope faded with each passing minute.

The nurse returned and signaled him to follow her. As their footsteps echoed down the long hall, he decided things had probably worked out for the best. Mitch had just suffered through a heart attack. The last thing his boss needed was more stress...which is exactly what would happen if Katie showed up and performed another freak-out like she had in the car.

The hospital hallway was like something out of a space movie. Everything that could shine, did shine. There was stainless steel, sleek floors, and the artworks on the walls were natural images in colors as bright as spring flowers. The air had a pure fragrance, not sterile, just clean. In the background, a myriad of beeps from monitors created a symphony.

"Here we are," she said, pushing open the subdued blue-green door.

John found the room plainer than the hallways. Simple cream walls, not peeling or dirty, surrounded Mitch who was lying on crisp but thinning sheets. His normal gruff exterior had been replaced by pale skin barely clinging onto his bones, dwarfed by the mass of tubes and wires attached to him. His eyes were closed; only the faint rise and fall of his chest indicated he was alive.

John cleared his throat.

Mitch opened his eyes and squinted. A second later, the older man cracked a wry smile. "Hey, there." He let out a weak cough. "I figured someone would be down here soon enough."

"How are you feeling?"

"Better. Though, they're holding me prisoner a few more days for observation and testing." Mitch coughed again. "How's Katie doing?"

An awkward feeling came over John. How could he let Mitch down gently to the fact that his only daughter was more concerned about herself than her ailing dad? His jaw tightened when he thought of easy it would have been for her to just pop in for a few minutes. "Yeah. Well, you see, Katie came with me, but—she decided to stay in the car." The sight of Mitch so helpless made his frustration surge back in full force. He bit back the rest of what he'd like to say. None of his opinions on Katie's prima donna behavior would do Mitch a lick of good.

Even from the hospital bed, Mitch was far too observant. He studied John's grim expression and slowly hoisted himself into a sitting position. "You're upset with her, aren't you?"

John glanced away from those knowing eyes and cleared his throat. "Sir?"

"With Katie, for not coming in?"

There was no avoiding answering this time. "I think it might have been nice if she'd made an appearance, yes," he said, choosing his words carefully.

Mitch nodded. "I figured as much. Take a seat." He motioned to the chair beside the bed.

John perched on the edge of the chair, wondering where this was going.

The hospital bed creaked as Mitch took a moment to settle himself. "I didn't expect Katie to come at all," he said.

John hadn't been sure what to expect. Even so, Mitch's response managed to confuse the hell out of him. "Not come at all? I'm sorry, I'm not following."

"I'm going to tell you something in confidence," Mitch said slowly. "And only because you have to work with my daughter and the doctors believe I'm going to need the two of you to keep the ranch running while my old ticker recovers. You can't share this information with anyone."

"Understood, sir." He leaned forward, his eyes fixed on Mitch's face. The monitor near the bed beeped a constant, reassuring rhythm but inside his body, alarm bells began to ring.

"Katie used to work at this hospital, did she tell you that? She loved her job and was one of the good ones—brought a smile to her patients' faces, going the extra two yards for them." Mitch paused for a breath and John's gut clenched. Waiting for the punchline he knew was about to come. "Up until July, anyway, when she was attacked--right here in this hospital." Mitch closed his eyes tight. Despite his obvious illness, John could see the pain and anger on his face.

The words hung in the air. The niggling suspicions he'd had, early on. The ones that he'd pushed aside, deciding instead to believe that Katie was just a snooty, spoiled brat. Fuck. He'd been right. Worse than that—he'd been right, but allowed his hurt feelings to convince him otherwise.

His throat swelled with emotion and he had trouble swallowing. Bile rose to his mouth. "Attacked? Here? How is that possible? I mean, it's a hospital—"

Mitch sighed. "Katie was working as a nurse in the community clinic. It was after hours. From what she told me, a patient returned and attacked her while she was finishing up some paperwork. He beat her up, bad. She ended up in the hospital for days, needed surgery. You should have seen her. My beautiful girl, what he did to her face..." The man broke off when his voice thickened with tears.

John's own eyes grew damp. The idea of Katie, black and blue in a hospital gown. Weak and scared…he could barely stand it.

His mind ran through memories of times where things had seemed off. The blank distant stare at the police station, and the worried looks Mitch and Linda always gave her. The way she retreated whenever he got too close.

His stomach turned sour. Her occasional limping and the faint scars and unevenness on her pretty face. The anxiousness that consumed her when they'd come home to find the door open, insisting someone had gotten into the house. The way she'd practically begged him to sleep in the same room with her, even though they squabbled a lot.

His fingers laced through the short strands of hair on top of his head and tugged. Someone had hurt her. Really hurt her. And that knowledge was like a sharp spike into John's own chest.

"No one knows why he did it. Apparently, he just took one look at my daughter, and—" Mitch looked away.

John remembered what his boss had said to him the day they'd met.

"Katie's been working on the ranch her whole life. Even during college and nursing school. But—things didn't work out. Now she's back here full time."

He'd hadn't given much thought as to why Katie gave up nursing, but when he did, he'd figured that maybe it was because the work was too tough for her. Or worse, that she was fickle—just like his ex. He wished he could go back in time and punch himself in the face. Even then, the thought hadn't been fair. Working a ranch was every bit as challenging as working in a hospital, and Katie had been more than pulling her weight there, doing the work of several employees.

"They catch the guy who did it?" John's hands clenched into fists. He'd love a minute alone with the bastard.

Mitch set his jaw and shook his head. "No. The guy used fake identification at the clinic and the police haven't been able to find him. He covered his face so the footage from the security cameras didn't help much either."

"So, he could be anywhere." No wonder Katie had been so freaked out by the open door.

"That's right. I don't think Katie will ever get past her fear until he's caught and put away for good."

John closed his eyes. He had to ask. "Did this guy—"

"No. He didn't get a chance to, thank God for small favors. The head nurse and the janitor heard a commotion. Scared the guy off. But Katie was badly beaten, nonetheless. I don't think there's any way she'll ever step into this place again. Not even for me." Mitch collapsed back onto his pillow, exhausted.

Silence encompassed the room, broken only by the faint beeping of the hospital monitors. He thought back to what he'd said to Katie in the car and he wanted to cry. One thought materialized in his head, repeating over and over again in a continuous loop.

I'm such an asshole.

He'd feel bad enough if he'd innocently misjudged her. The thing was, he knew that a big part of his reaction was because her perceived rejection the night before had pressed an old wound. And that was solely on him.

His therapist was right. If he continued on this way, letting his wounds fester, he'd never be happy. "So, if they haven't caught the guy by now, what are the chances they actually will?"

Mitch shrugged. "Not good, I suppose. Don't think I haven't wanted to grab my rifle and go hunting myself. Not that it would do any good. The cops are sure he's long gone by now."

"Yeah. Let's hope so." The hairs rose on the back of John's neck, but he kept his worry to himself. Now was obviously not the time to tell Mitch about the ranch's possible intruder.

"Listen," Mitch said. "Obviously, I'm going to need you and Katie to keep the ranch running while I'm stuck in this place. And after I come home, too."

John sat up straight. "You can count on me, sir."

Mitch offered John a weak smile. "Thank you, I appreciate that. And Katie will be fine once she's on the ranch and gets back to work there. We can talk about specifics tomorrow. Come by in the afternoon. I know Katie's glad to have you living out at the ranch. Between you and Koda, things will be plenty safe."

John nodded. His mind was already busy, making a mental list of all the things needed to keep the place running.

"You'll probably need to hire another hand or two," Mitch said. "I'm sure Katie can tell you if it can fit into the budget. Though I'm nervous about the weather holding—"

John held up his hand. "Don't worry about a thing, Mitch." He stood, leaning forward to carefully navigate the maze of tubes and pat the man on his shoulder. "You just take care of getting better. Katie and I will handle everything else."

He left a few moments afterwards, determined to make his last words to Mitch the truth.

Chapter 19

KATIE

The ride home from the hospital was long and quiet, except for the gruff, "Sorry for what I said before," that John had spoken when he returned from visiting her dad.

She'd spent most of the time in the car feeling like a giant failure, so the apology had acted like a balm to her guilty conscience. Not that she could blame him for thinking the worst. He'd updated her on her dad's condition, and then dropped into silence that was broken only by the soft spill of country music from the radio. Periodically, she'd catch him glancing at her. Almost like he was checking to make sure she was okay. Katie wasn't sure what to make of that, but she found his solid presence reassuring.

The landline rang as Katie fumbled with her keys on the front porch. *What now?* She dashed into the kitchen and picked up the phone on the fourth ring.

"Hello?"

Dad coughed. "Wasn't sure you'd be home yet."

She tugged at her hair at the sound of his voice, so weak and raspy. A lone tear traced down her cheek. She should have tried harder to go inside. Been braver, somehow. Instead of hiding out in the car like a coward. "Dad! Oh, Dad. I'm so sorry I didn't come in to visit."

The floor creaked behind her and she looked up to see John standing in the kitchen doorway, hovering with that same odd expression she'd noticed on the ride home. The sight of his familiar form made her feel obscurely better, like he was a rock of stability in this flood of confusion that had struck her family.

"They have to fix a blockage," Dad said.

"Did they say how aggressive they needed to be? Or how long you would have to stay there?" When it came to being a nurse, she'd always been able to keep calm in emergencies. That was one of the reasons she'd been in the top five percent of her graduating class.

John placed a cup of coffee on the table in front of her before retreating to the bench at the far end of the kitchen with his cup, keeping a respectful distance between them but there if she needed him. She wasn't sure if his positioning was deliberate, but she appreciated it either way

"They said minimally invasive. Just think of it as an extended vacation," her dad said. "Sure, I'd rather be spending it at the beach, but the nurses are taking *real* good care of me."

She picked up the coffee, inhaled. The distinct aroma took her back to the night shift at the wards. "Dad, eww! Thanks for the visual. Remember, I know most of them." She turned toward John and lifted her brows. Her eyes sparkled wickedly. "So, does that mean I'm in charge around here now? I mean, did our foreman even bother to tell you about the excitement we got into last night?"

John choked, sputtering coffee. He raised one palm and waved it in the air, trying to signal her not to say anything.

She bit back a laugh. She'd pay good money to know what was going on in that stubborn head of his right about now. Did he think she was going to tell her father about the suspected break-in here at the house? Rat him out for his arrest? Or—she gave a little shudder—fill him on the details of her little X-rated peep show? So maybe she was being a little cruel, watching John squirm like this. But he sort of deserved the payback, after his blow up at the hospital.

"While you were busy having a heart attack, I was busy bailing," she bit her cheek to keep from giggling when John's eyes almost bulged from his head, "those knucklehead dogs of yours out of trouble. They somehow got loose and were racing around the property when we drove up. Don't worry, they're fine. But they sure gave me a fright when they came out of nowhere."

John sagged against the wall in relief. Please. Like she was going to burden her bed-ridden dad right now with bad news of any kind. The intruder and John's arrest could wait. First and foremost, her dad needed to heal.

"I bet. Now, you make sure you're locking all the doors and gates before you leave next time, you hear?"

"Yes, dad, I know. I'll be extra careful, I promise." And that was the unvarnished truth. She had a feeling both she and John would be double and triple checking locks from here on out. John caught her eye and nodded. "John says, him too."

"See that you do. I'm not gonna be happy if anything happens to those rascals while I'm stuck in here."

"Well, make sure you listen to the doctors and nurses, so that you can get out of there faster. Don't want you enjoying your stay so much that you forget about us. Do everything they tell you to do and rest up. We'll take care of the ranch. All right?" She smiled listening to her dad grumble and watching the massive man in front of her pouring a second cup of coffee.

"Alright. Oh, and before you go—take it easy on John, would you?" her dad said. "I know he likes to play the tough guy, but I think he's hurting a whole lot under that exterior. He doesn't ever talk about what happened to him, but you can tell it was something pretty bad. Something more than just getting hit by an IED."

"I'll keep that in mind. He's been a big help around here, especially today. I, uh—I promise I'll take care of this place while you're resting up. Okay?"

"I know you will, honey. I hate to put so much pressure on you after...everything. I'm glad you have John there to help out." Her dad's voice was heavy with exhaustion.

"Me too. Get some rest now, you sound tired. I'll talk to you later." They said their good-byes and she hung up the phone with a definitive click. For a moment, she simply stood, staring at the wall. When she was talking to her father, she could pretend everything was okay. But as soon as she couldn't hear his voice, the fear flooded back.

"So, he's still doing okay?" John asked, breaking the silence.

She let out her breath. "He's gotta stay in the hospital for a couple more days while they finish checking him out. But, yes, I think he's doing okay."

"Good, glad to hear it." He hesitated, cleared his throat. Fiddled with the dishtowel hanging from a hook, before looking up to meet her square in the eyes. "Look, I really am sorry for earlier. I let my own personal history get to me, and I ended up taking that out on you. It wasn't fair or right, and I feel like a real ass. You've been nothing but dedicated to the ranch and a hard worker since I've arrived. I hope in time, you can forgive me for my outburst."

A lump formed in her throat. Until this exact moment, she hadn't realized how much she'd needed to hear those words. To know that he saw her as something other than a weak, broken girl. "Already forgiven," she said, and meant it. Yes, he'd been harsh back in the car, but she knew those emotions were at least partly coming from a place of genuine concern, over her father. The personal history part intrigued her, too, but she didn't think now was the time to ask.

"Glad to hear that because I think it's best we get back to work. I've got several ideas we need to discuss."

She laughed. "Excuse me, but who put *you* in charge?"

"Your father did," he said slowly. Cautiously. Waiting for her to overreact...only, she didn't feel like overreacting, for a change.

His unexpected apology and acknowledgment of her overall competence had caused her body to sing with giddiness.

That didn't mean she couldn't mess with him a little, though. She crossed her arms and scrunched her features into a scowl. "No, he didn't."

John put his cup down and eyed her like she was a wild animal, liable to pounce at any second. "Actually, he did, when I went in and talked to him, at the hospital. If you don't believe me, though, maybe you should call him, get this straightened out." He leaned against the counter, his arms folded over his chest.

She smacked her hand on the counter and then had to bite her cheek to keep from laughing when he flinched. "Let's settle this right now."

He squeezed his eyes shut and groaned, obviously thinking this would be a drawn-out battle. She snatched up the kitchen towel, twirled it, and snapped his butt with it.

His eyes flew open while he yelped and then gaped in disbelief. "Did you just swat me with that towel?"

He rubbed the spot on his ass with such indignation, a giggle escaped. His expression was priceless. She snapped the towel into the air a couple more times for good measure. "I'm cracking the whip. Letting you know who's *really* in charge."

"Wait. Are you...*messing* with me?" he said, still rubbing the back of his jeans.

She lifted her shoulders and smiled sweetly. "Wouldn't you like to know? Now, I'm going to make myself something to eat. I'm starving. You want some eggs, too?"

He shook his head, his lips parted and his forehead wrinkled. She had to admit, he was adorable when befuddled. "I...no thanks. But I think it's lunch time."

"Well, then I guess I should make it an egg sandwich," she said, opening the refrigerator and bending down to peruse the contents.

"Just let me know when you're done eating, so we can get some work done."

She placed the Tupperware of ham and loaf of bread down on the counter. She pulled a knife from the block, pausing before cutting into the bread. "Sure, you don't want anything to eat? You'll be less grumpy, old man."

She snickered as he fumbled with the files in his hand. "Your dad mentioned hiring at least one other employee while he's out. We especially need someone to look over these financial records."

"Financial records?" This time, her ire rose for real. "That's *my* job." She set a plate down on the counter with a thump.

"What's your job--doing the finances? Or making the call?"

She braced her hands on the counter, glaring at him. Her chest tightened into a knot like a cramp. Leave it to him to ruin what few moments of camaraderie they might have.

"According to your dad, we're both in charge. Which means we have to work together. Without fighting." When she just stared, struggling to subdue the critical voices in her head, he rubbed a hand over his head and tried again. "I'm not trying to offend you. Mitch—Mitch gave me a job. He trusts me. You've got no idea how much that means to me. Last thing I ever want to do is fuck that up. I just want a chance to prove myself again, show what I can do."

Her heart stammered. "Yeah? Well, me too."

"Then, this should be easy since we're on the same page. How about instead of bickering about who's in charge of what, we work together, as a team. Think you can meet me halfway?"

She scratched her forearm, her anger dissipating. "I can try."

"Good. No time to start like the present. So, boss, do you think we have the money in the budget?" he said. "For the new employee, I mean?"

She nodded. "We do."

"Good. I don't think we should use it to hire another wrangler, though."

"Oh? Why's that?"

"I figured I could help you with the wrangling."

Her eyes widened. "You? Sure you can work that in, among the rest of your duties?" She noticed him glance at the sandwich on the plate beside him. "That's for you. And in case you were worried, no, I did not add salt."

She pushed the plate closer and he picked up one half of the meal.

"Thanks, I'm starving," he said. "And yes, I can take care of the wrangling on top of everything else. You need to ride out, I'll go with you."

Her stomach growled and she squirmed, trying to hide the rumbling. She picked up her own food, pinching off a piece of the corner and popping it into her mouth. "If we aren't going to hire another wrangler, what do you suggest we use the money for?"

"A housekeeper."

She coughed hard, sending a tiny speck of cheese across the table. "A—*what?* Are you joking? Why would we need a housekeeper? I take care of the house!"

He held his hand up. "Whoa, slow down. We're a team, remember? And I figured your hands are already full running the ranch. Since your dad will need to take it easy when he gets home, a housekeeper could be useful. She'd be able to take care of the cooking and cleaning and leave you free for more important things. Simple as that."

The defensive retort that rose to her lips faded as she watched him pick up one of the folders in front of him and turn the page. She realized he really wasn't trying to piss her off. He was trying to help. Why was she always so quick to come out swinging, especially when his idea was sound? It wasn't like she took great pleasure in dusting or vacuuming, and having someone else to cook the meals? Well, that sounded like bliss.

Katie picked off another small piece of the sandwich. The moist bread and lightly salted ham swirled around her mouth. Each bite was careful, buying her time to calm down. "When you put it that way, hiring a housekeeper does make sense. I'm terrible at cleaning. We'd be doing my dad a favor."

His eyes twinkled when he looked up at her. "Great, glad we settled that. Now, think you'll be ready to go in ten minutes?"

Katie frowned. In all the excitement lately, had she forgotten about an appointment? "Sure, I guess, but what are you talking about? Go where?"

"Town. I'll meet you at the car." John took one last bite of sandwich before wrapping the remaining half in a napkin, putting his plate in the sink, and starting for the door.

Katie carried her own plate to the sink. "Care to tell me what it's about?"

"You'll see when we get there," he said over his shoulder.

Her throat began to close. The familiar swarm of bats beating around in her chest arrived. Sweat covered her palms. Since her attack surprises only caused her anxiety. She wanted to tell him, to relieve the chaos that erupted inside of her. But she couldn't. She didn't want to have that talk with him. Admit out loud what a big part fear still played in her life.

So, she focused on what she knew. Not only was she capable, but he made her feel safe. He was a soldier, and always seemed to have a plan. He was methodical and observant. Too observant. She needed to do this. She needed to learn to trust him...and herself. Completely.

For the sake of the ranch.

Chapter 20

JOHN

Outside, John listened to the distant lowing of a cow and went down a mental checklist while he waited for Katie to reappear. Better do a sweep of the barns tonight. Immediate surroundings too—once she was safely locked in the house. He welcomed the familiarity of planning security. He felt like he had a purpose.

I could make some excuse to take Koda with me. Just like being back in the field again.

Keeping Katie safe, even when she didn't know about it, gave him a good feeling. Keeping people safe was something he could do, and do well.

Except for Dirk.

"Okay, I'm ready." Her voice disrupted his unwanted memories. He watched her descend the porch stairs while cradling the manila file folders in her arms, her gait only slightly uneven. She seemed a little nervous, but the moment he stepped toward her, her hold on the folders tightened, as if daring him to try and take them.

His chest tightened, wishing he could comfort her, tell her everything would be all right, but he didn't want to embarrass her or shoot her straight back into defensive mode. *I can't mess this up. Not when we just came to a truce.*

"I'll drive," he said. To his surprise, she tossed him her car keys without a word and climbed into the passenger seat.

Pod-person? Alien abduction? Or was she finally beginning to trust him?

Barely five miles down the road, John found himself wishing for a sarcastic comment to remind him of what lurked beneath her surface. Without a caustic remark stinging his ego, his mind was free to notice how she was biting at her full lips. Her fingers clasped and unclasped around the files, and he struggled not to reach over and wrap his hand around hers.

At least when she acts all obnoxious, I don't keep thinking of how much I want to hold her.

"We'll stop at the feed store first. Then swing by my mother's house," he said.

"Your mother's? Why on earth would we need to go there?"

The car rumbled down the gravel road, heading toward the highway and the sprawling mountains in the distance. "I've still got a few things there. Since it looks like I'm needed at your ranch, I want to make sure I've got all my stuff with me."

She snickered. "Don't forget we still have to pick up your truck. Unless you plan on paying after it gets towed."

"Thanks for reminding me."

They rode the rest of the way to Laurel, Montana, in silence. And the silence felt good, calming. He even found himself whistling a few times.

At the feed store, Katie recorded all their purchases in the small account book she'd brought with her, entering them one after another with a stub of pencil. "You don't have to do that. We could just use the receipt to reconcile later." He tapped the piece of paper beside her on the counter.

She shot him a dirty look and turned her back to continue her record keeping.

He grinned. This was how he liked seeing Katie—all sassy and confident. And this was how things should be with the two of them. They were both so competitive, always ready to challenge each other and outdo one another. Her attitude made him want to stand up for himself, to prove himself to be worthy of her good graces.

When she finally finished with her painstaking task, he grabbed as much of the supplies as he could carry. "The rolled oats and the salt blocks will be delivered by Saturday?"

"Sure enough," the cashier said.

"You don't have much patience," Katie commented as they reached the car.

The sun was clear and strong today, the summer not ready to give up its grasp on the world. Only the changing colors of the trees revealed fall was on its way.

He shrugged, stowing the supplies in the back of the car. "I have enough when I need it."

"Wouldn't being in the military teach you a lot of patience?" She climbed into the passenger seat.

"What? That's the dumbest thing I've ever heard. Why would you think that?" He swung himself into the car.

"You were a dog handler, right? Doesn't that take a lot of time? Patience?"

He ran a hand along his jaw. "I guess. I never thought about it that way. I had already been deployed when I got my dog, and she'd already had two prior handlers. She was a great dog and knew her job."

"What happened to her?"

He fixed his eyes on the road and tried not to squirm in his seat. "She got adopted through the same program as Koda, after—after she returned to the States."

He hoped that would be the end of things, but after a few moments, Katie glanced at him again. "Wouldn't it have been weird if I'd gotten your dog instead of Koda?"

His breath caught. What did he say now? She'd presented him with the perfect opportunity to tell her the truth. To let go of the secret he was keeping, and get them to an entirely clean slate, once and for all. He squeezed the wheel. He wanted to tell her. He really did. But every time he tried, the words lumped in his throat and refused to come out. So, he grunted instead. Telling himself he hadn't truly lied.

Even though he knew he was deluding himself.

At some point, he would have to come clean about Koda, but this wasn't the right time, he argued silently. The dog played such an important role in her life. She relied on Koda. *The last thing she needs is to worry I'm gonna take her dog away from her.*

No, not now. Not right after they'd formed a truce, and especially not with her dad sick and the possible intruder on the property.

"So, where are we going?" she said, and his tension eased at the change of the subject. "Your mother's house, or to pick up your truck?"

"My house. Well, my mother's townhouse. We'll get the truck on the way back to the ranch."

"So, you've been living with your mom?" she said.

"Yeah? Just like you live with your dad," he said, and then flushed at her questioning look. She wasn't being snippy. It was a genuine question.

Now who was overreacting?

His guilty conscience probably wasn't helping much. "Sorry. Yeah. When I came back from my last deployment and was discharged, I moved in with her. I didn't have a place to live and I needed help getting around for a little while. She offered, so it just made sense for me to move in with her."

She nodded. "Makes sense. Um, we should probably stop at the grocery store, too. I don't think we've got any food."

He stole another glance at the beautiful woman to his right. She wound a lock of her dark hair around her finger, toying with it. A strong urge to pull the elastic tie out of her hair struck him. He wanted to see the fall of those dark strands across the soft skin of her neck. Or better yet, see it spread out across his pillow.

He shifted his legs in the seat to disguise the growing bulge in his pants. *She's not ready for something like that and even if she were, she's not my type.* Grimly, he compared her to the women he usually went for. She was tiny, slim. There was nothing to her. Her breasts were the size of teacups.

He imagined holding them, her skin unbelievably soft beneath his fingers. He glanced at her, saw her nipples had hardened from the chill in the air. "Dammit."

"What's wrong?"

"Nothing." His eyes focused out the windshield. If he played it cool, maybe she'd think he almost hit a pothole and wouldn't notice Mt. Everest in his pants.

"Nothing, huh" Her voice was sweet. Too sweet. "You know, you don't play the innocent well. At all. You think I wouldn't notice you checking me out? Not to mention, you just swerved."

She sounded entirely too smug. His cheeks flamed. "Do you really want to talk about playing innocent? After last night?"

"Oh, right, because you neve*r...play.*"

Her innuendo for play was clear, making his body feel feverish, like he was burning up. "No! Not in front of other people, I mean."

"What you're saying is you've never let a girl watch you jerk off?" Her tone was innocent, almost nonchalant, which made the words even more shocking.

And even hotter.

He shifted in his seat. There was no way to answer that question, not without going down a road he knew they had to avoid. Things between them were complicated enough without throwing *that* into the mix.

Like a lifesaver tossed to a drowning man, a beacon of light appeared on the horizon. His mother's house. "Hey look. We're here." He swerved into the driveway.

She snorted but let the subject change slide. "How long will you be?"

"I think you should come in with me." He turned off the engine. "I don't know how long I'll be. Mom will probably want to tell me off for not taking better care of myself, but you'll be more comfortable inside than in the car." As soon as he said the words, he saw she was staring at his pants. He looked down at the unmistakable bulge of his dick.

Goddammit.

He hopped of the car as fast as he could, catching the side of his head on the doorframe. Fuck. Rubbing his head, he jogged up the front stairs, his cock begging for relief from the unbearable pressure. As he rapped on the door of his mother's house, there was only one thought in his mind: *Please let Mom be home before I do something really stupid.*

No answer. He used his key to let himself in. "Mom?" he called. "You here?"

"In the kitchen, Johnny! Come on in."

Thank you, God.

He tucked his dick into the band of his underwear to disguise his erection, wishing it could instantly deflate. He turned around in the doorway and waved, inviting Katie to come inside.

His mother stepped out of the kitchen, drying her hands on a dishtowel. She wore an apron that rivaled the wallpaper in the sheer amount of flowers covering its surface. She tucked her grey hair out of her face as she greeted him. "It's a bit early for you to be home, isn't it?"

Before he could answer, Katie stepped through the front door. "Hello, Mrs. Rathborne."

"You didn't tell me you were bringing a guest." His mother squeezed Katie's hand. "Come on in. I don't get a lot of company. If I'd known, I would've made lunch. Or at the least, some tea and cookies."

Katie grinned. "That's all right. It's nice to meet you."

He quickly jumped into the conversation. "Mom, this is Katie Locke. Her father is my boss. We were out running errands, so I just stopped by to get some more of my clothes and stuff."

"Sure, sure," his mother said, still smiling. "It's all been washed and folded, up in your room. Now, Katie, you come in here with me and we'll see what we can put together for you."

Katie shot him an amused look, following his mother into the kitchen. He watched her look around the kitchen. Like the living room, it was pleasant, comfortably worn—if you could ignore the explosion of flowers on every possible surface.

"Mmm, the coffee smells good. Vanilla?"

"Why, yes. You've a good nose." His mother beamed, reaching for a fresh cup. "I like to add a teaspoon of vanilla extract over the regular coffee grounds before I brew it. Gives it a gentle touch of vanilla flavor. It's my little secret. And much less expensive than buying the flavored kind.

"That's so smart and sounds delicious--I'll have to try it."

John's mouth was hanging open. He slammed it shut. Who is this well-mannered woman and what has she done to Katie Locke? "I tried calling a couple of nights ago. You didn't answer."

"I didn't see your number, dear. You sure you called?"

"Yes...and it was late," he said.

"Must've been at Esther's playing bridge." His mother brought over a covered cake plate from the counter, set it on the small kitchen table, and lifted the heavy glass top to reveal three-quarters of a fresh yellow cake with thick chocolate frosting. "Have a seat while I find some plates."

"That late?" His mother was avoiding answering.

"Oh! That looks delicious," Katie said, lightly punching him in the shoulder.

His felt his stomach rumble in agreement. It had been a while since he had the ham sandwich. "I'll have a slice."

"Guests first." His mother's hand made a shooing motion. "Go and get your things together while I take care of Miss Locke."

"Call me Katie." She looked around the kitchen. "I'll help set the table. Where are the forks?"

"In the drawer right there." His mother reached past her usual entertaining plates for the good china, used only at Christmas. Was his mother trying to get rid of him to talk with Katie? Or to avoid his inquisition as to her whereabouts? Oh, god. Was she on a date?

Leaving his mother cutting huge slices of cake, he bounded up the steps to his room. Nope, not thinking of her on a date. Nor what the hell she would've been doing that late. Nope, no way. He grabbed the laundry neatly folded on the end of his bed, stuffing it into a duffel bag as though his life depended on it.

When he returned downstairs, Katie and his mother were sipping steaming cups of vanilla coffee, chatting about their favorite desserts and how they were both looking forward to the first snow of the Montana winter.

"I'm all packed up. Ready to go."

The two women ignored him, continuing their conversation.

"This is delicious," Katie said around a big mouthful of cake. "Mrs. Rathborne, if you'll give me the recipe for this, I'll actually learn to bake."

"Of course! I'll print out a copy for you."

His eyebrow arched. "You're going to learn to bake? Instead of just burning banana bread?"

Her eyes narrowed, promising retribution for the insult, but instead of commenting she turned back to his mother. "I hear you've got a recipe for lasagna that's pretty good too."

His mother flushed. "It's nothing special."

"Not according to John."

To his immense embarrassment, his mother leaned across the table to pat his hand, exactly as if he were five years old. "He's a good boy. Even if he makes his mother worry."

Katie shot him a sideways glance and giggled. Great. His mom always had the superpower of making him feel about five years old.

"My bags are upstairs," he said. "Katie, would you mind giving me a hand carrying them down?"

"Um, sure." She got up slowly and followed him toward the stairs.

"I'll just wrap up some more of this cake so you can take it with you," Mom called, happily bustling around the kitchen.

He waited until they were inside his room and shut the door. He turned around to find her studying his private space, just like he'd appraised hers. For a moment, he wondered what she thought of it. It was comfortable but plain, with few keepsakes. He'd never gotten around to unpacking properly, even though his mother had urged him to make himself at home and even offered to unpack for him. The house just didn't feel permanent.

She nudged the duffel bag at the end of the bed. "Please don't tell me you need help carrying this?"

He sat on the side of the single bed, elbows on knees and his hands hanging in front of him. "I wanted to talk to you. About my mom."

"She's nice."

"I've never seen her so happy,"

She walked over near the window. "It's not unusual for a mother to be happy to see her son."

"It's not me. It's you."

"What?"

"You heard me." John ran his fingers through his hair. "Though it's been so long since I've brought a girl home, I shouldn't be surprised she treats this like a special occasion."

She pressed a hand to her chest and pretended to gasp. "I feel so special. So, when was the last time you brought a girl home?"

He rubbed the palms of his hands against his jeans, his heel tapping the carpeted floor feverishly. "Five years ago. Her name was Morgan."

The teasing smile slipped from her face. "Wow, five years ago? That's a long time. Morgan, huh?"

"Yeah. I married her."

Her eyes widened. "Are you telling me—that—"

"No. I'm not married now, not anymore. We got divorced a couple of years ago. No kids."

"Oh, thank god!" She winced and tried again. "Not that your personal life is any of my business. I just...I mean..."

Her cheeks flamed bright pink, signaling that she was likely thinking about their kiss. The enhanced color only made her more beautiful. John shifted his gaze to the floor. "Right. I'm only bringing it up because my mom never warmed up to anyone as quickly as she did to you just now. Not even Morgan. Especially not Morgan."

"I see."

"No, you don't see." He rose and paced across the small bedroom. "Those two never got along. It was a huge point of contention between us. No matter how hard Morgan tried, my mother never accepted her. The three of us would sit through family dinners in total silence. Eventually, there weren't any more family dinners at all."

"Your marriage ended because your mother didn't like your wife?" He could hear the suspicion in her voice.

He sighed, turning around to face her. "No. My marriage ended because being a military wife was less exciting that my wife had envisioned it to be—so she ended up sleeping with another guy."

Her soft gasp filled the room. "And...you caught her?"

"No. I was deployed. A buddy of mine caught them."

Katie winced. "Sorry. Maybe your mom sensed something from the beginning."

He shrugged. "Maybe. More like, my mom could tell that Morgan was spoiled from the beginning. Her daddy always gave her everything she wanted, let her flit from thing to thing growing up, quit in the middle if she wasn't having fun. As it turned out, having a husband stationed overseas wasn't fun, so she quit our marriage, too. In that sense, I guess, she was at least consistent."

He stopped pacing and looked at her. Red face. Red ears. Arms crossed and toe tapping. She was mad. Madder than he'd ever seen. And though he wanted to question why, all he could do was pick up the duffel bag and an extra pair of boots.

"Give me those." She grabbed the boots. "Don't want your mother getting the idea we went up to your room for a *reason* or anything. Like some horny teenagers."

He gulped, following her out of the room.

His mother waited at the bottom of the stairs. "You're sure I can't get you some lunch?"

"We really do have to be going." He gave her a brief hug. "If you need anything, just call me. And don't forget to take your medication."

"Isn't that supposed to be my line?" His mother shook her head. "I've been doing just fine all these years while you deployed, dear." She handed Katie a huge portion of yellow cake in a large Tupperware container. "It was so nice to meet you. John, you make sure she eats something! She's so small."

Katie grinned and took the cake. "You can be sure I'll eat *this*, Mrs. Rathborne. Thank you so much."

"Oh, no, dear. Thank *you.*" To his amazement, his mother took her by the shoulders and enveloped her in a massive hug. "Just call if you need anything."

"Thanks," Katie whispered. "We will."

John's eyes settled beyond the women to a photo on the wall. Himself and Dirk in uniform—just the reminder he needed. His chest tightened. *Stay focused, soldier. You can't protect anyone if you get emotionally involved, so don't let your guard down.* He'd made the mistake of letting Katie under his skin. He wouldn't let it happen again.

Chapter 21

KATIE

Katie balanced the phone receiver on one shoulder and held the file open in her hands. "Is there a nurse around? I want to make sure it's safe to give you the week's report."

"Safe!" He took the bait. "Listen, you! I had a mild heart attack, and I'm recovering nicely. I'll be home any day now, so don't you get no funny ideas of treating me like an invalid."

If his retort was any indication, her dad was recovering fast. "Well, okay. But don't say I didn't warn you."

"Now you're making me nervous. What bombshell are you going to drop this time?"

Behind her the kitchen door clicked open. She just managed to suppress a flinch. Turning her head a tad she spotted Joanne, the new housekeeper, step into the kitchen. It had been three weeks since Joanne started working for them, and Katie still found herself surprised by the other woman's presence.

Joanne smiled. She was an older woman with two sons in school and was glad of the chance to earn a bit extra during the week. The woman held a tray of empty mugs and a plate with one slice of blissfully unburnt banana bread still on it and mouthed the word "coffee."

"Hang on a moment, Dad." Katie cradled the receiver against her chest. "Is this for me?"

"I've just been taking everyone a cup of coffee and a bite. You're the last. I couldn't find you in the stables."

"I was working in the office." Katie lifted the remaining mug of coffee and the plate off the tray, setting it on the bench beside her. "Thanks."

"I was just going to do the dishes," Joanne said. "Will that disturb you?"

"Not at all." Katie smiled and returned to her call. "You still there, Dad? That was Joanne."

"How's she working out?"

A wave of relief filled Katie as she watched the older woman bustle around the kitchen. "Honestly? I don't know how we functioned so long without her."

"Can't wait to meet her," her dad said. "When you first told me you were looking for a housekeeper, I was flabbergasted. But the more I think of it, the more I can't believe we never thought of this ourselves. John's a smart man."

As much as she loathed to admit it, John's suggestion about the housekeeper had been a good one. Since Joanne had arrived, Katie had taken on most of her dad's duties around the ranch. Between the two of them they'd accomplished more than she could've alone.

"Katie? You still there?" Her dad's voice interrupted her thoughts.

"Yeah, I'm here."

"Don't leave me in suspense! How are you doing?"

She decided to take pity on him. "Great, Dad. We've moved the cattle to the north pasture, strengthened all the fences on that side and are just about to start on the hill paddocks."

"All the fences?" Her dad whistled. "If this is how productive the ranch is with you in the saddle, we should have got a housekeeper a long time ago."

She grimaced. The rapid progress of the fences was nothing to do with her, everything to do with John, or rather his absence. He spent most of his days repairing the fences with Peter. She genuinely couldn't make up her mind if he was devoted to the job—or avoiding her.

That's absurd. A big soldier like that running from little old me?

But ever since they'd left his mother's house, there had been something ....

"What? But I'm not tired—yes, nurse, you're the boss." Her dad sounded resigned. "I've got to go. Anything else, Katie?"

"No. We got this, Dad. The ranch is in good hands."

"Don't I know it." Her dad's voice was replaced by an electronic beep. Call over.

She stood still a moment, savoring the warm feeling left by her dad's confidence. *At least someone believes in me.*

The sounds of splashing water reminded her of Joanne's presence. She replaced the receiver and turned around. Even up to her elbows in dishwashing water and her curves hidden beneath an apron, Joanne was an attractive woman. She was comfortably feminine, wearing sensible shoes, but with bright lipstick. The wedding ring she wore prominently on one hand did not stop her from teasing the ranch hands or them from enjoying her jokes. Katie liked her—although she couldn't help but feel that next to Joanne she came up short.

"Your father?" Joanne asked comfortably. "How is he getting on?"

"Good," she said. "He'll be home soon, I hope."

"You'll be looking forward to it."

Katie picked up her coffee cup. "Yes. The house feels different without him."

The other woman scrubbed a pot, making the bubbles dance. "I know the feeling. When my boys go away every year to their grandmother's, the house feels so empty. Like someone died."

Katie shivered. Her death seemed to be the central theme of her nightmares lately. When she was in the house alone, every creak sounded like a footstep. She found herself lying awake in the middle of the night, waiting for a blow to fall from an unseen hand. Some nights she'd look out the window to the bunkhouse, hoping John was still awake and on guard.

"You said everyone else had some banana bread but me? Does that include John?" At Joanne's nod, she stiffened. "Where is he now?"

"In his office," Joanne said.

At that news, Katie hopped to her feet, making the woman eye her cup.

"You're not finishing your coffee?" Joanne said.

Katie shook her head. "I've got to catch John before he heads out again."

"The weather's terrible. The hail is falling hard and fast. I just missed getting pelted."

"I'll be fine." She headed out the door and marched across the yard, the files clutched to her chest.

The weather was mild, but not pleasant, especially after the warmth of the kitchen. The hail had stopped but the lingering rain had a chill to it that warned winter was getting closer. Her chest thumped with a mixture of adrenaline and anticipation as she flounced into the equipment barn. She flung open the door to the foreman's office.

John scrambled to his feet as she stepped into the room, Koda running over for pets. "What—"

Perhaps he thought the rain would keep her trapped inside the house? Like some princess. Honestly, she wasn't sure why she was so upset, but she was. It couldn't be because he'd been avoiding her lately. She would be silly to care about that.

Silly or not, she somehow managed to smash the files on the desk so hard some of the mail within slid out. "I think you've been working on the fences too long."

He put a hand on the desk to steady himself as he slowly eased back into his chair. "What are you talking about?"

She plopped herself into the chair on the other side of the table. "Might be time for you to invest in some reading glasses. Your ordering's getting even worse. We're getting billed for two months' worth of hay, when it should only be one month."

"What?" He reached out for the receipt. "Let me see."

She handed it over to him. "Did you double-order again?"

He frowned down at the file. "I just don't understand your bookkeeping. It's all chicken scratch. How can you keep this straight? Look at this." He flicked the pages open, searching for the master record. "There. See? All your numbers straddle both lines."

She leaned across the table and studied her scribbles. She supposed they could be a little neater, so he might have a point. Didn't mean she had to admit that. She'd never hear the end of it. "So? I remember which is which."

He groaned and dragged a hand through his hair. "Which is great for you—but not for the rest of us." He tapped a number. "Did you pay in or out? You need to have a clear column for accounts paid and accounts receivable. It's just common sense."

She opened her mouth to speak but noticed his eyes were no longer on the file. Instead, they were glued below her neck. To where her shirt gaped open, exposing the tops of her breasts and the lacy fabric of her bra. Heat inched its way from her neck to her ears. Her nipples pebbled under his gaze, and her teeth sank into her bottom lip.

He shifted in his seat, coughing as he looked away. His face turned bright red and realization dawned. Maybe *this* was why he'd been avoiding her. Not because he liked working with Peter better or because he disliked her company, but because he was just as attracted to her as she was to him. A wave of confidence washed over her.

"You know," she said, in a husky tone that sounded more suited to a sexy movie than their accounting sessions, "maybe you'd like to show me what you mean."

His head whipped up in surprise and his throat bobbed when he swallowed. "Show you?"

She tilted her head, flashing her pearly whites at him. "You're always criticizing my methods. Time to teach me what you'd do instead." She licked her lips and twirled a lock of hair around her finger. "Unless you don't think your...*system* is up to it."

His focus zeroed in on her mouth while his fingers curled then flexed. Curled then flexed. With obvious effort, he yanked his attention back up to her eyes. Whatever he saw there made his own eyes narrow before he relaxed. His mouth eased up into a lazy, devastatingly sexy grin. "I assure you, my *system* is up to it," he said, his voice low as he leaned toward her.

Heat licked through her body. "Is that so?"

Anticipation made her itch to touch him. She hadn't felt this flirty since—since she'd been at nurse's college. As he inched closer, her eyes started to flutter closed...until he pulled open the desk drawer near her and pulled out a notepad. "What's that?"

"Paper, of course. I can show you my system."

She blinked and lurched away, surprised by the sharpness of the disappointed pinch in her gut. Her embarrassment was chased away by the twinkle in his eyes, though.

"As a matter of fact, I'd been meaning to talk to you about the accounting system soon anyway, so I drew this up on the off chance you'd have a moment to talk," he said.

Right. They had a ranch to run. Time for work. "Really?" She scanned the page and frowned. "But you've got three columns, not two."

"For notes. Let me talk you through it." He cleared his throat.

The system was simple enough, but she took advantage of the opportunity to lean over the notebook, looking down. She didn't miss the sudden tremor as her arm *accidentally* brushed his, or the way he sat stock still after, as if barely holding himself in check. Under the sweater he wore, his taut muscles were apparent.

Distracted by speculating what it might feel like to be held in those arms, she didn't realize he'd stopped talking, until her eyes fell upon his face.

This time he didn't look away, staring at her instead with a faint smile playing at his lips. "So, what do you think about my *system*?"

Busted. Saliva flooded her mouth, and she swallowed hard before answering. "It seems very nice...I mean, straightforward enough. I'm sure I can learn to handle it."

This time, she hadn't meant the double meaning, but that didn't stop her from grinning when he froze. He cleared his throat. "Sorry, wait. Just so I'm clear—you're saying...?"

"I'm willing to try your...accounting system," she took pity on him and clarified, "if only so we don't end up drowning in hay." She stood. "But if your system doesn't work, we go back to my way—the right way."

"Okay. But I promise you, my system works."

Their gazes met and warmth reignited, deep in her core. Her gaze traveled down to his lips. At this point, Katie wasn't sure which system they were talking about. What she knew with certainty was that her arm tingled where she had brushed against him, and that she found it difficult to tear her eyes away from his mouth. She couldn't stop imagining how that warm heat would feel between her legs. The image pushed her from damp to drenched, and her core twitched in need.

Time to get out of here before I do something stupid.

She turned on her heels when his calloused, warm hand gently clutched her arm. "Don't go yet. We need to talk about the north pasture."

She didn't want his hand on her arm. She needed it elsewhere. On her breasts. Or her ass. God, she needed to leave and fast. She flinched away, needing a safe distance between them to think coherently. "Someone needs to check supplies up there."

At her reaction, he reared back, and it was like a wall went up between them. He pinched the bridge of his nose. "It was on the top of your dad's list of things needing to be done this week. I don't think we can wait any longer." The earlier playfulness vanished. His tone was curt now.

She frowned and studied him. What had just happened? Had she upset him somehow? He'd switched from hot to cold in the space of a few seconds. Then, she noted the way he slumped in the chair and decided she was reading too much between the lines. He looked tired. No—make that exhausted. Taking on her dad's duties in addition to his own had been tougher than she'd realized. "You're right. After the frost we had last night, the water will be frozen soon enough. If any of the cattle stay up there for the winter, they'll need salt blocks and we'll need to move the hay feeders."

"Glad we agree," he said. "The only question is who to send out on a day like this."

She glanced through the window, noting that the skies had once again opened up. It was pouring rain. "Not Peter," she said at once.

"Peter's staying here to feed out. Linda can keep an eye on him. If you don't mind"— he hesitated—"I'd like you to take the truck and head out to do the inspection on the north pasture."

"Me?" She blinked rapidly. She must have misunderstood. "Not you?"

"Linda's asked me to head into town to pick up the antibiotic shipment that just arrived. She's got one weanling colt and a couple of calves showing signs of pneumonia and needs that shipment as soon as possible." He picked up the receipt that slid out of the file. "I can clear up this double order at the same time."

Katie still wasn't sure she understood. "So, wait. You're going to run the errands in town while I check the pasture?"

He glanced up from the file. "Yes. If that's okay with you...?" His expression was wary now, like he was afraid offended her somehow.

A smile broke across her face. "Yes. That's fine with me. In fact, I think that plan makes the most sense. I just figured..." *That you didn't think I was as useful on the ranch work.*

"...that I'd send you out to do the busy work?" He shook his head. "If I hired a housekeeper so you could take care of the ranch, what makes you think I'd have you wasting your time on errands?"

She blinked. Oh. When he put it like that... "I guess I still sort of thought you hired the housekeeper because you were sick of my lousy cooking."

He chuckled. "Well, I can't say the idea of a new cook in the kitchen didn't enter my head at all. But that wasn't the main reason." His expression turned serious. "Katie, you know the ranch better than anyone. Lots of people can cook and keep house—but you're the only one right now who can keep this place running. There's no one better to send to the north pasture." He said this all in a matter-of-fact way. Shorn of emotion, like he was delivering a report.

Somehow, that made his praise even more poignant. Because she knew he wasn't just trying to make her feel good or blowing smoke up her ass. John meant what he said. He believed in her.

A strange mix of emotions filled her, one that simultaneously made her shoulders go back while causing a hitch in her throat. "I'll head out after I finish some of the smaller errands around here."

"Good. Let me know how much hay is left and how the stock is doing in this weather. Especially make sure the run-in sheds are holding up. If anything's needed up there, we could haul it out tomorrow morning." John glanced through his open office door and rubbed his chin. "Be careful out there. It's coming down hard."

She rolled her eyes. "It's just raining. My dad's pick-up can handle it."

The corners of his mouth twitched. *Trying not to smile?* Arousal danced around her lower abdomen, her eyes unwillingly drawn to that mouth.

A forced cough pulled her back to reality. "Just be careful."

She nodded. "I'll take Koda with me."

"Good idea."

Koda stretched, displaying her teeth in a big yawn, and sat on her haunches. The dog's eyes darted between them.

"I guess I should get going," she said. Reluctantly.

"You have your phone, right?" His brow wrinkled. Right now, he sounded a little like Katie's dad.

"Why? You worried I'll get lost trying to find my way to the north pasture, cowboy?"

"Cowboy?" His eyebrow arched. "That might be even worse than 'old man.'"

"Aha! So, you're saying you prefer that I acknowledge your advanced years instead?"

He groaned and threw up his hands. "I can't win, can I?"

"Nope."

For several long moments, they grinned at each other, while Katie soaked up the warmth of their shared joke. Too soon, the rumble of a truck pulling up outside reminded them there was work to do. "If you aren't back by six, I'll come looking for you."

"Okay." She pulled the hood of her sweatshirt up as she sprinted into the rain toward the house. Koda ran alongside her, tongue lolling out of her mouth.

She grabbed the keys off the counter and dashed for the truck. She let Koda jump into the old blue Ford first, and then she followed. The engine roared to life and she set out for the north pasture. She would have preferred to be in the saddle, but with the weather as bad as it was, the truck offered more reliability and protection. Driving carefully along the dirt road that led to the north pasture, she steered the truck over the cattle guard that led to the pasture itself.

Koda rode alongside her in the front seat, sitting up and looking out of the window just like a person. The two of them on a little adventure. But her elation dissipated as a random thought intruded into her mind, bringing shadows with it.

Did he send me expecting me to fail?

She frowned. Most of the time, Mr. Take-Charge-Super-Soldier did everything himself. And with his obvious avoidance lately, she did find it weird he'd turn over such an important task so easily.

But then she recalled how drained he'd looked, and also, the words he'd spoken.

There's no one better to send to the north pasture.

No, he'd meant what he said. Any worries to the contrary had to be just that—her own anxiety, rearing its ugly head again. Messing with her confidence.

She gripped the wheel and inhaled a deep, reassuring breath. She could do this. John had faith in her. So did her dad. She just needed to keep working on her faith in herself.

As they reached the north pasture, Koda looked at her, ears up and tail thwacking against the door. Little squeaks came out of the dog's black muzzle as her front paws tap-danced on the seat.

"In this weather?" The dog loved the rain. But the cabin of the truck would reek of wet dog. And as much as she loved Koda, not even a mother can love that smell. But she couldn't deny her best friend and slowed the truck to a halt and opened her door, leaning back so Koda could leap out. "Okay. Just don't think I want you jumping all over me with your muddy paws."

As soon as the dog hit the ground she took off, tearing around the open field.

Katie laughed and resumed driving. The truck bumped along the field toward the first of the run-in sheds and was soon at the bottom of the steep, uneven hill. She dropped it into first gear, aimed it straight at the top, and gunned the engine hard.

She'd always liked this part. Her father had shown her how to do it when she was small, and she loved bouncing up the hill—just like riding a roller coaster.

Halfway up, a loud *bang* assaulted her ears.

The steering wheel yanked out of her hands. Katie didn't even have time to be afraid when the truck lurched and began tipping over.

The front end went up—and up—and up—and over.

Chapter 22

JOHN

Gravel flew as John's truck roared up the driveway. He gripped the steering wheel with white-knuckled hands. Peter had called to say Katie was in an accident. He didn't think his anxiety level could rise any higher, but each passing second proved him wrong.

Linda's truck was parked in front of the house. He pulled up next to it and jumped out, not bothering to close the door. *I have to see her. I have to know—know she's all right.*

John charged up the stairs, cursing himself the entire way. *Why didn't I go with her?*

He hadn't lied to her. Katie was the best person for the job. Plus, he'd been exhausted, and he'd figured she could use the confidence boost. But he should have known better. With the mystery of the intruder and back fence still unsolved, he should have taken the extra time and accompanied her. Just to be safe.

As Katie had pulled her sweatshirt up and dashed out into the rain, a strong urge to go with her had tugged at him. But he'd quieted the feeling and left the ranch. If he were being honest, partly to distract himself from his increasingly incessant desire for her. The same reason he'd been avoiding her lately. And now she was hurt. Possibly badly hurt.

And it's my fault.

A couple of nights, he'd noticed her looking out her bedroom window. And after she'd retreated, he'd leave the bunkhouse and sweep the property. Keeping her safe had become his main priority. He even sacrificed sleeping many nights to make sure no one broke in.

None of that mattered now, though. He'd failed in his mission. Again.

His boots thudded against the uneven wood of the porch stairs. Each step punctuated the worry building in his chest. He threw the door open, only to be greeted by a cacophony of barks from the dogs.

Nickel and Two Bits were plainly on edge, upset at the disruption to their usual routine. They barked, registering their unease. Koda sat silent and still. She gave one yelp when she saw him.

Heat drained from his body. He'd been on enough missions with Koda to recognize the dog had protected Katie from something far worse than a car accident.

"What are you in such a hurry for?"

Katie.

Her bossy tone didn't give him the usual prickles of irritation. In fact, his legs almost buckled from relief at the sound. He made his way to the sofa where she rested, an ice pack on her forehead. When she reached up to move it, he could see a nasty bruise on her forearm.

"Well?" she said.

"I heard you rolled the truck." The words came out harsher than he'd meant, and she flinched at the tone.

"I don't know what happened," she said. "I've taken the truck up the pasture hills a hundred times. Maybe I hit a hole or some mud or something. The last thing I remember was the back end sticking and the front end coming way up." She closed her eyes with another shudder. "I had my seat belt on, but I must have banged my head on the door frame. When I woke up, Peter was there. He was trying to get in but Koda wouldn't let him."

He frowned. "Koda was outside the truck? Is she okay?"

"She was following the truck. I let her out after the cattle guard so she could run. I'm just glad she wasn't inside it and didn't get hurt. It was her barking that woke me up."

He resisted the urge to bark the one hundred pressing questions he had, all at once. "What did you see?"

"I finally sat up and saw Peter out in the road. He waved at me, but Koda wouldn't let him get close." She stretched out a hand, settling over the dog's fur. "The truck was—is—lying on the passenger side." She groaned as she shifted her body. "Dad's going to be thrilled."

"The truck is the least of—will be the least of his worries. How did you get back?"

She sighed. "Adrenaline is a wonderful thing. I managed to push the door up and open enough to climb out. I started walking. I didn't get too far before Linda's truck appeared. Peter must have called her once he got to a spot with a signal. Thank goodness he saw me. Otherwise, who knows how long I would have been walking?"

The idea of her having to walk back to the ranch after a serious accident in this weather didn't sit well. Anger raged through his body. At himself. At Peter. At the goddamn truck. "Good God, Katie. I'm just glad you're all right."

"Thanks, me too." Her fingers dug into Koda's fur. "The funny thing was the way Koda freaked out. Was that her military training?"

He clenched his jaw. He wasn't one-hundred percent sure what to make of the dog's behavior, which frustrated him. "Sure, it could be. She's trained to sniff out dangerous situations, but she's also protecting you from any perceived threat." Every muscle in his body strained with the effort of not wrapping her in his arms.

Linda came in from the kitchen and handed her a cup of hot tea. "Joanne's arranged with her mother-in-law to pick up her sons from school. She'll be here to keep an eye on you until the evening."

Katie took the cup of tea with one hand and steadied it with the other. "That's great."

She seemed about to say something else, but changed her mind, blowing the steam of her cup instead.

John watched her, searching for something he could say to reassure. He turned his head and saw Linda was watching him.

The older woman leaned against the doorframe with her arms crossed over her chest. There was something in her expression that unsettled him. "Did you pick up the antibiotic?"

"Yes. It's in the bed of the truck, nice and cold. I'd appreciate it if you could put it away."

"Sure."

John stood. "I'm going to have a little chat with Peter."

He strode to the bunkhouse. He'd never liked Peter, but he supposed he owed the man his gratitude for now. Maybe the other man would have a better idea of how this all had happened.

He pushed open the heavy door, and found Peter sitting on the couch, beer in hand, watching television. He looked up when John entered the room.

"Oh, hey there. A little wet out there, huh?"

Peter's booted feet rested on the coffee table, a sight that triggered something in John. Katie was lying on the couch, bruised, and nursing an ice pack, while this jerk lounged around on the ranch's dime. His fists clenched, and he saw red.

Stepping closer, John kicked Peter's feet off the table, causing a sprinkle of dried mud to fall to the floor. He grabbed the remote control, pushed the power button, and threw the device across the room. It hit the wall, batteries exploding out of the case on the back, and clattered to the floor.

"Dude, what's your damage? I was just trying to relax a little after all the excitement. Chill."

Every word stung, only fueling the fire burning inside, hissing through John's body like a deathly poison. "Tell me exactly what happened up there in the north pasture. Don't leave anything out or I swear to God I'll punch you right through the walls of this cabin."

Pete shrugged and took a long swig of the beer. "There's nothing to tell. All I did was find the truck, dude. I tried to help, but that dog wouldn't let me anywhere close. I found a place with service and called Linda. That's it. That's the story."

John's gaze narrowed on the other man. He sounded honest enough, but John wasn't ready to let it go just yet. "You were supposed to be feeding out. Not anywhere near the north pasture."

"I was, but I saw the truck head out. When it didn't come back, I thought I'd take a look—just as well I did, too."

That made sense, John supposed. Some of the anger leached from his body as he realized he'd likely overreacted. Still. That didn't mean he liked Peter. "You didn't see anything else?"

"Nope." Spinning the beer bottle by the neck, Peter angled his head sideways. "Why are you so worked up, anyway? Katie seemed fine when I saw her. Unless..." A sly grin cracked his face. "Are you boning the boss's daughter? Not that I'd blame you. I've thought about tapping that myself, more than one lonely night."

In three steps, John crossed the small space and threw an uppercut at Peter's face. Peter's teeth clacked and he flew back. The other man yelped while blood spurted from his nose, splattering all over his Burberry flannel shirt. While sprawled on the floor, Peter wiped his nose with the back of his hand and then stared up at John, unblinking. Eyes hard as a rock.

John had seen that look before. That hardness, that callousness. Plenty of times, during deployments.

"You aren't going to talk about Katie. Not like that," he said, exuding an animosity that was like acid—burning, slicing, potent. His knuckles ached from the punch. But he would hit this guy again and again until every bone in his hand was broken if that's what it took to shut him up.

Peter lay back on the floor of the bunkhouse and pressed his hand against his nose. "So, that's a yes, I take it? Don't worry. Your secret's safe with me." He winked, like the two of them were old friends.

John turned away in disgust. "Get the fuck out of here and go home. You're done for the day and you aren't staying here anymore. Be gone before I get back." He stomped out of the bunkhouse before he ended up in jail. Again. He was so worked up, that he couldn't tell if he'd overreacted completely. Or if Peter really was that obnoxious. Maybe it was a mixture of both.

Either way. With everything going on right now, he didn't feel comfortable having the man stay at the ranch overnight. Peter sleeping elsewhere was just one less thing to worry about.

Night was rapidly approaching. He couldn't return to the main house just yet. Not this angry. And he still needed to do his daily perimeter check. His fingers flexed, throbbing. As much as he wanted to kill the creep, a modicum of sanity prevailed.

You know how to deal with guys like him.

And he did. He had been in the army long enough to know most of those assholes were full of hot air. If you punctured them just right, they'd quickly deflate.

Peter's time would come. Right now, John had other priorities. He continued to patrol the yard, taking the time to check the barns.

Linda was sitting in the living room, waiting for him once he finished his security detail.

"Katie's upstairs in the shower," Linda said, in response to his glance toward the empty sofa.

"Is she really okay?"

"She's fine. She'll have a nice bruise, but that's it. Katie's gotten worse injuries being thrown from a horse."

He collapsed into the armchair. "How's the truck? Damaged?"

She shook her head. "No damage beyond getting stuck, far as I can tell. Lucky. Good thing Peter was able to call me to come pick Katie up."

John scowled. "I guess. I like that guy much."

Linda cocked her head, about to speak, but paused. Her fingers drummed against her leg as her eyes scanned him.

"I'm heading out. Do you two need anything before I go?" she asked, grabbing her keys.

"No, thank you, ma'am. We'll be fine."

She huffed. "If you continue calling me 'ma'am,' I'll tell Katie to keep calling you 'old.'"

His jaw dropped. What else had Katie told the woman? "Will do, ma'am—I mean, Linda."

She winked at his correction and then headed for the door. Once Linda left, he looked around the room. Koda sat next to him, nudging his hand with her snout. He caressed her ears. "Good girl."

Even though he'd been sleeping over at the bunkhouse, Katie had left the pillow and blanket from the night he'd spent here in the main house. The small gesture warmed him.

The familiar sounds of a truck engine followed by spitting gravel meant Peter was finally gone. He sighed. He probably owed the younger man an apology at some point, but he'd worry about that later.

His eyelids grew heavy as tiredness overtook him. In the kitchen, Joanne fussed over the casserole she was making for dinner. She was there if Katie needed anything. Exhaustion consumed him. As did remorse.

I didn't protect her.

John's body was thrown back and forth as the Humvee traveled over the bumpy road. The engine roared as the vehicle climbed over the rocky terrain of Afghanistan. The men had to bellow to be heard.

He turned to his right. Dirk was speaking to him, but he couldn't hear a word he was saying.

"What?"

From the way his friend's face contorted, he knew Dirk was speaking louder, but no sound reached his ears. Dirk's eyes had a desperate quality to them that made a small shiver of dread snake up his spine.

The silence was more deafening than anything he'd ever experienced. Something was wrong.

Sudden darkness encompassed him followed by a painful burst in his chest. He awoke to find himself thrown face-first to the ground. His lungs burned and his bones cracked as he struggled to pull himself up into a sitting position.

A figure moved toward him. An intense flood of relief swept through him as he recognized Dirk's outline. Alive—he made it out!

But as the other man drew closer, he saw something was terribly wrong. Dirk's body was mangled and bloody. It only had one arm. The other was a fleshy stump, jagged and raw.

Dirk's body swayed and fell. Using the arm that was still intact, it inched itself over to John's ear.

Dirk's mouth twitched and shuddered. This time, John heard him clearly. "Why do you get to live? Why didn't you save me?"

Chapter 23

KATIE

Katie stood by the mahogany dresser, a towel around her shoulders. Her hand hovered over the contents of her make-up drawer. She'd just been in a serious accident. The last thing she should be worried about was lipstick.

She slammed the drawer shut when the rapping at the door reached her ears. "What is it?"

"It's just me," Joanne said. "Can I come in?"

"Of course."

"How are you feeling?" Joanne opened the door, her gaze falling on Katie's forehead.

She forced herself not to squirm under the woman's inspection of the rapidly developing bruise. As if she didn't have enough to be self-conscious about.

"I'm fine," she said.

"I'm glad to hear. Not that I wouldn't stay if you needed me, but—"

"You want to get home to your family," Katie said.

Joanne nodded. "And it looks like you'll have Mr. Rathborne here keeping an eye on you."

Katie's heart leapt. "John?"

"Fast asleep on the sofa in the living room," the housekeeper said. "Men! Well, there's casserole enough for both of you. All you have to do is heat it."

"You're spoiling us."

"Not at all," Joanne said, patting Katie's hand. "You're lucky it wasn't worse."

The two women walked downstairs and into the kitchen. Joanne grabbed her jacket off the hook by the back door and put it on. "I've gone ahead and made breakfast, too."

Once again, Katie gave an internal thanks for John's excellent idea to hire a housekeeper. "I really appreciate it. Please drive home safe."

Katie waved goodbye to the housekeeper from the shelter of the door, but the chill cast by that word stayed with her even after she was back in the warm kitchen. She sighed, shutting her eyes.

Now that she was alone, those "worst" possible outcomes flooded her mind. The truck rolling could've killed her. Dad's heart attack could've been fatal. And the attack in the hospital …

She gripped the edge of the counter, fighting off the anxiety pulsing through her veins. A warm body pressed against her. Koda's brown eyes gazed up at her.

"I'm being silly, aren't I?" It was weak to give in and indulge these fears—and if there was one thing she was not, it was weak. A loud snore punctuated her statement. Katie bit back a laugh, sharing a look with Koda. "Well, I'll say this much. He's an expert sleeper."

Remembering how tired he'd seemed that afternoon, she decided to let him sleep. She hummed as she washed her dishes, leaving a plate of casserole on the table with a note. As she did, the occasional sound from the living room reminded her she was not alone.

When she was finished, and he still hadn't stirred, she stuck her head in the living room. "John?"

He lay stretched out on the sofa, dead to the world—just as he had the night he'd caught her touching herself. Her cheeks heated at the memory. She couldn't believe she'd let herself go—in front of him of all people!

She covered him with a blanket. Koda eyed her. "What? He looks too peaceful to wake."

The dog followed her upstairs, lying on the floor at the foot of the bed. She climbed onto the plush mattress, her head resting on the pillow. Her eyes traced a small crack in the ceiling. She replayed the events from earlier and the way the truck bounced and swayed.

A guttural yell filled the house.

"John!" Heart racing, she swung her feet over the side of the bed, making her way downstairs with Koda at her heels.

Her feet slid across the wooden floor as she spotted him on the sofa. He'd kicked off the blanket and tossed about, moaning.

Her pulse returned to an easier pace when she realized. John was having some kind of nightmare.

She remained motionless, unsure what she should do. When he screamed again, though, instinct took over. She ran to the sofa, laying her hand gently on his chest. "John, wake up. John, it's just a dream."

He thrashed about and she pulled back; his elbow missed her face by an inch.

"No," he moaned. "No."

Katie swallowed a wave of panic of her own. *Come on. You've got this.* She took a firm hold of herself.

"John. John! Wake up!" She shook him by the shoulders.

He bolted upright, disoriented, his arms flailing as he reached for a support that wasn't there. Sweat coated his shaking body, and his breathing was heavy. He blinked, looking from one corner of the room to the next.

Her heart broke as the panic in his face was replaced by recognition. He stared at the blanket across his lap. Tears gathered in the corner of his eyes.

"Goddammit."

"And I thought I had bad dreams," she murmured.

He flinched. Apparently, she'd overestimated how aware he was of his surroundings. The horror with which he stared at her stated plainly he'd had no idea she was present.

"It was the TV." He motioned toward the blank screen. "I fell asleep with it on."

"No, you didn't. The TV wasn't on." She sat back on her heels, tucking her hair behind an ear. "It took me forever to wake you." Her fingers softly grazed his forearm. "I know you keep your stuff to yourself, but you cried out. I heard you. I wanted to help. The way you're here to help me."

She sat in front of him, looking at his face. Her fingers ran up his arm to his chest, and he sucked in a sharp breath as his eyes closed tight. His body shuddered beneath her fingertips, but not in fear. She moved closer, laying the palm of her hand flat over the center of his chest.

"Your heart's racing. I'll get you a glass of water."

She removed her hand and saw his lips part, as if in protest.

"Shhh. Stay there," she said.

Alone in the kitchen, she leaned against the sink. Her chest ached. His actions were all too familiar. She'd suffered the same way for the first few months after she was attacked. He needed her. After a couple of seconds of controlled breathing, she reached for a glass and filled it with water.

She entered the living room and stopped. Her feet seemed to glue themselves to the floor. John had swung his feet over the side of the couch, but that was as far as he'd gotten. His face was buried in his hands, and his...

She swallowed. There was a definite bulge in his Levi's.

"Here you go."

His head jerked up as she stepped closer to him. His pupils were dark, and his breathing still faster than normal. "Thanks."

His fingers brushed her own as he took the glass, sending a fresh jolt of electricity racing through her body. She cleared her throat and plopped onto the other sofa opposite him. She wrapped herself in the blanket, creating her own cocoon against the cold permeating the living room. Though she'd much rather have her body pressed up against his.

"Do you know where the remote is?" he asked. "You don't have to babysit me. You can go back to sleep."

Her pulse raced. Even now, emotionally shattered and vulnerable, he tried to subdue his attraction to her. And by the way his jeans bulged, he was attracted. Not to mention she'd been looked at with enough pity to know there was nothing sympathetic in the glances he sent her way.

"No, you are not fine. I've had nightmares, too. They don't just wear off as soon as you get up." This was more than she'd shared with anyone.

But he's not just anyone.

"I'm not going anywhere, so you'd better get used to it."

A tired smile crossed his face. "Fine." He dug into the cushion to retrieve the remote before tossing it over to her. He took a gulp of water, before settling back down.

She caught him glancing at her and she flicked through the channels at a rapid pace.

"Slow down, will you?"

"What? You mean, you want to watch something besides the back of your eyelids?" she joked.

"Something tells me agreeing on a show to watch is going to be more difficult than agreeing on the bookkeeping."

"That's because you make everything difficult," she said. "Although, come to think of it, I do know something you'd like to watch."

"What, this crap?" He stared at the screen. She'd stopped on some show about housewives with big, fake tits. "I hate reality TV. I thought you would, too. I guess you're just full of surprises."

Inside, Katie smiled. He had no idea. But he was about to find out.

As he sucked his teeth, she inconspicuously removed the soft pink satin pajama shorts and threw back her blanket, hitching one leg over the arm of the sofa. At least she'd put on a pair of sexier panties. She bit the corner of her lip, waiting for him to turn toward her.

"Hey, Katie, are we really gonna watch—"

His jaw dropped and his eyes widened. She grew wetter as his eyes dropped to her fingers, tracing the front of her blue nylon panties. Her body hummed. The nerve endings between her legs were on fire. Her thin camisole top brushed against her hard nipples.

"No kitty underwear this time," she said.

He gulped, groping for his pillow, too slow to hide the immediate reaction of his body. "Katie, what are you doing?"

Her breath became ragged. The nerve bundle between her legs swelled with need. "I told you. I know what you like to watch." She slipped her fingers under the lace-trimmed fabric.

She stroked her swollen folds, moving her hands back and forth. A soft moan escaped her lips when she brushed against her clit. Her other hand traveled up her firm belly and began stroking her breasts, pinching her already-hardened nipples. Her eyes remained firmly affixed to his face.

"Fuck, Katie." His voice cracked. He hadn't moved, but every breath he took signaled he was having a harder and harder time holding his arousal in check. His eyes were dark and hungry, and as she watched, he swallowed. He hadn't moved, not even to touch his clearly urgent erection. No, he was watching—watching her drive him crazy.

She spread her legs wider as her fingers slid in and out of her folds. Her head fell back against the sofa, her eyes half-closed. Soft whimpers escaped her full lips as she used her first and second fingers to rub on either side of her clit. What started out as a show for him, turned into a pleasuring activity for her. She'd never been this turned on, never enjoyed getting herself off as much as she was now. But she wanted more.

She lifted her head, her eyes scanning his body. "You really never let anyone watch?"

"Huh?"

She clamped her lips to confine the small giggle threatening to escape, watching him try to make sense out of her question.

"Um—no. I haven't," he said.

Her tongue traveled slowly across her upper lip.

"Show me," she demanded, her voice a husky whisper.

Her stomach knotted when he recoiled, his eyes darting to the floor. Had she misread his desire? Misread the way he'd trembled as she brushed against him in the office? And when her palm had rested on his chest?

"It—the IED left scars. It's not—it's not pretty."

The insecure waver to his voice was something she could relate to. Whenever someone tried to sympathize, it only made the feeling worse. So, she remained silent, focusing on him. Determined to show how sexy she found him.

Using the thumb of one hand she pulled the fabric of her blue lace panties over to one side, showing him her sex as the fingers of her other hand circled her swollen clit.

"Show me." Her voice remained firm, revealing a side of her she hadn't felt since that night at the hospital. She'd never thought she'd feel it again. It both thrilled and terrified her all at once.

He unzipped his jeans and eased his cock out of his shorts. The angle didn't look comfortable and he seemed to be trying to show as little of his skin as possible. At the sight of his cock, erect and wet with desire for her, she arched her back, her hips giving a little thrust.

"Oh, fuck, Katie." An uncontrolled hurricane of firing nerve endings tore through when he gripped his straining length, the tip gleaming. Her mouth salivated watching his cock grow as he spread his legs, his hand pumping his thick erection.

"John," she moaned. Her eyes were halfway shut, but still focused on him. Her fingers rapidly stroked her clit as her hips gyrated. "I make you that hard."

"You have no idea how hard you make me," he growled. "I'm hard all the fucking time. And I think you know that."

She didn't think she could possibly feel any hotter.

"I want to watch you come," she said, her voice low and laced with longing.

A low, rasping moan rumbled from his chest at her words. His grasp tightened and his pace quickened. Her brown eyes remained on him, drinking up every impassioned movement as he stroked himself, faster and faster, until he was unable to hold back his moans. His body shuddered. She watched breathlessly, her own body quivering, as his seed spurted out onto his abdomen and dribbled down his hand.

She closed her eyes and tilted her head back. Her hand began working even harder, stroking her clit at a frantic pace. She lifted her tank top, exposing her stomach and breasts. His needful growl filled her ears.

"Oh, God, John!"

She wanted him to touch her but knew he wouldn't. Not until she asked. The muscles of her abdomen flexed, and she tightened around her fingers. Her breath stopped as an orgasm rippled through her.

"Fuck." His words sounded like they were ground out from clenched teeth. "You're so beautiful."

She took a deep breath, luxuriating in the pleasure still pumping through her body. She removed her hand from her panties, her fingers glistening with her moistness. She looked up to see him staring. His mouth was slack, as if it wanted to wrap around her fingers.

She smiled as he closed his eyes and he made a visible effort to catch his breath.

All the excitement too much for you, old man?

She stood, taking advantage of his inattention to pull up her clothes and slip out of the room.

In the bathroom she splashed water on her face, attempting to cool her burning cheeks. Arousal was fading replaced by a sudden, unnecessary feeling of giddiness.

Never in a million years would I have thought I would do that.

And she'd done it. And John—he'd appreciated it.

She eyed her reflection. She was looking at a Katie she'd never seen before. Sure, before the attack, she'd been more confident. Flirty. But not like this.

Her heart began to beat faster. She wasn't what one would call an angel, but brazen wouldn't be a word someone would've used to define her sexually. Brazen Katie existed in her fantasies. And in the pages of the books she read when she substituted herself for the main female character. Yet somehow, thanks to John, her fantasy-self had become real. And she was thrilled and terrified.

Chapter 24

JOHN

John sat on the sofa, his eyes shut and a faint ringing in his ears. Well, that was different. Katie made him come so hard his ears rang. A wide grin spread across his face and he felt lighter than he had in years.

He was enjoying the sensation when something hit him in the chest.

John's arm curled up automatically, trapping the object. His eyes flew open, and he stared at her, standing in the doorway wearing a devious expression.

"Figured you'd need to clean up." She darted out the doorway, as if expecting him to return the gesture.

He looked into his hands and laughed. She'd just flung a roll of toilet paper at him. He pulled off a couple of sheets and cleaned himself off.

Heading into the kitchen, he glanced up the stairs. The door to her room was closed and the lights were off. He yearned to lie next to her, but she hadn't given any inkling she wanted the same. And he didn't want to push.

He placed his glass in the sink, noticing the plate and note on the table. A smile hovered on his lips. He heated the meal and took it back into the living room to eat. He grabbed the remote and started flicking through the channels, determined not to go back to sleep. He didn't want her hearing him scream again tonight.

Or any night.

His eyes turned up at the ceiling, but there was no noise. After rolling the truck, she needed the rest. A touch of sadness filled him when his eyes fell upon the empty sofa across from him. But it was quickly replaced by the memory of the bold show he'd just witnessed.

If I hadn't seen it, I'd never have believed it.

She had done more than put on a spectacular show. She'd bared a vulnerable side of herself to him. As he did to her. The two of them, together, who would have guessed? After weeks of bickering, maybe now they could bring out the best in each other.

It'll never work. Remember Morgan? She'd thought he was fun, too. For a time.

His fists clenched. Despite the superficial similarities, Katie was nothing like Morgan. But that fact didn't change anything. After what she had been through, Katie deserved someone strong. Not someone broken who could barely take care of himself. A man who couldn't save his friends when it mattered the most. John's teeth ground together with such force, he was afraid they might break.

Her safety was in his hands and he wasn't going to let anything happen to her.

Because you've done such a good job of that so far.

He wanted to punch his own brain. But it spoke the truth. When her truck overturned, it hadn't been him who'd come to her rescue. It was Peter. He grimaced. And Koda.

Koda.

Her toenails clicked against the floor as she walked over to him. "Hey, girl."

Koda jumped up on the sofa and lay in his lap. His hand ran over the soft fur of her belly as his mind spun. Something still didn't seem right about the accident, and even though he had no reason to suspect Peter, the other man made him uneasy. He shook his head, annoyed with himself. If Peter had been involved, why bother to call Linda to help? Besides, much as he disliked the man, he had no motive. "If only you could tell me exactly what happened, girl."

The dog's brown eyes were darker than usual in the dim light of the living room. With a sigh, he removed his hand.

"Go on. Back to Katie." He motioned to the stairs. "*Schützen* Katie."

There was no proof it had been anything but an accident. Nor proof there'd been an intruder the night they'd come back from the police station either, except for the damp sink.

But the ruined fences. Those were deliberate.

Someone had a grudge against the Lockes, and he was going to make sure whoever it was didn't hurt anyone.

This time, I'm not going to fail.

He stared at the TV without seeing it. He hadn't protected his brother—but he would be damned if he would fail Katie.

Snow. *Just what we need.* John stood in the ranch house kitchen looking out at the sky covered in thick clouds as far as the eye could see. It wasn't just monotonous, it was oppressive. Despite the warmth of the kitchen, he shivered.

The day had a dull, muted light, making it hard to judge time. To him, the night stretched on and on as he sat in the living room waiting for dawn to come so he could act. Now he stood, coffee in hand, weighing the best thing to do.

He'd called around the neighboring ranches for help righting the toppled truck, but everyone seemed to be busy scrambling to get ready before the bad weather hit. He and Peter could try using the tractor to tow it back onto its wheels, but after their confrontation yesterday, John wasn't sure he was willing to work with the man on so delicate a task. But the longer they left the truck out there, the bigger the chances of it incurring serious damage.

There was the sound of footsteps on the stairs, followed by Katie's voice. "What're you up to, Nicky? Where are your two buddies?"

He grinned, looking into the hall. Trust Nickel not to miss the opportunity for tummy rubs. She lay on the floor, her tail wagging, as Katie bent down to pet her. "I've already let them out."

She let out a little squeal and turned hard on her knees.

"Sorry." He took a step toward her. "Didn't mean to scare you."

"Thought you'd be out working. I'm surprised you didn't pound on my door yelling 'it's eleven already'." She fidgeted with the collar of her shirt.

He coughed, hoping his face wasn't giving his feelings away. "I made coffee."

"Yes, grandpa." She grinned and stepped into the kitchen. "What's this?"

His fingers ran through his hair. "I also made breakfast."

"You did?"

"Figured it was fair. You did cook me dinner after all."

"Unhappily for you, Joanne told me she left breakfast last night. What do you say to that, ranch foreman?" Her eyes sparkled; she was pleased with herself.

He groaned. "Okay, you caught me out. But I'll have you know, I heated everything myself."

She sat at the table, looking around the kitchen. "Where's Joanne?"

"Couldn't make it in. The weather's bad and there's a chance we might get cut off. I told her not to risk it." He cast a look at her.

To his relief, she merely nodded. "She can't chance being separated from her sons. Good call."

For a moment, he caught himself wondering what kind of mother Katie would make—and took a hasty sip of coffee. He must be seriously overtired if that was where his mind was going. "It gets worse."

"Oh?" She looked up from her own cup of coffee.

"I have been trying to get a group together to retrieve the truck, but no luck. Seems like this sudden shift in the weather caught everyone by surprise. Two of the ranch hands have called to say they can't come in, and the third isn't answering his phone."

"And the fourth?"

"Peter." He grimaced. What were the odds the only one of their ranch hands to show up was the one John least wanted to see?

She pursed her lips. "Why does that not surprise me?" She leaned against the kitchen counter. "And Linda?"

"Sent me a message saying she'd be late. She had to go into town for a..." He glanced at his phone. "Special delivery."

"At a time like this?"

"She left me instructions to take care of the sick calves. I've already been out to tend to them." He straightened and took a plate of hash browns and omelet out of the microwave. "Now it's your turn."

"Hope you're not proposing to dose me with medicine." She stuck her tongue out, before sitting at the table. "Mmm. Got to say, the housekeeper was definitely one of your better ideas."

John cupped his ear. "I'm sorry, I'm not sure I heard that, can you speak louder? Are you saying I have good ideas?"

Katie sniffed. "Only occasionally. Don't let it go to your head."

"With you around to keep me in place? Not a chance."

She grinned at him and kept eating.

He sipped at his coffee. The atmosphere between them was companionable. It was different from the moment they'd shared the night before, but just as intimate. Almost like the two of them were a family.

"Morning Two Bits, Koda." She smiled as the two dogs joined Nickel in the kitchen. "Isn't Koda well behaved? Look at her. The other dogs are shameless, but I've never seen her beg for food, have you?"

He froze. He should tell her. He had to tell her.

"Must be her training." Her eyes fell on him and she sat up, putting her fork down. "John?"

"There's something I haven't told you." John's chest tightened. He knew this was a big mistake. She'd opened up to him. Trusted him. And what he was about to do would rip it all away. But she deserved his honesty. He'd made a mistake, not confessing on day one. "Something I should have told you a long time ago."

"Nothing good ever came from a statement like that." She tried to laugh. "It's too early in the morning to be this serious."

"I am serious." He took a deep breath. "I—"

There was the sound of a truck pulling up outside.

"Someone's here."

"Forget them." He knew if he didn't do this now, he never would. "Look, Katie. I—"

The front door was flung open. "Isn't anyone going to welcome a poor man home?"

"Dad!" She was on her feet and racing for the door, Nickel and Two Bits chasing after her in a mad race to greet Mitch first.

Goddammit!

John couldn't be mad at the man for his recovery, but if only he'd timed it better. He counted to ten before making his way to the porch where Katie was still hugging her father.

"And here's our foreman." Mitch freed a hand to shake his, grinning widely but still looking pale and thin.

"Welcome home, sir." He looked past him to Linda, leaning against her truck, arms crossed and with a satisfied expression on her face. "This is the special delivery?"

She nodded. "He wanted it to be a surprise. And with the weather turning, well, it was now or never."

"Dad! If you knew the weather was bad, you should have stayed at the hospital! What if something goes wrong?"

"Nothing will go wrong. I feel fit as a fiddle."

She steered her father toward the door. "Inside. Now."

John chuckled. If Mitch had thought the nurses at the hospital were hard work, he was about to get a shock.

Linda carried a suitcase past him. "I took the liberty of picking up some supplies in town. Help me unload this stuff, will you?"

He walked over to her truck and picked up a jug marked "chlorhexidine gluconate" and dragged it out of the flatbed. Some of the fluid splashed, running down the sides of the jug and over his hand.

The acrid scent of the liquid burned his nostrils. His damp forearm tingled from the cold. His vision clouded but he knew exactly where he was. Back in the medical tent at the makeshift base thousands of miles from home, with the bastards who had set the IED out there waiting for a chance for a second go.

Consciousness threatened to slip away from him. He fought the darkness flooding his vision. Nausea nearly overwhelmed him but was drowned out by sharp, burning pain in his chest and shoulder. A pungent metallic odor flooded his nose—blood. Something cold and wet touched his skin. A medic. One of our guys.

The medic worked fast, with no time to be gentle. John breathed in antiseptic. The smell triggered his nausea. Bile rose in his throat. I can't move! *He gagged, struggling to breathe.*

An unseen person grasped him with strong hands, rolling him onto his side. "Suction, dammit, suction!"

He vomited over the side of the table he lay on. As he struggled to clear his vision, there was a gurgling roar beside him. Something pushed into his mouth, probing his throat. What's the matter with my throat?

He screamed but nothing came out. I'm awake! I'm here! I feel that!

The screaming in his head was deafening. Something razor sharp sliced into his flesh, leaving the agony of a firebrand in its wake. Please—please let me pass out. I can't take any more of this. The mind was supposed to disconnect, to protect itself from the horror flooding his senses. He tried to lift his arm, push the razor away. Tried to open his eyes. What's wrong? Why doesn't my body work? He failed.

Stop—stop!

The pain went on for hours. By the time he felt the darkness creeping over the edges of his consciousness, wrapping his mind in emptiness, he was too tired to do anything but give in.

"John!"

The voice seemed to come from miles away.

He breathed heavily, staring at the gravel beneath his fingers. It was too regular to be desert. His mind struggled to place it, and then he caught sight of a tire in the edge of his vision. *Linda's truck.* His body heaved, as though he was going to be sick again. He was on all fours at the ranch—and he had an audience.

"*John!*" Katie collapsed onto her knees beside his hunched form.

He shut his eyes. The gasps wracking his form momentarily subsided only to be replaced with great, sobbing gulps of air. His shirt clung to his back with sweat. It was cold.

"Katie, don't touch him." Linda's voice. She stood at a distance.

"John, we're here." Katie sounded scared.

He tasted salt. The dampness on his cheeks wasn't sweat but tears—his tears. *Fuck me.* He couldn't move.

A sharp bark and the clatter of paws kicked up dust from the gravel. Koda pushed her nuzzle past his fingers, whining as she licked his face. *Move, dammit, move!* As if his strings had been cut, he slumped back against the wheel of the truck.

He screwed his eyes shut, reaching for the side of the truck to pull himself up. Once on his feet, he headed for the bunkhouse, Koda at his side. The flashback had been bad enough, but being seen at his weakest was a nightmare all its own. He worked so hard to keep the barriers in place that protected him from this sort of humiliation, and with a few splashes from a bottle of skin scrub solution, it was all ripped away. The woman he'd fallen in love with had just seen him fall apart on the ground. Not the kind of image you could remove from someone's mind. She'd accepted most of the rest. But this—even he would run.

The realization sank in, shaking him to his core. He was in love with Katie Locke. When had that happened? How had he been so stupid?

"John, please don't block me out." Katie had followed him. "Tell me what's going on."

Her presence, on top of everything else, overwhelmed him. He couldn't handle this. Not right now. Maybe never. "Leave me alone!"

"I won't," she said, in that stubborn way of hers. "I'm here for you."

Only because she didn't understand the extent to which he was damaged. When she did, she'd reject him. Anybody would. His heart ripped open. "I don't need you, just go away!" He slammed the bathroom door. He heard Katie sobbing but when he saw his reflection, inhaled the smell of urine, it was just too much. His fist crashed through the mirror, shards of glass clanking into the sink.

"John?"

"Get the fuck away from me!" His knuckles connected with the wooden door. The force of the blow split them open. He heard her stumble backward. His gut twisted. Bile filled his mouth. He'd scared her. He could feel it. *This is the monster I am.*

He flipped the nozzle to turn on the shower. It took a minute or two for the water to heat up, and he could hear other voices outside. *Mitch and Linda.* He stepped in, burying his head under the cascade of scalding water to drown out the world. He concentrated on the burning sensation as he sank to the floor. *I should probably adjust the water's temperature.* But the thought was dull, disconnected from the rest of him. He wanted to feel something other than the pain inside.

He stayed in the shower until the hot water turned ice-cold. When it became unbearable, he stepped out and wrapped himself in a towel. He threw on his shirt before walking out, making sure he was covered.

Outside the bathroom, Mitch, Linda, and Katie sat on the couch, waiting for him. His muscles tensed, preparing for what was inevitably going to come. There was no way they were going to keep him on after an outburst like that.

Katie instantly rose to her feet. Before she could say anything, he stalked off to the bedroom and shut the door. He knew he'd lost his job. Once he got himself dressed, he stuffed his belongings into his pack.

When he emerged, duffel bag over his shoulder, Mitch glared at him.

Here it comes.

He braced himself.

"Where do you think you're going, son?" Although it was a question, Mitch's tone was stern.

"Home. I know I'm fired." His eyes focused on the door. His exit.

"Did I say that?"

God, really? Now he was being treated like a child.

"Son, take a seat. You're not being fired."

"Why?" He still couldn't look at the man. Or anyone else.

"Besides the fact you're a damn good foreman? John, we all care about you."

"John, we know you're suffering. Katie's told me about the nightmares. We see it in Koda too," Linda began. "We see the commercials. Read the stories about soldiers returning and what they go through. The reality is none of us really understood—until we actually saw it. It doesn't mean we look at you any different."

"But you do." John's eyes went right to Katie. "Look, I don't belong here anymore. Katie, yesterday was a mistake. *We* are a mistake. It will never work."

"Why would you say that?" Her bottom lip quivered.

"Because you're not the only fucked-up one." He cringed the moment the words left his mouth. "I didn't mean it like that."

"Yes, you did." Her eyes were swollen, her cheeks stained with tears. She turned toward the door, but not before her stricken expression etched itself on his soul.

Desperation tore through him. He had to make her understand. "You need someone strong who can protect you without going to pieces over some goddamned chemicals." He looked down. His hands shook. "Look at me. I'm pathetic. Thought I could help—and I've only made it worse. Like I always do."

"Look, son. You're upset." Mitch was practical. "We can talk this over when you've had time to calm down."

"No need." He hefted the duffel bag. "I won't be back."

"You're not fired."

"I quit." He turned to face Mitch. "Sir. You gave me a chance when so many others wouldn't have. I hate to prove them right, but I'll never forget what you did for me."

"Then stay," Mitch said. "We need you."

"You need someone who isn't broken. Someone who won't let you down."

"Let me down? You and Katie took care of the ranch while I was laid up."

"He wants to go, let him go." Katie didn't sound like herself. Her voice was oddly detached. "It's like I said from the start, we don't need quitters on this ranch."

He swiveled his head to stare at her.

"If you want to run away, that's fine," she said. "But don't try and pretend you're doing it for our good. Admit it, John. You're scared. You're scared of putting yourself out there, taking a chance. Too afraid that now that you're no longer a soldier, you're not worthy anymore. Well, that's bullshit. You're so wrapped up in feeling sorry for yourself that you don't even recognize how important you are to other people."

"You don't know a single damned thing about it," he growled, but his voice lacked venom.

She folded her arms. "I know I'm right. And you do, too."

He turned away but it was too late. He couldn't escape her words.

"You can't run, John. Not from yourself."

Chapter 25

KATIE

Katie's body shook. Every muscle was on edge. She wanted to cry. To scream. To shout. Instead, she focused on holding her body still. Her eyes stung, but she resisted the urge to wipe them. She was not giving John the pleasure of seeing her distress. "You can't run, John. Not from yourself."

Trust me. I know.

John spun around unsteadily, making for his truck.

They watched in silence as John threw his duffel bag into the back of his truck. He's really leaving. Katie drew a deep breath. Every instinct she possessed screamed at her to go to him, to beg, to cry, to do anything to stop him leaving. The gentle pressure of her father's hand kept her where she was. *I can't stop him.* Until he saw the truth of her words, there was nothing she—or anyone—could do.

I'm not enough. She looked at her feet, unwilling to see the moment when he drove off, leaving her behind. *I'm weak—too weak.* If she'd been stronger, he wouldn't have pushed himself to the point of breakdown trying to protect her. And he wouldn't be leaving—

"So, our foreman is leaving?"

Peter.

She stiffened but didn't raise her face to look at him. She took a deep breath, concentrating on getting her expression neutral. She'd be damned if she let Peter see her upset.

Out of the corner of her eye, she saw Peter step out of the barn. His coat was damp, and his boots splattered with mud. Clearly, he'd been out and about on the ranch already.

Her mouth flew open when he emerged more clearly into her line of sight. His entire left eye socket was black and blue. Looked like their newest employee had been on the losing end of a fight.

Her father murmured something conciliatory, but Peter didn't wait for him to finish. "He's not taking his dog with him?"

She raised her head. "What are you talking about?"

Peter's eyes widened. "What—you didn't know?" He looked between her and John. "That's what I was worried about. He might have cozied up to you, but he didn't bother to tell you the truth about why he came here."

"You little shit." John began stalking back toward them. "Don't listen to him, Katie."

"What the hell are you talking about?" she asked Peter.

"Sorry, it's just...after our last *encounter*," he winced, touching his bruised eye socket gingerly, "I decided to do a little research on our trusty foreman." Peter fished his phone out of his pocket. "And I happened to stumble across this."

Her stomach twisted. Was Peter implying that John had punched him? If so, why? What was going on here? There was bile in the back of her throat, but she held out her hand for the phone.

"What's all this about?" Her father glanced between the two men, his brow furrowed.

Peter turned toward him. "Our foreman and I had...some words last night. Made me a little worried about his stability, what with your daughter here and all, so I wanted to know what his deal was." He flicked his wrist in John's direction. "Turns out he's been keeping secrets from us."

"Katie." John's voice sounded close by. He sounded utterly miserable. "I can explain."

She couldn't take her eyes off the post. There was a photo of John, a man she recognized from a photo from his mother's house, and—

Koda.

"You posted this months ago." Her head swam. "About wanting to find your dog. The dog you'd been assigned to work with overseas. The dog named Koda."

John tried to grab the phone. "Katie. Listen—"

"She's *your* dog? The one you've been looking for? Why didn't you tell us?" Her voice was breaking with the shock and pain she felt.

"She *was* mine." John sounded anguished. "In Afghanistan. We worked together. By the time I met you, she was yours. I'm just glad to be around her again. That's what I was about to tell you, before your dad and Linda came home."

"Is that why you stayed on?" Her voice trembled. She raised her eyes to his. "Because we had your dog and you figured you could at least be around her again?"

"At first, yes. Legally I had no option on getting Koda back. And I needed the job, so I kept my mouth shut."

"Son, you thought we'd fire you?" Mitch asked.

John pressed his lips together, digging his hands into his pockets. "I did. At first. But then I saw the bond Katie had with Koda, and I couldn't say anything. I didn't want to disrupt that. And I like working here. Three Keys Ranch is a wonderful place. And I love—I like being around you, Katie."

"Make sure you check out the comments section. I found it enlightening." Peter ducked back as John stared at him. "What—going to punch me again?"

She scrolled down. The words swam before her eyes. Only a few rose up out of the sea of text to register.

"Look, Katie. You have to understand this was months ago." John extended a hand toward her, pleading.

"I understand, all right." She stepped closer and lowered her voice. "Did you see those comments? People—your friends—called me a selfish bitch, a heartless monster who wouldn't give a wounded veteran his dog back!"

"I posted later, updating people to the situation—" He fell silent as she glared at him.

"You could update your Facebook, but you couldn't tell me the truth." She practically spat the words, holding the phone back to Peter. "I trusted you."

Her voice cracked. She felt raw, as if she'd been turned inside out and exposed to the cold November air.

"I'm sorry."

"I don't want to hear it." She pointed to his truck. "Just go."

John's shoulders slumped and then he stiffened. "If that's what you want." As he turned again, making his way back to the truck with heavy steps, Koda sat in the yard. She looked from Katie to John, her brown eyes puzzled.

Katie drew a deep breath.

"Guess that explains some things," Peter said. "All the weird stuff that's been happening was a front so you'd keep him around."

"Weird stuff?" her father asked.

Katie and her dad both turned to Peter, whose brows lifted in surprise. "John didn't tell you about the north fence being vandalized?"

"He might have said something to that effect," her father said. "But I didn't listen. I can't believe anyone round here would do something so low. I don't believe that John would, for sure."

"I didn't want to believe it either, but what's the saying? Twice is a coincidence, but three times ...?" Peter nodded and folded his arms.

Katie's stomach dropped. "Three times? But the fence has only been broken twice."

"Got bad news." Peter glanced at the ground. "I've just come from the north pasture. Fence is down and some of the cattle got out last night—pregnant cows."

Her lungs felt like old, stretched-out elastic, with the way they struggled to contract for her next breath. "Where I wrecked the truck just yesterday?"

"Hold up," her father said, his mouth tipping down at the ends. Red blotches appeared on his face. "What wrecked truck? Why am I just hearing the first of this now?"

"Don't you go getting yourself all wound up for nothing, Mitch. You can see for yourself, Katie is fine," Linda said. "And you know what the doctor said about you exerting yourself."

Her dad made a disgruntled sound, before pivoting and striding toward the barn, kicking up mud in his wake. Katie and Linda exchanged uneasy glances and followed.

"Forget the doctor," her dad said. "This is my ranch, and if my cattle are out..." A deep, rattling cough caught him off guard. Linda darted forward and grabbed his arm, supporting him as he regained his breath.

"I'm fine." Her dad tried to wave Linda away. "Let me go."

"You're doing no such thing." Linda's voice was stern. "The doctor said you'd need rest, and that's what you're getting."

Once she ascertained that her dad was okay, Katie turned and hurried into the ranch house. Her head beat in an angry rhythm, in time with the pounding of her heart. Luckily, it did not take her long to get what she needed. Joanne had left the fridge well stocked with groceries, and it was the work of a few minutes to put sandwiches and fruit into the saddlebags. She added two bottles of water and pulled on her coat and scarf.

When she walked outside, Peter was giving her dad a more detailed description of the damage done to the fence. John's truck was still parked in the yard. She wondered why he hadn't left, then caught herself. Don't know. Don't care. He'd lied to her—lied to them all.

When she stepped into the barn, John straightened up from inside Snowbird's stall.

"What are you doing?"

He stepped back and she could see Snowbird had been fitted with saddle and riding tack. "Getting her ready. You're riding out, aren't you?"

She raised her chin, meeting his gaze defiantly. "Try and stop me."

John looked as if he was tempted, but instead he looked down, as if it were painful to meet her gaze. He looked older than ever, his eyes filled with an exhaustion she couldn't imagine. "I won't. But I don't think you should rush off on your own. Take someone with you."

"I don't need anyone." She took Snowbird's reins. She ran her hands over the horse, checking the saddle sat correctly. "I'm not afraid."

Before he could protest, she swung herself up onto Snowbird's back, directing the horse out of the stables.

Her dad, Linda, and Peter looked up as she rode toward them.

"Riding out?" Her dad took a step toward the barn. "I'll join you."

"You'll do no such thing." Her voice was firm, anger at John's betrayal giving her strength. "You need to rest, or you'll land yourself right back in a hospital bed. Tell him, Linda."

"Katie's right. This is no time to be stubborn, Mitch." Linda placed her hand on his arm. "I'll make sure he gets some rest."

"I'll come with you," Peter said quickly.

Katie shook her head. "You'll get to work repairing the broken fence."

"Wait. We can ride together—"

"No time," she said. "If I don't get the missing herd back inside the ranch, who knows where they'll end up once the snow's over."

"I don't know about this, Katie." Dad eyed the sky with the thickening clouds. "The weather doesn't look so good."

A chilly gust of wind swept over them just then, causing goosebumps to erupt across Katie's skin. "We can't be losing those cows and a big piece of next spring's calf crop. This ranch runs on beef. You know that as well as I do." She used her heels to urge Snowbird. "I'm going to go. I've got cattle to find."

She turned automatically to call Koda. Instead, her eyes fell on John. He stood in the shadow of the barn, his eyes fixed on her.

Even through her anger, she felt a sudden surge of pain. It was as if someone had stabbed her in the gut. She swallowed and urged Snowbird into a gallop.

His muscles rippled and his powerful limbs thundered over the tightly pressed dirt of the yard. The wind wisped his mane into the air like flames. In moments they were clear of the fence, riding across the pasture towards the hills.

The dry arctic air froze her nose hairs and stung her cheeks, filled with the cold, dusty scent that preceded a snow. Her anger faded, replaced by numbness. Above her head, the solid gray clouds seemed to be lowering toward the earth, drawing close.

I don't have much time.

Already snow was falling, rapidly accumulating on the ground. By the time she'd reach where the fence was cut, any tracks would be covered up. Time for a change of plans.

The cows had escaped from the north pasture, but if she rode up McCullum's Ridge, cut over the high ground toward her dad's old hunting cabin, she could circle back and intercept the cows before they got too far—provided they weren't already in the ravine.

They're range-raised animals. They've got some sense. *Unlike me.* She took a deep breath, pushing back a feeling of alarm.

Did she really think she could find and bring the cattle back, all by herself? Her head throbbed, her headache returning. She was so weak, she couldn't even drive a truck up a goddamn hill.

Before her, a massive shape rose out of the snow.

The truck. Snowbird came to a halt. She didn't blame the horse. The last thing she wanted to do was approach the truck, be reminded of just how badly she'd stuffed up. She opened her mouth, intending to urge Snowbird onward.

We don't need quitters on this ranch. Her mouth snapped shut. She'd said those words to John. His reply still stung. She'd never forget the defeat in his voice as he turned away.

You don't know a single damned thing about it.

"You're wrong. Dead wrong—and I'm going to prove it." She swung down from Snowbird's back. She approached the truck.

A nagging voice at the back of her mind urged her to hurry, said she was running out of time. Something urged Katie onwards. *I have to do this. I can't give into fear.* For a few glorious hours last night, she'd been free—free of the fear haunting her since the accident. She couldn't lose that.

The truck was mostly covered in drifts of snow. She walked around it, looking it over, the ground crunching beneath her feet. There were no obvious signs of damage. *I guess I just stalled in some mud.* She crouched by the back tire. *There was a bang. I wonder...* She brushed snow from the tire, revealing a puckered hole in the rubber.

The crisp, cold air felt like water filling her lungs. Her eyesight started going blurry, and her heart pounded so hard her chest ached. No. A stone wouldn't puncture a tire like that. No, the hole was too neat to be anything but deliberate. But that meant—

Someone had purposely shot the tire out on the truck. Maybe even tried to kill her.

Her mind flickered to what Peter had said, just a short while ago. How he thought John was to blame. Katie's body jerked at the alien thought, rejecting it. No. No matter what secrets John had kept about Koda, there was no way he would have done this. She knew him well enough by now to know that was impossible. Even in her anger, she knew that John had a strength of character that would never allow him to deliberately hurt the people in his care. In fact, just the opposite. John did everything he could to protect them.

She shook her head. She couldn't get distracted now.

The police—she needed to call the police.

But she couldn't move from the spot.

She didn't know how long she crouched by the truck. The snow fell thicker, the landscape around her becoming even gloomier and more impenetrable. Snowbird whinnied, flicking his tail as he drew closer to Katie. The horse wanted to be out of there. She ran her hand over Snowbird's neck. "We need to move."

But where?

A bark broke the uncanny stillness of the hills. She stood motionless, hardly daring to raise her head. She saw a dark shape streaking across the fields toward her.

Koda? But—

As she stared, she saw Koda pause to nose the snow. The dog evidently had Katie's scent. She barked once before taking off in her direction.

She looked back the way the dog had come. Behind her was a familiar figure swaying in the saddle. *John*. She swallowed back a rush of warmth—*he hadn't left her after all*—and then Koda was upon her.

"Yeah, you found me. Good girl, Koda." Katie patted the dog's ears. She waited for John to arrive. When he reached her, she noted how fast Redwood was breathing. They'd ridden hard to catch her.

"Katie." He needed a moment to catch his breath.

"I'm fine." She tightened her hold on Snowbird's reins. "What are you doing here? Didn't you quit?"

"Yeah, I did." He took a deep breath. "Look. I've been a jerk, and I've let you down when you relied on me. But I had to see you again." He looked at Koda. "I had to bring you your dog."

"My dog?" She couldn't believe her ears—or her eyes—as Koda padded up to her. "But you're her partner."

"Some partner." His expression twisted. "I couldn't keep her safe. Couldn't keep anyone safe. You—well, look at her. You think she'd be anywhere near this happy with anyone else? No, she's your dog."

She looked at Koda. The dog gazed up at her with steady brown eyes. As she always did around Koda, she felt calmed by her presence. She ran a hand along Koda's back. The dog was so much more than a companion to her. But the same held true for John. Koda was his everything. His only link to a past he'd been cut off from forever.

She bit her lip. There were many things she could say to him, but as she studied the lines on his face, only one came to mind. "Help me find the cattle?"

Hope lit his eyes, made him straighten to his full height. "You want my help? After...everything?"

"I didn't give you an easy time," she admitted. "And I'm still mad that you weren't honest with me sooner. But—whatever happened, I know you aren't doing anything intentionally to hurt me. Besides, Koda adores you and trusts you," she gave the dog's soft head a pat, "and that's good enough for me."

John's eyes darkened and he cast his gaze onto the ground. "You think—you could ever trust me again?" His tone was harsh, the words ground out through gritted teeth. "I swear on Koda's life that I had nothing to do with the fences."

She felt a rush of warmth. She knew how hard the question was. "I do trust you—I know you would never do something like that, to hurt me or my dad."

He stared at her. "How?"

"Because I see the pride you take in your work. The care you take in our animals—the dogs, the horses, and Koda. I don't think you could ever put our cattle in harm's way. And I see you at night, patrolling to make sure I'm safe."

His jaw twitched with some unnamed emotion, but he didn't say another word. Instead, he swung himself down from Redwood's back and held out his hand to her.

Wordlessly, she took the hand he offered, squeezing it tightly. "Come on, partner. We've got work to do."

Chapter 26

JOHN

The swirling storm of screaming silver had forced Katie and John to abandon their search for the cattle and take shelter in the hunting cabin. The gale whipped each flake, so pretty on its own, into a projectile that hurt unguarded skin. They'd dismounted in the run-in shed. He rubbed down Redwood, while she unhitched the saddlebags from Snowbird.

"What happened to you over there?"

John swallowed. "Excuse me?"

"Overseas." She hesitated. "When we adopted Koda, we were told about an IED."

"I got hurt," he said in a low voice, still looking straight ahead.

She took a step back from Snowbird. "Is that what you dream about?"

He clasped the reins in his hands. "I don't need sympathy right now. We need a plan and a fire."

"Well, I can work on one of those." She picked up the saddlebag. "Dad makes a point of keeping these cabins stocked in case of emergencies like this. There's plenty of firewood. I'll start a fire if you finish the horses."

"Leave it to me." As soon as the cabin door shut, he took a deep breath and got to work removing Snowbird's saddle, relieved to be alone.

But her question haunted him. *What happened to you over there?*

The tone of her voice was almost tender. John grimaced. *The last thing I want is her pity.* It was hard enough catching the pain in his mother's eyes when she looked at what he'd become. To see the same gaze on Katie was more than he could bear.

After he'd rubbed the horses dry with a burlap sack, he grabbed a bucket to bring water to the tired animals. The pump beside the barn was creaky from the cold but worked just fine after a few quick motions. He threw plenty of hay into the trough and then locked the gate on the fence around the shed.

He slipped into the warm interior of the cabin to find Katie with her hands stretched out to the fire. Koda had already staked her claim on a sheepskin just in front of it. "Don't think I've ever been happier to see a fire before."

She looked at him. "It's just a little snow," she said. "Haven't you been out in worse?" Her hair splayed out at the bottom of her knit hat. There were still a few snowflakes caught on the wool.

He felt an urge to reach out and pull off the hat before they melted. "Sure, I have. But those clouds are heavy. This could easily be way more than just a little snow."

She shrugged. "It's the beginning of November, you know. Montana weather's crazy." She added another log to the fire and sat back in one of two rough chairs before the flames.

He looked over at her. It surprised him how tender and protective he felt toward this woman. It had been years since he'd felt this way for any woman.

As he watched, she dropped her gaze to the floor.

"What's wrong?" he said, tensing.

"It's just that up here we're more secluded. Isolated. From everyone," she said, refusing to look up.

Pain sliced through his ribcage. Was Katie afraid of him now? He inched closer, his socks padding softly on the hardwood floor. "You're safe here. You're safe with me. I swear." He paused, but she still couldn't look up.

"You don't understand."

He placed a finger underneath her chin. She winced but didn't move away. He gently lifted her face up to meet his gaze. Her eyes were brimmed with tears, and he could see the humiliation creep over her face.

"Katie, don't. Your father explained what happened. Why you couldn't go inside the hospital. I wanted you to tell me when you were ready, but it just didn't happen that way. And I'm glad he told me. But I don't want you being scared. Or making yourself anxious because you thought I didn't know." He hoped his voice conveyed what he felt. No pity. Just empathy, pure and genuine.

"I didn't feel anxious because I thought you didn't know. You made me anxious by hiding whatever you're hiding." Her voice was quiet. "You don't have to tell me, but—"

"The reason I couldn't tell you was because I thought there's no way I'd be allowed to stay at the ranch if you had any idea what a failure I am."

"Failure?" She frowned at him.

"Yeah." He hesitated, but the woman in front of him had trusted him with her innermost self. Could he really hold back? "I'm the reason Dirk died."

"Dirk?" When she spoke her voice trailed slowly, like her words were unwilling to take flight.

Hearing the name on her lips was both a blessing and a curse. "He was my best friend, my brother in arms. We were heading out on a mission." He hung his head, his heartrate ramping up as the images came flooding back. "I noticed Koda's harness was loose on one side and I switched seats with him to adjust it. But I stayed."

The familiar pain was a cyclone, tearing through his insides and leaving him hollow. Still, he forced himself to meet her gaze. "It's my fault he died. I should've caught the harness issue before we loaded up. I should've switched back to where I was sitting. The IED should've killed me. I'm the one who should've died."

Her soft gasp was almost too much to bear. This was it. This was when she finally looked at him with the disgust he deserved. Instead, he felt the gentle warmth of her hand, covering his. "All this time—that's what you've been hiding?"

He nodded. "I'm broken. I'm no good for the army. But that was the only thing I ever wanted to do. The only thing going for me now is people think I'm some kind of hero. If they knew the truth." He took a deep breath. "So, you see. I want to protect you, want you to feel safe."

"And you think after hearing your story, I would forget all the times you came to my aid? I saw you patrolling the yard the night the dogs got out. I didn't think I'd ever feel safe in the house again after that night, but I did. And it wasn't just because of Koda, John. It was because of you."

There was a trace of her usual stubbornness in her tone—but just a trace. "Me?"

"Yes," she said, in a tone that didn't allow for argument. "And right now, I don't know what I'd do if you weren't here."

She glanced at the door and shivered, sending a prickle racing along the back of his neck. "What's wrong, Katie? Is something worrying you?"

"What, apart from the missing cattle, the snowstorm, and everything else?" She hunched her shoulders and wrapped her arms around her waist. "The truck. John, I don't think it was an accident."

"What do you mean?"

As she described what she'd seen, his pulse built to a loud drumming that drowned out every thought but one. Nothing—nothing—was going to happen to her on his watch.

Nothing.

He pinched the bridge of his nose. "After the night someone entered the farmhouse I did some checking. Seemed a little too convenient to happen the one night you were alone on the farm."

"And you didn't say anything about your suspicions?" Her voice rose.

"I didn't want to scare you." He held up his hands. "Thought maybe I was being distrustful again."

To his surprise, her eyes filled with tears. "If you hadn't come along when you did, I'd probably still be there by the truck."

"You're kidding. Without my elderly ass holding you back, you'd have the cattle rounded up and back at the ranch by now."

She smiled but it didn't reach her eyes. "What if something happens to you? No one else is here. I don't want to be alone."

"Koda is here. Together we won't let anyone get to you. I promise. I won't let anyone hurt you again. Ever." The severity of his tone took him off guard. And he realized there wasn't a line he wouldn't cross to protect her. He swallowed hard. "You can trust me."

"I know." There was a faint smile on her lips and a hint of her usual sparkle in her eyes. "I figured it out during our first sleepover. You...you didn't do anything. Most guys would have at least made a move." She shot a sly glance below his waist. "Especially with the bulge you had going on."

Heat crawled up into his cheeks. The woman actually made him blush.

"It's coming down pretty hard out there, isn't it?" She looked past him to the window.

He followed her gaze. He could just make out the shadowy shapes of the trees through the driving snow. Despite it being the middle of the afternoon, the day had already descended into darkness. "It is."

She took an audible breath, and when he turned she was standing up, brushing her hands off on her jeans. "We're probably going to have to stay here overnight, so I guess we should see about getting something to eat. Dad always keeps loads of canned stuff here. I'll see what we've got."

"Sounds good. Do you need any help?"

"No, thanks. I've got it." She dug through the wooden cabinets in the kitchen nook at the north-facing end of the room, pulling out cans and boxes of non-perishable goods. She opened a can of soup and dumped it into a pan. "You make sure the fire stays going."

"Yes, ma'am." He stood a moment watching her. Despite the stress of the last forty-eight hours and the tension of their current situation, she'd bounced back to her usual manner. *How can she think she's weak?* He shook his head, tending to the fire.

Before long, the soup was bubbling. She grabbed a couple of bowls and ladled out the soup. She brought in a tray with crackers and granola bars, disappeared one more time, and came back with two bottles of water. "Behold! I've made us a feast."

"Thanks for making this," he said. He took a big spoonful of the soup and felt the warm liquid pour down his throat, warming his belly as it progressed. He let out a contented sigh. He could stay like this with her forever.

She joined him on the couch, tucking her feet beneath her. "I don't mind cooking. Not that this is really cooking. Although I do recall *you* claiming you can cook."

"I can," he said to her, glad to see she was poking fun at him. It brought a smile to her face.

He was suddenly aware how close she was to him. Aware of the vanilla and almond fragrance of her body lotion. And of the warmth radiating off her skin.

He set down the bowl and his eyes searched hers.

Licking her dry lips, she lifted her chin.

"John. Kiss me." Her voice was steady and clear.

His heart pounded as he cleared his throat. "Are you sure?"

"I wouldn't have asked otherwise. Do you really need a second invitation?"

He leaned forward, intending for this to be a simple kiss. As soon as their lips touched, he knew there would be nothing simple about it. He cupped her face as his mouth consumed hers.

She didn't pull away but met him with the same ferocity, sliding into his lap.

He suddenly froze. He wasn't sure if he was ready for this, ready to let her see him—all of him, even his ugly scars. This time, there would be no hiding anything.

His hand wandered over the length of her body and his fingers hooked under her waistband. But she flinched and he withdrew his hand immediately.

"Are you okay?" He paused, searching her eyes. "Katie, are you okay?" He shifted under her, and she leaned in and kissed him again.

"I'm okay. It's just been awhile."

Her fingers trailed down his chest and tugged his shirt from his pants. Her lips traveled down his neck as his hands slipped under her shirt and felt the heat of her skin. She was on fire.

For me.

She removed his shirt and unhooked his belt. His body instantly went rigid from fear, the hard flesh from healed gashes and shrapnel exposed for her to see. But they were nothing compared to the horror show she'd find beneath his jeans.

But she only looked at him with the same concern he'd shown her. "John?"

He gazed at the fireplace. "I was hurt bad. An IED. Burns. Not so pretty to look at." Shame consumed him and he avoided eye contact. He braced himself for the disgust he knew was coming, or even worse—the pity.

"You told me I could trust you. Well, maybe you can try to trust me?" Her tone was soft. Her lips gently kissed the side of his mouth. "From one fucked-up person to another?"

He whipped his head up. "I didn't mean that."

"I know. And now I know why you hide." She tucked a strand of hair behind an ear. Her eyes rested on him. There was no pity in them. Just—compassion. "You don't need to apologize to me. I just hope someday you'll be able to trust someone with your scars, the way I trust you with mine."

He breathed in deep and stood up. He took her hand and pulled her up, too. Then placed her hand on his chest. "I do trust you."

She gently trailed her fingers over his body, unbuttoning his jeans. He closed his eyes as he felt his pants drop. But he craved her warmth when she pressed against him and her lips gently kissed every part of his chest and belly.

He allowed his eyes to open until her fingers hooked into his boxer briefs. Then they slammed shut again. *Moment of truth.* He felt her gently remove them. He didn't want to see her reaction.

"John?"

His tongue was stuck to the roof of his mouth. He wasn't certain if he was even breathing. The shame was almost too much. Not only of what he looked like, but because he was also aware of how flaccid he was.

"John. Open your eyes, please," she said softly.

He swallowed hard and looked at her, allowing the tears to fall down his face. She reached up, kissed him, and stepped back. Away from him.

She doesn't want me.

"I don't see anything wrong with the man in front of me. You volunteered to sacrifice yourself to protect your men and your country. Nothing could be more honorable. No one could be more perfect, wounds and all."

Nothing could have made him love Katie more. No one had ever made him feel more accepted, as if there was no standard to live up to, because to her he was already everything he needed to be.

Before he could respond, to let her know what her words meant to him, she removed her shirt. Her pale skin glowed against the backdrop of the snowy light. Even through his tears, he couldn't help gazing at her perfect body.

She stared back at him. "Are you going to make fun of me?"

The question threw him for a loop. "I'm standing here naked. Limp. Fucking crying. And you ask me if I'm going to make fun of you. For what?"

She unbuckled her own jeans and pulled them off. Standing in front of him was the most beautiful girl he'd ever seen. Topless. Hands on her hips.

In Superman underwear.

From deep inside his chest came a great shaking motion and his face muscles grew tight. The laugh erupted like a busted water main arching into the summer sky. He massaged his cheeks, the muscles aching from the wide grin.

She frowned.

"Sit," she commanded, pushing him onto the couch with her fingertips. He watched as her lips parted and her pupils dilated at the sight of his suddenly straining erection.

"And to think I was going to wear my lacy pink panties." She straddled him, grasping his rigid length as she invaded his mouth, their tongues entwining.

He groaned as she stroked him, gently swiping her thumb over his head of his cock to spread the slickness. His hips jerked up in response and he grabbed her thighs.

He released his grip and his hands traveled against her smooth skin. He wanted to touch every inch of her body but his need was too strong. He stood up from the couch, lifting her off her feet.

She gasped and wrapped her legs around his waist. She ran her hands through his hair, scratching her fingernails along his scalp and neck.

"God, Katie!" He wanted her so fucking badly. He pressed her up against the rough wooden wall, pinning her body with his own. He felt her buck against him, as if her body wanted to challenge his strength.

"I need you inside me." She scratched her nails down the length of his back.

Growling with desire, he laid her on the thick woolen blanket they had been eating on. She thrust out an arm, knocking aside the bowls of soup and crackers. He frantically pulled off her panties, stopping to gaze at her. She was perfect.

"You're so goddamn beautiful," he whispered.

She smiled up at him, her dark hair pillowing around her face. "You're not so bad yourself." She lifted her hands and pulled his face to meet her own. "Now shut up and kiss me."

And kiss her he did. Their lips met frantically, as if each were starving for the other. Her tongue flicked in and out of his mouth, prodding and exploring. He groaned, his dick almost painful from the swelling. He pushed against her, feeling the wetness that had instantly sprung from her pussy.

He kissed her neck and stomach, pausing only for a moment to take a rosebud-pink nipple in his mouth. He sucked and swirled his tongue around it, feeling her writhe underneath his weight.

As he kissed his way to her belly toward her wetness, he grabbed her hands in his own and entwined his fingers around hers. He wanted to make her feel beautiful. He wanted to make her feel safe.

When his mouth finally enveloped her pussy, she cried out with pleasure. He flicked and stroked his tongue around her clit, feeling it swell within his mouth. She clutched at his hands, bucking and dipping with every flick of his tongue. She tasted so good, like vanilla and soft leather and pine and sugar, all at once. He could taste her innermost wetness forever. But she couldn't last as long. She gave one final thrust toward his face and went rigid as an orgasm shuddered through her body. He slipped his tongue inside of her, wanting to feel every muscle ripple and roll as she came.

By the time she had finished, his dick felt like it would explode.

"Katie—condom," he managed to get out.

She reached down and dragged his jeans over, pulling a condom from his wallet. As he rolled the latex over his cock, she kissed him, licking at the wetness that clung to his lips.

He pushed her back down and thrust his cock inside of her. Her slick, warm pussy felt like heaven. As he thrust, her muscles clamped tight around his dick. It was like a fist squeezing him as he ground against her.

The corner of her mouth curled into a devilish, sexy smile. "Harder," she panted. "I need you."

He hammered into her, watching his length disappear. His thumb circled her clit and her nails dug into him again as she gasped. He felt a strong surge travel through his stomach, down his legs, and up his neck, as if his whole body was prepared to come. He rubbed her clit with more insistence.

"Come with me," he moaned. "Katie, come with me."

When her body bucked and shuddered in response to his commands, John felt himself explode in wave after wave of pleasure and relief. He moaned, clutching her legs as he came before collapsing on top of her, panting and smiling.

She brushed her hand against his cheek and smiled. "I don't think it will be so bad being snowed in together."

He laughed and leaned over to kiss her.

Chapter 27

KATIE

Katie woke the next morning, a chill blowing over her exposed skin. For a moment, she was confused about where she was—and a small sigh brought the previous night rushing back.

John lay curled up against her, an afghan wrapped around his body. Did he actually sleep? Really sleep? He looked like it, more peaceful and content than she'd ever seen him.

There had been no terrible dreams last night.

She looked around the cabin. The fire had died down to embers. The furnace, though she could hear it chugging away, wasn't doing enough to keep the cold at bay. They'd have to move and get dressed quickly. With the cows still missing, they needed to get back to the ranch for reinforcements.

"Hey," she whispered into his ear.

He opened one eye and looked at her. Then he squeezed his eyes shut. "Five more minutes?"

"Five more minutes. Then time to get to work, buddy." She leaned down to kiss him. She hadn't been happy in so long that the sensation actually felt strange.

But he groaned and extracted himself from her arms, shivering as he stood to put on his jeans. "I'll see if we can get this fire going again."

"Sounds great," she replied.

While he lit some fresh kindling, she opened the door for Koda to run outside. Then she returned and stood behind the couch. "Want first shower?"

"There's a shower?"

"You'll find soap, shampoo, and towels in the little closet," she called to him, rolling her eyes as she plopped into a chair with her phone to check her email and social media. "About the only thing we don't have is phone reception."

He grunted. "I'll take hot water over checking Facebook any day of the week."

He paused as if about to say something else, then disappeared into the bathroom.

Her fingers punched in the phone's code and she opened the app. It would take time before he was fully able to trust she wasn't going to be frightened off. Now that she understood why he hid, she no longer felt threatened.

The sound of ferocious barking made her jerk straight. Her phone slid through her fingers and hit the ground. The bathroom door opened behind her, and she whipped her head around. "What the hell could that be?"

"I don't know. Get dressed." John pulled his jeans back up then scooted past her.

She headed over to the couch and grabbed her clothes from the floor, yanking on her sweater and jeans, her heart slamming into her chest as if it were a boxer looking to knock out its opponent. *Dammit! Won't this ever end?*

"Maybe it's just coyotes. She hates it when they come around the house." She pulled the sleeves of her sweater over her hands.

"Hey, dog! Get back!" It was a man's voice.

Every muscle in her body tensed. "That's Peter!"

John's arms went rigid, muscles and veins popping out from under his skin. "Yeah. Koda was right. A skulking coyote. But she and I will take care of it."

"Are you sure?"

"Go in the bedroom and lock the door."

"But—"

"Go. Koda and I will take care of this."

She took a couple of small steps back as he strode across the room. She spun and hurried into the bedroom. She closed the door and stood with her ear pressed against it.

The front door creaked open.

"Koda! Come!" John called.

Peter's boots thunked against the cabin floor so loud Katie imagined they echoed to all within a several hundred meter radius.

"That's better." She pulled away from the door as Peter spoke, his voice causing the hairs on her arms and neck to stand erect.

"What the hell are you doing here?"

The high-pitched note to Peter's laugh made her skin crawl. "Not much of a way to greet a friend who's trying to help you. Old Mitch is worried. I volunteered to go look for you. And here I am."

The front door shut and the wooden floor creaked as two sets of footsteps walked across it. Katie cracked the door of the bedroom and looked out just in time to see Peter slam the butt end of his rifle into John's temple. Her hand clamped over her mouth as she screamed.

John crumpled to the floor, grabbing the side of his head.

Koda, still outside, barked like a mad wolf. Katie could hear her ninety-pound body slamming against the front door.

Peter kicked John in the ribs as he crawled across the floor, trying to get up. "So much for the big army guy. Too fucking easy to take you down. "

"Try it again," John gasped, still on his hands and knees.

"Why? Look at you. Helpless. Worthless." Peter shook his head. "No wonder the army kicked you out. But you weren't kicked out—my mistake. You were human scrap. They threw you in the junk heap and here you are."

I have to do something. The sight of John fighting against his pain gave Katie the strength to push past her fear. Her eyes darted around the room. *If I can climb out the window, I can open the door for Koda—*

But her movement caught Peter's attention. He raised the rifle. "Get out here. Right now. Sit on the couch or he's dead. *Move!*"

Gritting her teeth, she inched towards the couch. She had no choice.

"And you." Peter pointed the rifle at John again. "You get your sorry ass off the damn floor. And take this"—he reached into his jacket pocket and pulled out a roll of duct tape—"and tape up her hands behind her back. Do it or I'll shoot her first."

As John struggled to his feet, Peter kept talking, enjoying the captive audience. Katie forced herself to think how to use this to her advantage.

Peter's piercing black eyes watched her like a wolf observes its prey. "I've tried three times before to get to you. The first time—in the hospital—"

"That was *you?*" Her every word was clipped, punching into the air.

"No." A grin lit up Peter's face like a sallow candle in a dirty paper lamp, wide and open, showing his over-whitened teeth. In this moment, he looked nothing like the prep school man-child that she'd hired. "I hired someone that time, but you know what they say. If you want something done right, do it yourself. So—"

"But why?" Sweat drenched her skin, as her nails dug into her palm. *Calm down.* She needed to keep him talking. Keep him distracted. "What have you got against me?"

"Well, now." Peter's eyes glittered. "It's not you personally, little lady. More like your father."

John stood up straight. He struggled to keep his balance, his expression calm, and gave her a faint nod. *Keep talking,* he mouthed.

"My father? But he—he's been nothing but kind to you! He welcomed you onto the ranch."

"Because he knew I could make things damn unpleasant for him if he didn't." Peter exuded cold malice with a tinge of arrogance. Perhaps he'd been a baby left to cry too often or suffered from a personality disorder doctors couldn't fix. Either way, he had as much empathy as a medieval mace. She should have trusted her initial gut feeling about the man. Or at the very least, she should have trusted John's gut.

"What are you talking about?"

Peter grinned. There was something feral about it, like the coyote she'd first mistaken him for. "He killed *my* father."

Shocked silence followed Peter's accusation, followed by a dull ringing in Katie's ears. His claim was outrageous. "You can't really believe that, can you?" She struggled to keep her voice calm. "They were business partners! They started Three Keys Ranch together!"

"Yeah. They sure did. But it didn't end up that way. Mitch crowded him out of the deal. Took his money. Took everything. Left him out in the cold. My father died of a heart attack at the age of forty-one. The stress and the deception just killed him, no different than if he had pulled a gun on him."

Katie shook her head. "Not true! It's not! I know that story. My father—"

"Shut up, bitch!" Peter raised the rifle. "Your father killed him and now he's going to pay. He's going to know what it feels like to lose a family member. And he's going to find it out today!"

Her brain stalled. She couldn't think of anything to say.

"I tried myself when your father went into the hospital, and again when you drove out to the north pasture alone. But both times your attack dogs got in the way—one named Koda and the other John." His smile was lazy but didn't meet his eyes, which lit with a disturbing, vicious gleam. The combination made Katie's skin crawl. Something was wrong with Peter. He was sick in a way that went far beyond her anxiety or even John's battle trauma.

"You broke into the house," she said. Delay was her only tactic right now. She had to keep him talking. "You thought I'd be there alone. And out at the pasture—what'd you do, shoot out my tire?"

"Of course. And if that damn dog hadn't been there, this would have been over already. Looks like the third time's the charm, doesn't it?"

There was a crash as Koda threw herself against the door, barking wildly.

"Damn dog. All right. You get over there and tape her up, like I said. Remember. Any trouble and I shoot her first, not you."

John took the duct tape and walked over to the couch.

"You and I are gonna have fun, Katie," Peter sing-songed. "We have unfinished business."

"You're a fucking lunatic!" Spit built up in the corner of her mouth, muscles and veins straining against her skin.

John's hands directed her to stand up—and then, before any of them could blink, he whipped the roll of duct tape right at Peter's face.

The man ducked but staggered back as the roll bounced hard off his head. In one move, John shoved her over the back of the couch so she fell to the floor and launched himself at the man with the rifle.

But Peter moved fast and stepped back. John caught him by one ankle and forced him to the floor.

Peter struggled to bring the rifle up and turn it around as John strained to grab it, too.

"I'll open the door!" She scrambled to her feet. "I'll open the door and let Koda in!"

"You stay right there!" John yelled. "You stay there—trust me!"

"Thanks, Army." Peter had the upper hand when it came to leverage. She watched with horror as Peter brought the rifle around to point right at John's face. "With you out of the way, I can finally finish what I started."

"Koda!" John yelled.

The barking stopped.

"*Hopp Fenster!*"

Before her eyes, the window smashed into a shower of glass. A snarling brown blur launched at Peter, clamping its teeth shut on his arm, shaking it violently.

John grabbed the rifle and aimed it at Peter's head. "Koda! Come!"

The dog let go. She went to John's side, growling viciously, her eyes fixed on Peter.

Slowly Peter got up to a halfway sitting position. "Fucking beast—"

"Your turn for the duct tape." John kept the rifle trained on Peter. "Take off the coat so I can search you."

"Sure, boss." Peter grinned, his face white and his eyes glassy. "Anything you say." He moved one hand under the coat and drew a small pistol from its fold. Before he could raise it, John fired—and Peter fell back with a jerk to the floor. In one fluid move, John snatched up the pistol, and cracked Peter over the skull with it. He slumped to the floor.

"John. John! You're alright!" Propelled by a rush of relief, Katie didn't wait for an answer before launching herself into his arms.

"Fine." John pulled her in tight. She stood safety of his arms, soaking up his warmth and strength. "Guess there's fight in this old man yet."

Katie could have cried. She shuddered, letting John pull her even closer. "Peter—"

"Unconscious," John growled. "He's going to prison. This time, he's going to pay for what he's done."

She inhaled through her nose. "All this time ... it was him. But now—between you and Koda— it's over. It's finally over."

A shudder wracked John's body. "You trusted me."

She raised her eyes to look at him. "I said so, didn't I? You and Koda." She stretched out her hand to stroke Koda's body.

John grabbed her hand. "Look," he whispered.

Katie looked down and her heart stopped. Blood. Her hand was painted red with blood.

Koda's.

"No," she gasped, desperately seeking out the dog...just in time to watch Koda slump to the floor. The dog released one weak yelp, and then didn't stir.

Chapter 28

JOHN

Koda. John slumped on the couch. He hung his head and looked at his shoes. *I can't lose you.*

It had taken hours for the police to be finished with them, but he and Katie were finally back at the ranch. Linda was tending to Koda's gunshot wound in the barn. The vet had taken one look at him and banished him to the house, saying the last thing Koda needed right now was stress—and he was radiating nothing but anxiety.

He cradled his head in his palms and just sat there, not sure of what to say or how to feel. His muscles twitched, as if they were propelling him to grab his duffel bag and leave the ranch once and for all.

"Don't even think about it."

Katie's voice. He looked up to see her scowling at him from the living room doorway.

"You're not going anywhere. And neither am I."

He smiled faintly. "When did you learn to read minds?"

She folded her arms. "You've got that hiding look on your face again."

He winced. She had him. She was stubborn and he knew she wasn't going to back down. Hell, he'd done nothing but square off with her since day one—and here she was, threatening, or was it promising—to stay by his side. "Why would you want someone like me?"

"Because, old man, I happen to love you."

His head jerked up while his heart leapt into his throat. Barely daring to believe.

She smiled at his surprise, reaching for his hand as she sat next to him on the sofa. "I was scared to death when you threw yourself between me and the gun. Scared I'd never get to tell you how I feel."

He stared at her fingers resting over his. His mind struggled to take in everything she had just told him. She loved him—all of him. She'd seen him break down, and instead of running, she only wanted to build him back up. She accepted all of him, broken parts included.

He turned his hand, catching her fingers. A stunning realization swept over him, so powerful it felt like drowning. But even as he struggled to breathe, it was the best feeling he'd ever had.

"I love you, too." His voice broke. He couldn't believe he was saying those words again.

She nestled against him. "I know."

He offered a bemused smile, slipping an arm around her.

"I just went to see Linda," she said. "Koda's out of danger. The bullet wound gave us all a scare, but Linda says it looked much worse than it actually was."

He breathed out. "And she couldn't just say that?"

"With you scowling at her like she'd personally hurt your dog?" She nudged him. "She wanted to make sure Koda got some rest."

The last of his tension melted away. "She's really going to be okay?"

"She'll have stitches and need to rest, but she'll make a full recovery."

Koda would never be the dog she was before the IED. But she'd adjusted to ranch life so well he couldn't imagine being at Three Keys without her.

He bit his lip. "You think your dad would take me back on? Not as foreman, but maybe—"

She started to laugh.

"What's so funny?"

"You saved my life, John. You and Koda. Don't you realize? As far as my dad is concerned, you're a hero. He'd probably give you the ranch if you asked—though don't get any funny ideas." She dug his elbow into his side. "Three Keys is mine."

"You got it, boss."

She resettled against his side and closed her eyes, falling asleep in mere minutes.

As he got up to place a blanket on her, he smiled. He loved her. Fiercely. And he didn't want another day to go by without her in it. *Which means it's time to stop running from my problems.* Watching her ride off alone in search of the missing cattle had been a slap in the face. He'd realized at that moment if he didn't stop running, he was going to lose the most important person in his life. That had given him the strength to admit the extent of his brokenness to her. And now?

John traced the curve of her face with his fingers, careful not to wake her. No more hiding. No more faking being all right. And no more running.

For the rest of the winter and into the spring, the horses and cattle and people of Three Keys Ranch thrived. The missing cattle were recovered safe and sound. Two more top-drawer stock horses joined those already in the barn. The new calves all hit the ground healthy and those from last year sold for excellent prices.

Koda never left his side while he spent his days chasing after cattle, mending fences, and mucking out stalls. She even accompanied him to some of his therapy sessions with Dr. Evans. At night, the two of them curled up with Katie. They were a family, the three of them, and they would never be apart again.

On a beautiful Sunday afternoon in mid-April—one of the few sunny days in Montana's notoriously rainy spring—Koda ran up the front porch steps of the ranch house ahead of him. She barked at the front door.

"Not so fast." He adjusted his tie and shushed the dog.

Koda cocked her head to one side as she looked up at him. Her tongue lolled out as she panted happily.

He started to knock, and grinned when he realized Katie was already there waiting for him at the door. She tossed her hair over her shoulder and smiled almost shyly at him.

Her father was right behind her. He placed a hand on her shoulder. "Ready?"

"Ready for what?" Katie's gaze bounced between the two of them. "Aren't we stopping by your mom's and then going to The Fieldhouse for lunch?"

"Yes. That's right. Lunch." He tried hard to keep a straight face. "And I've never been more ready for anything in my life, although I have to say it's scarier than being in combat."

Mitch laughed. "It'll be a bigger adventure, I guarantee."

"What on earth are you two talking about?" she demanded. "Oh, never mind. It doesn't matter. I just want some food. I'm starving!"

"Right this way," John said, and stepped back to pull the screen door open for her.

"Have fun, kids," Mitch said, with a wink.

They climbed into his old truck and headed toward the main highway. A country song about love lasting forever played on the radio. John stole a glance at the woman in the passenger seat beside him.

Appropriate.

Over the winter, she'd supported him every day, helping him confront the many demons still haunting him. He'd struggled, but every time he'd felt hopeless, she reminded him he had a reason to stand his ground. As time passed, he'd become comfortable in the life he was leading—and she had joined him on that journey to find healing of her own.

Before long, he pulled off the road and drove beside the stream they had discovered while moving some of the cattle to a new field a couple of months ago. It had quickly become their special spot. He saw a smile of delight as she recognized where he was taking her. He parked the truck and both of them got out. The bubbling of the water made the perfect background music as they walked to stand beside the stream.

He leaned over to kiss her.

"This past year, this place—this ranch—this home—has healed me in ways I never thought possible," he went on. "*You* have healed me. I never would have believed that could happen, but it has."

He reached into his pocket.

"I have something to ask you."

A tear ran down her cheek.

He gently touched it away with his fingertip before easing himself onto one knee. "Katherine Locke. Will you do me the honor of becoming my wife?"

"Yes. Oh, yes, absolutely!" she cried, flinging her arms around him. Their lips met again.

"And in case this isn't enough," he said, "I have one other surprise for you."

He placed his hands on her shoulders and turned her around to face the stream.

"This place means a lot to both of us. And now it's where we will build our home."

Her mouth parted and her eyes widened. "What?"

He laughed. "Really? I have to spell it out for you? I bought the land, Katie. It's ours. Our spot is now *our* spot."

"Oh, my God, John," she gasped, her hands flying to her mouth once again. "I can't believe this. I can't believe it!"

"Believe it," he said, laughing. "And of course, this moment wouldn't be perfect without a certain someone for us to share it with."

He turned towards the truck. "Hey! Koda! Get your furry butt out here!"

Koda leapt out of the back of the truck and raced toward the couple, barking happily as she barreled into their legs. They laughed as they fell to the ground, their limbs entangled with Koda.

"This is our family now," he said, gazing into her eyes. "You will always be safe, Katie. I promise you." She bent her head to his and their foreheads touched. Koda gently poked her nose in between their faces to nuzzle them both.

They remained beside the river for the rest of the afternoon, eating fresh cherries that stained their lips and pointing with reddened fingers at the land where their house would come into being, until the first twinkling star appeared in the Montana sky.

Epilogue

John

This is it. The real test. John grunted as he stepped out of the passenger side of the car and onto the quiet residential street. He placed his hands on the small of his back and arched it. The drive to Colby, Kansas had taken well over ten hours, with only a couple of short stops along the way. It had taken him far longer to build up the courage to make the trip at all. Working with Dr. Evans, *really* working with Doc, helped him find that courage.

"Hey, now. The drive wasn't that bad," Katie said, sliding out of the driver's seat.

He rolled his eyes. "A roller coaster would've offered a smoother ride."

She pulled her cardigan tighter around her body. "I don't think your truck would have made it out of Montana."

"Nonsense," he said. "My truck would have made it just fine."

She laughed. "Your truck is old, just like you." She came around the front of the car and smiled at him.

He smiled back, but his hands balled into fists and he dug them into his thighs.

"You okay?" She rubbed his shoulder. They gazed at the two-story home, painted a bright yellow color with cheerful white paneling.

It seemed strange to him the house could look so relentlessly sunny, despite the grief and despair that must have existed within its silent walls.

"I'm fine. I'm just surprised she agreed to see me. I haven't visited her in a long time. The last time was back when Dirk was still alive, long before we deployed, and he told me before the mission she was mad about that."

"I think she's going to be happy to see you. She wouldn't have agreed to it otherwise."

Talking to Dirk's mother had always felt easy, warm, and friendly. But now, the thought of speaking to her filled him with dread.

"She's got no reason to be nice to me after what happened," he murmured. "She can't forgive me for not taking care of her son."

Katie stood quietly, just letting him go on.

He ran a hand through his hair. "I don't know how I can possibly sit in her living room and talk to her about Dirk—not when it should've been me sitting there—"

She stopped him with a hand on his arm. "Look. She's there in the doorway, waving to you."

And so she was. He raised his hand to Mrs. McDonald.

"John, are you ready?" Katie's touch on his arm became more insistent.

No. I'll never be ready for this. But it was too late to slip away now. "Let's go."

The two of them walked up the driveway, their shoes clipping on the pavement. By the time the door opened for them, he'd broken into a cold sweat.

"Oh, I'm so glad to see you!" Mrs. McDonald gasped. "John! It's been forever!"

And Dirk's mother wrapped him up in the tightest bear hug he had ever received in his life.

"You still give the best hugs," he murmured, as she squeezed his rib cage.

"We grow 'em strong here in Kansas," she laughed. She finally released him and turned her attention to Katie. "And who is this beautiful young lady?"

Judging from the way she was smiling, she approved heartily of the woman beside him.

"I'm Katie Locke. I'm John's fiancée." She glanced over at him, flushing with excitement.

They were still getting used to the official labels on the relationship, but he wasn't worried. In the last few months, they'd grown so close she already felt like his wife. The idea both exhilarated and terrified him all at once—feelings he couldn't get enough of.

"I'm so pleased to meet you," Mrs. McDonald said, enveloping Katie in a warm hug. "You can call me Gail." She stepped into the house, motioning them to follow her. "Come on in. I've just finished baking a batch of chocolate chip cookies."

She nodded toward him and then caught Katie's eye.

"I don't mean to boast, but I can tell you they happen to be *this* man's favorite cookies!"

He held his hands up. "Guilty as charged."

"Come with me, Katie." She ushered Katie into the kitchen leaving him to wander into the living room.

His heart broke again.

Pictures of Dirk covered almost every wall and table in the house. A picture of him in his uniform hung on the wall in the foyer. His high school cap and gown sat on a table near the couch.

Up on the mantle of the fireplace was an American flag, folded into a triangular shape and placed inside a triangular glass case. Right beside it was a photograph of Dirk and himself in desert camouflage, standing proudly together beside a Humvee, Koda between them on the hood of the vehicle.

Hot tears burned behind his eyes. *It's not fair. It's just not fair.*

"John, do you want—" Katie's voice stopped short as she stepped into the room with small plates and napkins. Mrs. McDonald was right behind her, holding a large tray filled with cookies.

He couldn't help himself. He started to break down in huge, body-wracking sobs. He picked up the picture with Dirk and Koda and himself as everything he'd tried to suppress for the past year suddenly came bubbling to the surface.

He couldn't make it stop. He gasped for breath between sobs, becoming aware Mrs. McDonald stood next to him.

"I miss him so much." He turned his face away from the two women. The sudden surge of emotion shamed him. He should've reached out to her sooner. Dirk should've never been taken from his mother. He felt ashamed of everything.

Mrs. McDonald set the tray on the coffee table and rested her hand on his shoulder. He turned around, bracing himself for what was to come next.

"He misses you, too, John," she said gently. "Dirk was always writing to me about you and the rest of the guys. You were his closest friend."

She picked up a photo of Dirk in his high school cap and gown, and her eyes grew bright as a wistful smile spread slowly across her face.

"He was such a handsome boy. All the girls loved him."

John let out a short laugh. "Yeah. I remember." He wiped away a tear with the back of his sleeve.

Finally he walked over and collapsed onto the couch, exhausted. He ran his hands over his face and tried to collect himself. *Inhale. Count to five. Exhale. Count to five.*

Katie set the plates and napkins on the coffee table and sat beside him on the couch. The warmth and sensation of her body comforted him. He gave her a small smile and made himself look at Mrs. McDonald.

"I—I'd love to try a cookie, Mama D." He smiled tightly.

"Of course!" She served them each a plate with three enormous chocolate chip cookies and sat in chair across from the couch. "Oh,

I should get us all big glasses of milk. You see, my cookies just don't taste as good without—"

"Mama D." He cleared his throat before continuing. "I've been wanting to apologize to you for the longest time. I just didn't know how."

She set down her small plate, her eyebrows shooting up into her hairline. "Why in the world would you want to apologize to me?"

He tried to take a deep breath but the air just wouldn't go in, like his lungs were surrounded by metal bands. "Because—because Dirk was sitting in the wrong spot when we were hit by the IED. I was supposed to be sitting where he was—but we switched places. If I hadn't asked him to switch, he might be still alive. Oh, Christ, I'm just so, so sorry." The tears built up again, pushing on his eyes.

She held up her hand.

"John, you have to stop right there." Her eyes locked onto his own, her gaze intense. "You have nothing to apologize for. It wasn't your fault this happened. No one's to blame but those terrorists." She smiled warmly at him. "You gave him brotherhood and the army gave him purpose." She walked over and sat on the other side of him, gently embracing him. "Please don't ever think I once blamed you for his death."

He wrapped his arms around Dirk's mother and buried his face in her shoulder. "God, I miss him. I miss him so much."

On the other side of him, Katie placed a gentle hand on his arm. A rush of emotion finally freed him from the terrible burden he had carried for so long—but no longer carried alone.

Acknowledgments

First and foremost, thank you to my Heavenly Father for blessing me beyond all measure.

Thank you to my family for your support and encouragement. For picking up the slack and adjusting your lives so that I could get this manuscript done. Thank you for the laughs we shared about how I was writing a romance book, yet how you pushed me to finish it. Thank you to my dogs, who are pure psychopaths with never-ending energy, and never-ending love. Thank you for showing me what "drive" really is, for demonstrating what pushing past your limits means. Would I have a nicer house without chewed moldings, broken doors, and tumbleweeds of fur? Of course, but I wouldn't have the abundant laughs and stories to share about you two.

Thank you to Jami Nord and Emmie Mears at Chimera Editing. I don't think I would have ever gotten this book to where it needed to be without you. And Emmie, I truly appreciate all the Minnesota information you provided me. It was destined for me to find you.

Thank you to Michael Mammy, who, two years ago, read this story to help make sure my scenes were authentic. He made me promise to keep pushing forward with this story, to not stop. And that promise pushed me, and it's what I reminded myself of every time I was close to giving up.

And lastly, THANK YOU with all my heart to those men and women, their families and friends, and to those four-legged soldiers who voluntarily sacrifice their lives, well-being, and time to defend this great country we live in. Your sacrifices and memories will never be forgotten.

About the Author

Paris Wynters is a multi-racial romance author whose stories that celebrate our diverse world. When she's not dreaming up stories, she can be found assisting with disasters and helping to find missing people as a Search and Rescue K-9 handler. Paris resides in New York along with her family. For fun, she enjoys video games, and watching hockey. Paris is a graduate of Loyola University Chicago.

Connect with Paris Wynters online:

Website: www.pariswynters.com

Facebook & Instagram: @ParisWynters

Tiktok: @ParisWyntersBooks